OUTLAW VALLEY

Thomas Thompson

BALLANTINE BOOKS • NEW YORK

Library of Congress Catalog Card Number: 87-13689

ISBN 0-345-35717-5

This edition published by arrangement with Doubleday, a Division of
Bantam, Doubleday, Dell Publishing Group, Inc.

Manufactured in the United States of America

First Ballantine Books Edition: November 1988

*To my granddaughter Lisa June, who likes to
collect family items.*

CHAPTER ONE

IT WAS THE THIRD NIGHT OPAL SPRAGUE HAD GONE WITHOUT sleep. She couldn't blame it all on the prison break, for that had happened only late yesterday afternoon, and in spite of the fact that whatever happened at the prison up there on the rocky bench affected the lives of everyone here in the sparsely settled northern end of the Owens River Valley, Opal Sprague had more to face.

The enormity of the task of driving fifty mules across the high Sierra Nevada without adequate help loomed larger and larger, and the passing of each fall day increased the chances of snow in the high passes from a possibility into a probability. And then there was the fact that Rupert Cunningham still hadn't said whether or not he would give her credit for the supplies she needed . . .

She got out of bed, shivering slightly against the dawn chill, and as always she went first to the window of the little cabin by the glacier-fed creek and she saw the encroaching dawn splashing its deceptive softness on the White Mountains that rimmed the eastern edge of the valley. For a moment she looked at the now familiar sight, the line of yellowing cotton-woods along the river, the sagebrush flats that ran to the hills . . . The mules grazed contentedly in the precisely fenced pasture and Big Blue, the lead mule who had become her personal pet, stood at the gate, waiting for her morning oats. *You don't have many problems, Big Blue*, she thought. She

1

glanced at the empty bed and for the first time in a year of widowhood she missed her husband.

The fact that she thought so rarely of her husband was another source of worry. It wasn't normal, she was sure, to feel more relief than grief, but there was no way she could control her innermost thoughts. And thankfully, no one need know. She was a person who was totally honest with herself. She had made a marriage of convenience with a man three times her age and she had done it for one reason only. She had wanted to get away from her family, and she hoped to God she would never see any of them again. But she would. Her cousin Lee Kirby was being paroled this very afternoon from that blister of a prison on the rocky bench and she needed him desperately to help her drive those fifty mules across the mountains.

She slipped off her nightgown and stood naked in front of the full-length, gilt-framed mirror, the most elegant piece of furniture in the two-room cabin, and she thought of what her husband, Frank Sprague, had said when he had given it to her. "Women like to look at theirselves," he had said. "Reckon you ain't much different. I brung you a present." She remembered the exact words because it was the closest thing to a love speech he had made to her in their two years of marriage.

She was beautifully formed and not unattractive, she told herself with the inherent honesty that was so much a part of her. Twenty-three years old: two years married and one year a widow. Still young, and a woman with dreams, but the practical side of her told her that unless she delivered those fifty mules across the Sierra the flimsy dreams she clung to so desperately would be at an end. She reached for the denim jeans and the man's shirt that hung on the back of the chair and she slipped her feet into half boots. Outside Big Blue rattled the poles of the corral, a signal that another day had started.

Frank Sprague had been a Spartan man, the best head guard the prison had ever known, some said, but deep inside there had been a softness, and he had installed a hand pump in the kitchen as a convenience for his wife. Opal pumped a basin of water, sloshed it on her face, and touched her long, blond hair into place before tying it tightly in back with a blue ribbon. She wasn't hungry, and she went outside into the coolness of morning. A promise of heat was in the valley air, mocking the permanent white streaks of glaciers that slashed the bullet-gray granite barrier of the Sierra that rose steeply from the west side of the valley. Big Blue snorted a morning welcome.

She went to the corral and stroked the muzzle of the blue roan mule. "Gonna be another hot one," she said. She thought nothing of speaking aloud to the animal; she had few friends. "I suppose you want a bait of rolled barley?" Perhaps she only imagined it, or perhaps she was starved for communication, but she believed the mule nodded its head.

She smiled, and her face was pleasant and young, but worry had etched lines above the bridge of her well-formed nose long before they should have been there. She went to the barn and opened the door, and the man was standing there, pressed spread-eagle against the wall, his chest heaving from exertion. She recognized the often washed, faded denim of the prison. The convict said, "It's me, Opal."

A flood of memories swept over her, suffocating her with their intensity. The constant moving—at least six "stepdaddies," most of whom had tried to get in bed with her. The hiding; the fear of the law; the loneliness of the isolated valley in the high country. And this man who stood in front of her—the one man who had truly loved her as a child and had tried so hard to be decent to her. "You were a damn fool to come here, Uncle Fenton," she said.

"Opal, I don't want to cause you no trouble, you know that," the man said. He was in his sixties, a sparse man who had never known the press of extra weight on his bones. He was tired and he was afraid, but he had that open grin and a sense of understanding seemed to emanate from his every movement.

"I won't give you a gun," she said. "I won't give you a horse."

"Don't want a gun, honey," he said. "Guns can get you in big trouble. As for a horse—" The puckish grin she knew so well spilled across his seamed face. "You ever known a time your old uncle Fenton couldn't get a horse?"

She felt tired and depleted. The very thing she had tried to escape was back again. Her family. Her bloodline. She said, "They'll catch you. You haven't got a chance."

"Hardware clerks," he scoffed. "Shoe salesmen and bartenders. Hell, Opal, they don't worry me none."

"Will Baker's with them," she said.

Fenton Hoover cocked one eye in a way that was so familiar to her. "I thought on that, Opal," he said. "Baker's got Lee Kirby to worry about. Those two are gonna help you with them mules."

She was whipped and she knew it. This man had meant more to her, growing up as a child, than anyone else on earth. He was lovable and totally incorrigible, and she knew it as well as she knew her own name, and she knew she'd try to help him. There was desperation in her voice when she said, "You only had a few more months to go. You could have gotten a parole, like Lee—" The thought struck her hard. "This won't hurt Lee's parole, will it?"

"You know I wouldn't do anything to hurt Lee," he said.

She felt a surge of relief. There was a chance that even with Lee Kirby's and Will Baker's help she couldn't get those mules across the mountains in time. It was a certainty she couldn't do it without them.

"Maybe if you gave yourself up," she said.

The old man shook his head. "I can't take any more," he said. "I'm used to open country and sky. I ain't goin' back inside them walls."

"I've been away from it three years, Uncle Fenton," she said, her voice breaking. "You're the one who told me to get away from it. You're the one told me to marry Frank Sprague!"

"You done right, Opal," Fenton Hoover said, and now it was the voice of a treasured uncle, a man who had taken the place of a father she had never known, a man who had protected her and believed in her while she grew up with an endless string of "stepdaddies." She remembered so clearly the night he had held her in his arms and said, "Your mama loves you, honey. It's just she's got a wild streak in her like all the rest of us Hoovers. But you ain't got it, baby. You're different. You're gonna have a good life . . ." There had been few kind words in her life. She couldn't forget those. That was the last time she had ever seen her mother.

"I'm not getting back into it, Uncle Fenton," she said.

"I don't want you to," he said. "A little grub. That's all I need. I'll take my chances."

Still she hesitated, knowing full well that eventually she would give in. She said, "You'll go back to the valley?"

"It's the only home I know," he said. She started to turn away and he said, "Opal, about that prison riot last year when your husband was killed . . ."

She turned quickly. "What about it?"

"I didn't have nothing to do with that, Opal. Frank Sprague was a hard man but he was fair. I tried to help him, but it wasn't no use."

"I knew that," she said. "I got a full report from the warden."

The old man's voice was totally honest. "That means a lot to me, knowing you know I didn't have nothing to do with it." He swallowed hard and now she couldn't tell if he was being sincere or only being the consummate con man she knew him to be. "I wouldn't do nothing on earth to hurt you, Opal."

"Then why did you come here?" she said desperately.

"A little grub, honey, that's all. A few biscuits . . . maybe some jerky . . . I won't be able to build a fire for a few days."

"But if they catch you and they find out I've helped you . . ."

"They'll never find out, Opal," he said, and this time he meant what he said.

"I'll see what I can find," she said.

She started to leave, still not sure she'd go through with it. Fenton Hoover said, "You keep hearing things in prison. A new man comes in . . . he knows somebody that knows somebody else . . ." She wondered what he was leading to. She didn't wonder long. "Rance Overton's back in the valley," he said.

She felt her heart skip a beat. She thought it was all over. She had been married two years. She was a widow. But the memory was there, and fight it as she would, it was a fantasy that rose to haunt her. The jet black eyes . . . the utter masculinity of the man . . . And she had been so young and so lonely. She wondered if any woman ever forgot her first lover. . . . She said, "It means nothing to me." She hoped she sounded convincing.

"I wanted to be sure," Fenton Hoover said. "He's rotten, all the way through, Opal. You did right getting away from him. Don't never give in to him again."

There was no way she could answer. Words would have choked her. She left the barn and went toward the cabin and the gray dawn had moved aside to let the first fingers of sun lift over the White Mountains to splash against the granite cliffs of the Sierra.

That same dawn found Larrabee Lucas Stone mounted up and leaving his camp there on the bank of the Owens River. He was a saddle-lean man on a blood bay horse with a gun on his hip, a rifle in a scabbard, and a meager bedroll behind his battered saddle. Those items, plus the three silver dollars in his pocket, constituted the entire assets of his twenty-six years of living, and Larrabee Stone was right contented with his accomplishments.

Wyoming was a long way behind him, but he still glanced over his shoulder from time to time. It wasn't likely a county sheriff would follow him across three states, but you never knew. Sheriff Harry Brockwell didn't have too good a sense of humor, and finding his prisoner gone and a hole in the side of his jail probably wouldn't improve his disposition none. Larrabee put the thought aside. If Sheriff Harry Brockwell wanted to find him he wouldn't have any trouble. The fracas had started at Larrabee's going-away party and at least fifty people knew he was heading for the cow town of Millerton on the west slope of the Sierra at the edge of the San Joaquin Valley in the golden state of California. The thing that had led Larrabee Lucas Stone to pick that particular spot was the fact that he had never been there.

So far, the trip had been right to his liking. He had taken a job for a few days in Colorado and another for a week in Utah. Nevada hadn't promised a hell of a lot except promise. The mining town where he had spent three days and too much money was filled with men who had either been millionaires the last week or were going to be millionaires the next week. Some of them had offered him some golden opportunities but Larrabee Stone had turned them down. He was sort of gun-shy about any job that couldn't be carried out from the back of a horse.

And he had spent two nights camping out with an old Paiute Indian who had told him wondrous tales about those towering Sierras he would have to cross and of how there were valleys no white man had ever seen, and of the vagrant lakes and streams, and the ground that spewed steam through the blankets of snow. Looking at those barren, granite cliffs that rimmed the opposite side of the valley, Larrabee wondered if maybe the old Indian hadn't been out in the sun too long. From here, the bullet-gray peaks splashed with patches of first sun looked as if they couldn't support a jack rabbit, let alone lakes and timber. Larrabee didn't much care. He knew that hordes of miners and even wagon trains had crisscrossed those mountains not too many years back. If they could do it, so could he.

He had camped at the mouth of a creek where it emptied into the Owens and he followed along that, skirting willow thickets and strands of cottonwood, until he came to the fenced-in pasture and ran a practiced eye over the handsome bunch of mules that cropped grass near the precise line of fence posts. A well-kept little spread, but why would a man raise mules when this verdant valley would be a paradise for cows? From his earliest days in Texas and the last drives to Kansas and the moving of stockers to Montana and Wyoming, Larrabee Stone's thoughts had never been far from

cows. It was then he saw the sign on the gate. HELP
WANTED. Larrabee scratched the six-day growth of beard
on his face and squinted at that sign. Those three silver
dollars in his pocket sure as hell wouldn't go very far.
Larrabee Stone took a sudden liking to mules.

The sign was hung by a wire looped over a post. Larrabee
leaned down from his saddle and lifted the invitation free. He
rode on to the gate and again, without dismounting, unlatched
it, rode through, closed it behind him, and rode into the yard
between the barn and the cottonwood log cabin. It was then
he saw the man in the open barn door.

The man ducked back quickly, but not before Larrabee had
gotten a look at him. He was old. Sixty . . . maybe more.
Scrawny cuss. And that faded denim shirt and denim pants
looked just one hell of a lot like a prison uniform. A girl,
dressed in worn pants and a man's shirt came out of the
cabin. She had a flour sack in her hand. The flour sack was
bulging, as if maybe with supplies of some kind. She stopped
dead still.

"What do you want?" she said.

Larrabee Stone was suddenly aware of his appearance. The
almost week's growth of beard and clothes that hadn't been
changed for a lot longer than that weren't exactly the way he
would have chosen to present himself to a pretty young lady.
And she was pretty. Her hair was blond and pulled back, but
it didn't make her features severe. Her waist was tiny and in
spite of the loose man's shirt there was no doubt at all that
she was a woman. He lifted the sign and said, "I'm lookin'
for a job, ma'am. Says here you're lookin' for help."

He had sensed a terrible tenseness about her, but now she
seemed to have better control of herself. She said, "The job's
been filled."

"By the man in the barn?" he said.

Again he saw the uncertainty in her, a tired slump of her
shoulders, almost a look of defeat. "It's none of your business," she said.

"Reckon I can't argue that," he said. He jerked a thumb
toward the horse trough. "Mind if I water my horse?"

She was becoming desperate. She looked at him and her eyes darted toward the barn and she glanced at the ever-rising sun, then she turned and froze. Larrabee followed her gaze. A dozen horsemen had broken out of the cottonwoods and were headed for the mule ranch. They were less than three hundred yards away. Her breath caught in her throat. She said, "I've got to feed the chickens!" She made a dash for the barn. That wasn't chicken feed in that flour sack, Larrabee knew, and he hadn't heard a rooster. The riders came on and one of them leaned down and opened the gate and they rode into the yard between the cabin and the barn, leaving the gate open behind them. The man in the lead was big and he was wearing a badge. He was staring intently at Larrabee Stone. "Who the hell are you?" he said.

Again Larrabee was made conscious of his appearance . . . the beard, the trail-stained clothes, the worn holster, and the gun on his hip. He thumbed back his battered Stetson and turned on what he hoped was his most disarming smile. "Name of Larrabee Lucas Stone," he said. "My Norwegian mama always called me by both names . . . Larrabeelucas. But that makes quite a mouthful so most folks call me Tex."

"Where's Opal?" the man with the badge said. He sounded as if he were used to getting straight answers.

"I'm new here," Larrabee said, "so I don't know folks by name . . ."

The girl came out of the barn. There was no color in her cheeks.

The man with the badge said, "Who the hell's this jasper?"

"A drifter, looking for a job," the girl said. "Nothing more."

The man with the badge dismounted. By his movements Larrabee knew he was older than he had first supposed. He was a bulldog of a man, square of face, a man with broad hands and a face that looked as if it had seen too much of the wrong side of life. When he moved over toward the girl, Larrabee realized that whatever his small part had been here it was over now. The man with the marshal's badge was ignoring him completely. "You all right, Opal?" the man with the badge asked. There was an unexpected softness in his voice.

"Of course I am, Will," she said.

Larrabee glanced at the rest of the riders. They were an ill-assorted group, most of them in town clothes. They certainly weren't cowboys and he doubted they were lawmen. He had no way of knowing, but they looked as if they might be butchers or hardware clerks or livery barn keepers or bartenders. His observation was exactly correct. They were a makeshift posse, rounded up on the spur of the moment by Deputy U.S. Marshal Will Baker.

"I worried about you all night," Marshal Will Baker was saying. "I wanted to come by but I couldn't. All hell's busted loose up at the prison and every guard's on duty . . ."

There was one man who stood out from the others. He was well dressed and he looked like a man who would be called upon to play Santa Claus at the local school's Christmas program. He said, "You can't say we didn't respond to your call, Will. We saw our duty as citizens and we responded."

"Yeah, Rupert," Will Baker said. There was a tinge of annoyance in his voice. "I knew I could count on you."

"A man has a civic duty to a town that supports him," the Santa Claus said. "What happens up at that prison affects all of us."

"Save your speech for next Fourth of July, Rupert," one of the men said.

"Have you caught them?" Opal asked.

The marshal shook his head. "They split up. Two of them went down river. We'll get 'em. The other one . . ." He shrugged.

The girl sounded as if her throat had gone dry. "The one who split off . . . ?"

"I don't know if it was your uncle or not," Will Baker said. The bulldog of a man had suddenly lost his composure. "Damn it, Opal," he said, "I don't like doing this, but I'm a lawman. You, of all people, ought to understand that. Your husband was a lawman and a damn good one, long before he became head guard up at the prison." He took a deep breath.

"Look, Opal. I got to ask questions. Have you seen Fenton Hoover?"

Larrabee could sense the turmoil in the girl but she wasn't showing it outwardly. The words came out almost as a laugh. "He'd be a damn fool to come here," she said.

A good answer, Larrabee thought. *Answer a direct question with a statement and you might get away with it.* He felt a sudden admiration for the girl.

"I don't like this, Opal," Will Baker said, "But I got to look around."

She couldn't answer. She just nodded her head. Will Baker drew his gun and moved off toward the barn. It seemed he was gone an eternity and Larrabee never took his eyes off the girl. She was rigid, her hands clenched into tight fists. In time Baker came out of the barn. He had holstered his gun. "Did you know the back door was open?" he said.

Larrabee saw the relief run through the frame of Opal Sprague. "That latch," she said. "It's been broken for a long spell."

"I could fix it for you, ma'am," Larrabee said. "I'm right good at fixing barn door latches."

He had called attention back to himself. Will Baker turned on him. "You . . . Tex . . . or what the hell ever it is you call yourself. What way'd you come in?"

"Nevada side," Larrabee said. "Over the Whites. Camped out last night on the riverbank."

"You seen anybody?" Will Baker asked.

Larrabee looked at Opal Sprague. Her eyes were closed. Larrabee stroked his bearded chin, squinted one eye, pursed his lips, and glanced upward, a picture of a man in deep thought. "Let's see," he said. "Come off the White Mountains last night . . . made camp about dark. Got up at daylight . . ." He glanced at the girl. He could have sworn she was praying. He shook his head. "Nope," he said. "I can truthfully say I ain't seen a soul between here and the White Mountains. Saw some mighty fine mules, though."

He didn't look at the girl. He didn't need to. He could feel her relief.

"Been a prison break," Will Baker said. "Three of the bastards."

"I look like one of them?" Larrabee asked. There was a streak of perversity in him that made him push his luck. It was the same feeling that had made him bust the wall out of the Gillette jail rather than spend three more days there.

"If you looked like one of them you sure as hell wouldn't be standing there without handcuffs on you," Will Baker said.

"Guess that lets me off the hook then, don't it?" Larrabee said.

"Not by a damn sight," Will Baker said. "There's a state prison in this county and we got one hell of a tough vagrancy law around here. If you don't know what that means, it means we don't want no drifting gun-hung saddle tramps around here. You get back on your horse and just keep riding, the faster the better."

"He's not a vagrant, Will," the girl said. Her voice was barely audible.

"What do you mean?" Will Baker said. "You said yourself he was."

"He's got a job," Opal Sprague said. "I hired him to help us drive those fifty mules across the mountains."

CHAPTER TWO

THERE WAS NO WAY TO KNOW WHO WAS THE MORE STARTLED—
Deputy U.S. Marshal Will Baker or Larrabee Lucas Stone.
Larrabee had played a lot of poker in his time and he figured
this was a good time to hold his cards close to his chest. Will
Baker, on the other hand, was a man who laid his cards face
up. "What the hell you talking about, Opal?" he blurted.
"You can't hire the first drifter that comes along."

"I just did," Opal Sprague said.

Baker's voice softened some. "Opal, listen to me. I told
you I'd find some help for you, didn't I?"

"You've been telling me that for the past month," Opal
said. "I'm out of time, Will. I've got a contract date on
delivering these mules."

"You need half a dozen hands at least," Will Baker said.
"How the devil you think three men can drive fifty mules
across those mountains?"

"Four," Opal said. "I'll be there."

Baker sounded a little desperate and Larrabee had the
feeling he wasn't a man used to giving in to desperation. He
said, "It can't be done. I'll scout around. Give me a week or
so more."

"I haven't got a week or so more," Opal Sprague said. "The
minute Lee gets out of prison you bring him over here. Nobody
knows those mountains better than Lee Kirby does. As soon
as I get the supplies, we're leaving. You with me or not?"

"I got no choice," Will Baker said. "My job is to stick with Lee until he gets to Millerton."

The name of the town almost made Larrabee overplay his hand. It was the place he had promised himself he would go. Rupert Cunningham, the man who looked like a beardless Santa Claus, had suddenly taken a keen interest in the conversation "If you ask me . . ." Cunningham started.

"I didn't," Opal said.

Larrabee felt a surge of admiration for the girl. He was beginning to realize she was in one hell of a tight spot but she sure showed no intention of backing down from it. Larrabee liked that. What he didn't like was the idea of four people, one of them a woman, trying to handle fifty loose mules in rough country. *This might be a good time to fold my hand,* he thought to himself, and then he remembered what Will Baker had said about that vagrancy law in this county. The three silver dollars in his pocket wouldn't go too far. . . .

"Now don't go getting your back up, Opal," Will Baker was saying. "We're all trying to help you, you know that." He went across and swung into the saddle with an easy, fluid movement that belied his obvious age. He turned to the mounted posse and said, "Come on, we got a few more hours before I have to get on over to the prison and go through that damn legal mumbo jumbo."

One of the riders said, "Will, I got to be getting back to my shop." He had a nasal twang in his voice.

"We been up all night," another said.

"You're apt to be up a few more nights," Will Baker said. "We got three convicts loose. You want your wives' throats cut in their sleep?"

Larrabee thought of the old man he had caught a glimpse of in the barn and he thought of how Opal Sprague had protected him. He didn't know why, but he had a strong feeling that the man in the barn wasn't one to go around cutting women's throats in the middle of the night.

Rupert Cunningham, the Santa Claus, said, "You boys go on. I'll catch up with you. I've got some business to talk to Opal about."

"You listen to him, Opal," Will Baker said. "Rupert's just trying to help you."

Larrabee saw Opal stiffen, and he saw her hand clench at her side. Rupert Cunningham got down from the saddle, awkward and laborious, a man who was not used to riding. "Don't take too long, Rupert," Will Baker said. He wheeled his horse and the ill-assorted posse followed him out through the open gate. Rupert Cunningham stood there, facing Opal Sprague.

"Well, Opal?" he said. "You thought it over?"

"I have," she said.

"Good," Rupert said. "I brought the papers. Like I told you the other day. It's just a formality."

"That's what I've been thinking about, Mr. Cunningham," Opal said. "Those formalities of yours have led to your owning most of the ranches in this end of the valley."

Larrabee thought he saw a flicker of concern in the fat man's eyes but if he did it wasn't there long. This was a man who was supremely sure of himself. "I'll admit this valley has been good to me," he said.

"Frank always said you were a mighty shrewd businessman," she said.

"I take that as a compliment," Rupert Cunningham said. "I had a lot of respect for your late husband. He was a shrewd businessman himself."

"And he never signed any of your papers," she said.

The eternal avuncular kindness left Rupert Cunningham's face and Larrabee got the distinct impression this man might well play Santa Claus at the annual school program but he could also carry the sting of a scorpion. "Frank Sprague paid his bills," Cunningham said.

"And he taught me to do the same," Opal said.

There was a tenseness growing between these two that Larrabee could really feel. They acted as if he didn't even exist. It made him uneasy and he moved over to his horse, hooked a stirrup over the saddle horn, and loosed the cinch. He heard Rupert Cunningham say, "Frank Sprague's dead, Opal."

"I'm not," she said. "He left me this ranch and it's paid for. I got a bigger mule herd now than when he died. The railroad's coming and they're prospecting for borax over in Death Valley. The mule business is going to be big and this sale's going to put me right in the middle of it."

Larrabee glanced over his shoulder and he saw a glisten of perspiration on the fat man's forehead. His voice had become lower. It was hard and flat. "I'm not giving you those supplies without security," he said.

"Then I guess I won't get 'em," the girl said, "because I'm not signing your damn note."

A slow smile grew on Rupert Cunningham's face but it wasn't a pleasant smile. "Just how do you expect to feed yourself and three men?" he asked.

"I'll kill one of the mules and make jerky out of him if I have to," Opal Sprague said.

For the first time, Rupert Cunningham turned to Larrabee Stone. "Good luck, stranger," he said. "You're signing on with a paroled convict, a marshal who hates his guts, and a girl who's too damn stubborn to move out of the way of a brushfire. You must need a job real bad."

He moved over to his horse, laboriously thrust a foot in the stirrup, and made three tries before finally hefting himself into the saddle. He reined the horse and didn't look back as he rode through the gate to follow Will Baker and the posse.

For a moment the girl stood there, her back turned to Larrabee, then, without looking at him, she started walking slowly toward the cabin. Larrabee said, "We haven't talked much about that job you offered me, ma'am."

She stopped, but she still didn't look at him. "You mean you'd take it?" she said.

"Well," Larrabee said, "I reckon I'm somewhat like you. I'd like time to think it over." He could tell just by the rigidity of her shoulders that she was choking back a sob, fighting not to let it go. He said, "While I'm thinking, mind if I water my horse and maybe borrow a bait of oats from you?"

She turned and her lips were set in a straight line, and he

saw the tears in her eyes but they weren't spilling over. The girl had one hell of a lot of control. She said, "Go ahead. While you're doing that I'll put a pan of biscuits in the oven and stir up some gravy." She didn't wait for an answer. She couldn't. She turned away from him abruptly and started toward the cabin, her pace quickening with each step until she was nearly running. She fumbled with the door latch as if she couldn't see well, and when she got the door open he heard the muffled sob and then her emotions broke. She slammed the door shut and he knew she was standing there against it, all the tension of the past hour breaking at once. He felt an urge to go to her . . . to try to help . . . but he knew there was nothing he could do.

He went over to his horse and picked up the trailing bridle reins. He led the horse to the barn and removed the saddle, the blanket, and the bridle. Taking the pitchfork that was there, he tossed some fresh meadow hay into the manger. "Might as well eat, Snort," he said to the horse. "Might be we'll be leaving here sooner than we thought. It don't sound to me like it's the best job we've ever been offered." He gave the horse an affectionate slap on the rump. "But damned if I'm gonna pass up biscuits and gravy," he said.

No more than a mile from the barn, the glacier-fed creek that ran through Opal Sprague's place made a long, sweeping curve through a thick stand of willows. Heavy winter runoffs had cut deeply into the bank here, forming an overhanging shelf. The water was waist deep on Fenton Hoover and it came to his chin as he squatted down and pressed himself against the dirt wall. The hoofbeats were getting closer and now he could hear the men's voices plainly. A man said, "Damn it, Will, we been up all night and ain't had nothin' to eat . . . ."

"Quit your damn whinin', Floyd," Will Baker's voice said.

Another voice said, "Will, Rupert Cunningham's comin' up on us."

"You think I didn't see him?" Will Baker said.

"Not unless you've got eyes in the back of your head," the voice said.

"He has," the first voice said.

Fenton Hoover heard them giving their soft "whoas" and knew they were reining up, right there above him. His legs were starting to cramp from the coldness of the water and he felt if he didn't change positions soon they'd go out from under him, but he knew he didn't dare move. He had recognized the name of Rupert Cunningham. He was the man who owned the big general merchandise store there in town and it was said he was one of the richest men in the valley. He wondered why none of the Hoover bunch had ever tried to rob Cunningham's store, but it was only a fleeting thought. He was through with that sort of thing, he told himself. If he ever got out of this mess and back into the valley he'd content himself with doing the cooking and cutting wood. Leave the business of rustling and robbing up to the younger ones. *I'm getting too damn old for this,* Fenton Hoover told himself.

He heard the arrival of the other horse, a muttered exchange of greetings, and then Will Baker's voice saying, "Get things straightened out with Opal?"

The new voice . . . that must be Cunningham . . . said, "That woman's more stubborn than the mules she's raising."

In spite of the misery that was creeping through his bones, Fenton Hoover smiled. *That's my girl,* he thought to himself. *Don't let nobody push you around.*

"Well, come on," Will Baker said "They had to leave some kind of tracks. I got a couple of more hours before I go over to the prison."

Rupert Cunningham said, "Will, the boys and I have been talking. We've got stores to run . . . business to take care of. We pitched in and helped you as best we could because it was our duty, but this county's got a sheriff. Damn it, this is his job. Let him round up a regular posse and take care of this."

There was an unmistakable muttering of approval, and one voice said, "Yeah, we elect a sheriff and don't see him once in three months. Where in hell is he, anyway?"

Will Baker's voice was as explosive as Fenton Hoover knew

he could be. "He's down at the county seat tangled up in a court trial, that's where he is! That's what being sheriff means nowadays. Back when Frank Sprague and I were lawmen together we would have run these three convicts down by now and had 'em strung up to a cottonwood and it would have been over with. Nowadays even if you catch a man red-handed, the damn lily-livered courts will turn him loose. . . ."

"Now you just calm down, Baker," Rupert Cunningham said. "We've got a mighty fine justice system in this country. I'm a county commissioner, don't you forget that. You got no real jurisdiction over me. I was just doing my civic duty . . ."

"You make me sick, the whole bunch of you," Will Baker said. "Go on back to town, if that's what you're so set on. I don't need you."

There was more muttering and grumbling and then the jangle of bit chains and the squeaking of saddle leather and gradually the hoofbeats grew dimmer. Fenton Hoover let a low moan of pain escape from his lips. Apparently they were gone, but he still couldn't take any chances. He knew Will Baker . . . both in person and by reputation. It would be just like him to hang back . . . take one more look at this creek. . . . A horse and rider pushed through the willow thicket, not fifteen feet upstream from where he was hiding Fenton Hoover didn't take time to see who it was. He slowly ducked his head completely under the water.

It was a matter of seconds, undoubtedly, but it seemed like hours. He felt his very guts tightening and cramping and every bone in his body was howling with pain, and his lungs were about to explode and blow out his ribs. . . . He couldn't take any more of it but if he moved too fast he knew he stood a chance of getting a bullet right between his eyes. He had no physical part in making the decision. Slowly his mouth and nose came out of the water. He wanted to take in great gulps of air but that would make a sound. He hunched down there in the shallow stream, his head pushed back so far he thought his neck would break and the life-giving air trickled softly into his distended nostrils and escaped through his open mouth.

The weight of the horse upstream from him had dislodged a large clump of moist earth and thick grass. It floated downstream and lodged against the side of his nose, then moved and covered his mouth. He could taste the wet earth and smell the newly crushed grass, but he was breathing. Upstream the horse lifted its head abruptly and noisily blew water from its nostrils. The saddle creaked. The horse turned and the horse and rider went back through the willow thicket. Only then did Fenton Hoover reach up carefully and brush the clod of earth off his face. He was, by God, alive, and the rider was gone.

With the immediate danger momentarily out of the way, the foxy cunning that was so much a part of him returned to Fenton Hoover full blown. As long as he wasn't inside those walls there was a chance, and a chance was all he had ever asked of life.

He moved slowly along the bank, still staying in the stream, and he sorted out the things he had heard. First of all, Opal was all right. That was the most important thing to Fenton Hoover. She had helped him, as he had known she would, but even if he was caught . . . even if they tore off his arms and legs . . . no one would ever make him say Opal Sprague had helped him. Then he thought of the stranger who had ridden into the yard. There was no doubt in Fenton's mind that the stranger had seen him. Why hadn't he said anything? Was he a man on the run too? Or was he a bounty hunter, saving the kill for himself? Fenton had no idea what sort of a price might be on his head but there would be something. The Hoover family was pretty well known in local law circles.

Most of all he had learned that the sheriff was down at the county seat. That meant maybe a few more hours before the sheriff could round up his deputies and form a posse. That was a break. After a long time he carefully climbed out of the stream and onto dry ground. He had trouble making his legs work and he reached down and tried to rub them to get his circulation going. Peering around, he got his bearings and went unerringly to the overturned stump and retrieved the sack of provisions he had hidden there. The mere feel of that sack of food Opal had given him gave him a surge of confidence. If he could keep hidden during the day, gradually working his way toward the mountains . . . Getting a horse and saddle was the least of his worries. *Hell,* he thought to himself, and now there was a grin on his face. *It was me taught the Indians how to steal horses in the first place.*

Fenton Hoover crawled under a thick clump of elderberry, dragging the sack with him. He reached inside and lifted out a biscuit. The grin was still there. Opal always did make the best damn biscuits. He bit into one of them and started to chew. As far as he was concerned, he was a free man.

Larrabee Lucas Stone would have to agree that Opal Sprague made fine biscuits. And her gravy was more than passable too. It had been a long time since he had had a woman-cooked meal and he did more than justice to it. Beyond knowing this and the fact that she looked right pretty leaning over a cookstove, Larrabee had found out very little about the woman who had offered him a job. Either she wasn't the talkative kind or she didn't feel like talking to him but, whatever it was, she hadn't said more than a dozen words during the entire meal.

Larrabee was a man who could adapt to any situation, but he was doing a damn poor job of it here. For one thing, he had been overly conscious about his appearance. He had caught a glimpse of his reflection when he had washed his face in the horse trough and he was a scroungy-looking devil to say the least. Every time he moved and got a whiff of the clothes he had been wearing for a month, his confidence slipped one notch lower.

"You sure are a fine cook, ma'am," he said.

"It wasn't nothing," she said.

He should have known she would say that. Every woman said that when you complimented her on her cooking.

The silence in this cabin was getting downright oppressive, and in time there was nothing to do but push back his chair and stand up. "I sure do thank you," he said.

She nodded without even looking at him.

"From up there on the slope I saw what might be a town

over yonder," he said. "Thought maybe I'd ride in there and take a look-see."

She turned then and faced him squarely and the light from the window spilled across her face. She was downright pretty, and those eyes were the softest blue he had ever seen. She said, "You did me a favor this morning, Mr. Stone. That man who was out there in the barn means a whole lot to me. You could have told the marshal about him. You didn't. That means I owe you."

"No need to feel that way," he said.

"We got a sort of code in our family," she said. "Somebody does something for you, you do something for them."

"You offered me a job."

"That's right. I did. That marshal wasn't fooling about the vagrancy laws around here. They could clap you in jail just for not having a job. So I said you had one."

"I haven't said I'd take it," Larrabee said.

"You don't have to," she said. "You did me a favor, I did you one. The slate's clean, Mr. Stone. You don't owe me a thing."

The conversation was over as surely as if she had slammed a door in his face. He stood there a moment, his hands feeling awkward and big as he worked his fingers nervously, then he turned and left and went straight to the barn. His horse nickered a welcome.

There was a brush and a curry comb on the wall, handles thrust through leather loops. He took the instruments and gave the blood bay's back a good massage, then he carefully smoothed the saddle blanket and tossed on the saddle.

He flipped a stirrup over the saddle horn and pressed himself against the side of the horse as he tightened the cinch. There was a turmoil going on inside him and, try as he might, he couldn't push it aside. That girl in there needed help and she needed it bad, but why in hell should he get himself mixed up in something that was none of his business? The man in the barn was an escaped convict; common sense would tell you that, and he, Larrabee, had helped that man escape the law. Aiding and abetting, they called it, and the law took a dim view of such things. And that turned his thoughts to Sheriff Harry Brockwell of Gillette, Wyoming. A nice enough fellow, but a damn bulldog when it came to enforcing the law. Harry Brockwell probably hadn't been too happy when he came back to find his prisoner gone and a hole in the side of his jail. What the hell. It was a long ways from here and a good two months back. But still, you couldn't tell about a man like Sheriff Harry Brockwell. It would be just like him to send a telegram to the sheriff in Millerton telling him to pick up one Larrabee Lucas Stone, escaped convict. He had known exactly where Larrabee was headed. And he had known Larrabee would get there, because when Larrabee Stone said he was going to do something he did it, and everybody in the town of Gillette had known Larrabee was heading for Millerton, California. That's what the farewell party had been about, and then some of the boys had started getting a little rambunctious . . .

He kept telling himself that that was all that was on his mind, and while he told himself that he knew he was lying. Thoughts of the girl in the cabin kept getting in his way and he remembered the desperation on her face when that posse had ridden in and the stiff-backed rawhide spine she had shown when she had faced the man who looked like a beardless Santa Claus. She was quite a woman, and she needed help, but she had said herself he didn't owe her a damn thing. . . . He led the horse outside and swung easily into the saddle. He felt at home here, and the miles were out there ahead of him, just waiting for him to ride them down. He looked around and the girl was standing in the cabin door. Larrabee Stone touched the brim of his hat. "I sure do wish you luck, ma'am," he said.

"I've found out you make your own luck," she said.

"Reckon that's so," he said. She had shut him out again and there was no way to reason with a woman he didn't even know, and he'd be a damn fool to get mixed up with her anyway—

He rode through the gate and he didn't look back, but he knew she was still standing there, looking after him. He just hoped to God her chin wasn't trembling and that there weren't any tears in those eyes that held the softness of spring flowers.

To the horse, but not out loud, he said, "Hope you got your nose in that hay, Snort, because you and me might be moving on a lot sooner than we thought."

The valley was there before him and the invitation of the town, but beyond that, shooting straight up like a wall, were the towering granite masses of the Sierra Nevada.

CHAPTER THREE

IT WAS MIDMORNING NOW AND THE SUN WAS BUILDING UP TO the pinnacle of noon heat that it had borrowed from the long miles of desert behind him. As he rode through the shade pools of the cottonwoods, he felt the cool wash of a vagrant breeze, but in the open the sun rays found him again and reminded him that this was a land of challenge, a place that tolerated no mistakes. The sheer escarpment of the mountains seemed to say, "You've whipped the desert, now let me have a try at you."

It wasn't as if Larrabee hadn't known those mountains would be there. Even back in Wyoming men had talked of them and of the gold they guarded so fiercely and of wagon trains that had fought their way through them. Some had made it; some hadn't. It was the awesome nearness of them now that startled him. It was as if after all these miles a master builder had erected a wall across his path. He thought of the girl and her determination to drive fifty mules through that seemingly impenetrable wall of stone.

There was no kindness in the appearance of these dull gray peaks that pierced a cobalt sky. He had crossed the Rockies, but the Rockies offered a man a gentle reminder of what was ahead. Leaving the Mississippi the table-flat land rose steadily, letting a man's lungs become accustomed to the altitude. Well-worn ruts in the prairie grass marked where immigrant wagons had passed and settlements had sprung up, and hun-

25

dreds of sweating men had pushed a railroad ever westward toward manifest destiny. But here there was no warning. From the floor of the lush valley, the mountains rose abruptly, saying simply and clearly, "Try me if you must." They offered nothing in return except the siren song that told of a long valley beyond their westward slopes, a valley where cattle grazed in belly-high grass and a man used to the saddle might find a job to his liking. Larrabee Lucas Stone rode on toward the cluster of trees that marked the town. Beyond the town were the mountains.

The old Paiute Indian with whom Larrabee had shared blankets and a meager meal had also talked of those mountains. He was an old man, faded and wrinkled with the curse of a broken dream in his eyes. Late into the night he had rambled on about the old days when all this domain was the rightful land of the Paiutes and the Shoshones and with the drone of his voice floating through the thin wall of campfire smoke, his rambling tales had turned to legends. He spoke of broad valleys no white man had ever seen, and some, he said, were valleys where warm water bubbled up from the ground and steam melted away the snow. Truth or legends? Larrabee didn't know. What he did know was that the town of Millerton lay on the other side of those mountains. He would have to cross them to get there, and get there he would.

He reined up briefly and took a new look at the strange escarpment that cut across the valley. He had noticed it first from a vantage point on the slopes of the White Mountains, now at his back. It looked as if in some time beyond recall a giant had smitten the valley floor with a huge sword of vengeance. It was as if the lower valley had dropped away and the far upper reaches had retained their level. It was a scar of stone several hundred feet high, and crouched on that rocky rim was a cluster of buildings, rising like a blister from the virgin land. He knew now that those buildings must be the prison. *A hell of a place to be locked up,* he thought to himself. He felt suddenly uncomfortable . . . perhaps from the thought of being locked inside walls, perhaps from the uneasiness of feeling there were eyes boring into his back.

Imagination, he told himself, and he rode on toward the town.

But it wasn't all imagination. The eyes of Fenton Hoover, the escaped convict, had never left the back of Larrabee Stone while he stopped there, reined up, looking off toward the escarpment and the cluster of buildings on its rim. Fenton Hoover knew those buildings well. He would die before he went back inside those walls.

He crouched behind the root mass of a big cottonwood that had outlived its time and given way to the winds that sometimes howled up this valley. Soil clung to the roots and formed a natural hiding place. Fenton Hoover had been here for more than an hour, crawling on his hands and knees from one thicket to another, dragging the flour sack of supplies behind him. He knew the rider was the same one who had ridden into Opal Sprague's yard. He knew nothing about the man beyond that, but he sized up the easiness with which the drifter sat his saddle and he saw the meager bedroll tied behind the cantel. *Just a drifter riding to someplace,* Fenton Hoover thought to himself. He wished the drifter well. There had been so many times when he himself had kept riding to some place. He felt a twinge of sadness for the man, for he knew now that some place was no place at all. He risked a quick glance at the sun and accurately measured the time as along about noon. Anytime now the gates of that prison on the shelf would swing open and Lee Kirby would step out a free man. The thought gave Fenton Hoover a lot of solace. If Lee Kirby and Opal Sprague were both all right, then the world was all right with Fenton Hoover.

The gates of the prison at the top of the escarpment swung wide and Deputy U.S. Marshal Will Baker rode through to meet the small reception committee that was waiting for him. He recognized the warden and the chaplain and he tried to avoid looking at the tall, slim youth who stood between them. Will Baker had had a son once. He would be just about the age of the one who stood there between the warden and the chaplain. This one had served his time and was being given another chance. Will Baker's son was dead.

Will Baker reined up in front of the three men, thickset, tough, relentless, a man who couldn't let the past be the past. The young man met his eyes and held them. He wore new-issue blue jeans, a blue chambray shirt, and a battered broad-brimmed hat he had saved from yesterday. This was Lee Kirby, a handsome young man with the prison paleness still in his cheeks, a parole paper in his pocket, and the bitterness of remembering in his blue eyes.

"My son, the world is out there waiting for you," the chaplain said.

"You've been a model prisoner, Lee," the warden said. He offered his hand. "We're all counting on you to make good."

Will Baker spit across his saddle horn. "You're all whistling in the dark," he said. "Goddamn bunch of bleeding hearts, turning criminals loose so they can go back and do it all over again. Who in hell thought up this parole system anyway?"

The warden was a small man with a turkey neck, but he had lived a long time with cruelty and toughness and there was a lot of sinewy fiber in him that didn't show on the surface. "The boy has lived up to every legal rule there is, Will," the warden said. "He's got a job waiting for him over in Millerton. He's got a job until he gets there. Your orders are to see he gets there, no more."

"I've read the goddamn orders," Baker said. He glanced at Lee Kirby. "This all he's got? I mean what he's wearing?"

The warden was a bit tired of Will Baker and he had been for some time. He said, "If you've read your orders you know that Mrs. Sprague has guaranteed to provide him with heavier clothing, food, whatever he needs until you get those mules delivered to Millerton."

The chaplain had kept silent until now. He said, "If I may express an opinion. . . ."

"I don't care how many opinions you express," Will Baker said, "but get on back inside those walls to do it. I've watched those sons of bitches in there. They've screwed up their lives from hell to breakfast and people like you come along and put a Bible in front of 'em and all they see is that Jesus is going to forgive everything they ever done so they jump up and down and yell, 'Hallelujah,' and the bleeding hearts say, 'Ain't that fine,' and they give 'em a parole and turn 'em loose and they go right back out and kill somebody because Jesus is gonna forgive 'em.''

Lee Kirby stood there, every ounce of remaining color drained from his face. He kept clenching and unclenching his hands, as if the muscles of his hands were having spasms and he had no control over the movements. The chaplain said, "After two years the adjustment won't be easy, son.''

The warden put out his hand. "I trust you, Lee,'' he said.

For a long moment Lee Kirby stood there, a young man, barely into his twenties, but he had been knocked down enough times to fill the quota of a man of sixty. He hesitated a long moment, then wiping the palm of his hand on the front of his shirt he reached out and gripped the warden's hand. "I won't let you down, Warden,'' he said. "My family kinda goes along with if somebody does you a favor you got to pay that favor back. I ain't never gonna make you look bad, Warden.''

"Let's get going, damn it,'' Will Baker said impatiently. "There's still three convicts loose out there, Warden, or did you forget about that?''

There was a flush of anger in the warden's cheeks but his voice was calm. "When are you going to retire, Will?'' he asked.

"Any day,'' Will Baker said. "I don't like the way the law's being run.''

Lee Kirby said, "Should I go on over to Opal's place, Mr. Baker?''

"You will like hell,'' Will Baker said. "You'll go there when I take you there and not before. Swing up behind me. You're staying in the hotel in town tonight where I can keep an eye on you.'' He kicked a foot out of the stirrup.

Lee Kirby swung easily up behind Will Baker. He sat

there, staring at the broad back of a man he knew hated him. There was nothing personal in it. Will Baker hated convicts. Everyone knew that. Maybe it was the thrill of being outside those walls that did it, but Lee Kirby felt a little moment of perversity. "Ain't you afraid I might try for your gun, Baker?"

"I wish you would," Will Baker said. "I wouldn't mind having an excuse to gut shoot you."

Lee Kirby didn't answer. The thrill of being outside . . . the fragrance of the air . . . the unobstructed view of the long valley from here . . . That's all that mattered. He had a good job waiting for him on the other side of the mountains. And there was a girl. *Try your damnedest, Will Baker*, Lee Kirby thought. *I've been inside walls for the last time*.

Will Baker turned the horse and they rode toward the town of Twin Pines that snuggled peacefully in its grove of cottonwood.

Larrabee Stone rode into the town. It was a peaceful place, cooled by the cluster of trees that surrounded it. The town wasn't much different from a lot of others he had seen in his time. The main street was broad, as if the town had figured it would grow a lot more than it had. The two most prominent buildings, he noted, were Rupert Cunningham's General Merchandise Store and directly across the street a two-story building with a railing-enclosed balcony on the second floor. A sign that covered most of the false front proclaimed it to be Dolly Varden's Hotel. He noted the swinging doors and envisioned a saloon on the first floor. Down the street a bit was a gun shop with the inevitable bright red wooden rifle jutting up like a finger. A horse that looked vaguely familiar was tied at the hitch rail in front of Dolly Varden's place; two buckboards were in front of the general merchandise store. The thing that held his attention was the red-and-white spiral striped pole and the sign that said Baths. He went directly there.

He took his meager bedroll from behind the saddle and laid it on the board sidewalk in front of the barbershop. Hooking a stirrup over his saddle horn, he loosened the cinch a bit. The horse looked around and nudged him lightly. Larrabee grinned. "Don't worry, Snort," he said to the horse, "I'll smell different when I come back." He made a half hitch with the reins around the hitching rail, picked up his bedroll, and opned the door to the barbershop. The small bell on top of the door announced his arrival.

The barber was asleep in his chair. He came alive at the sound of the bell, snatched the cloth from the chair, and gave it a sharp snap. "You're next," he said, and Larrabee wasn't too surprised. There was no one else in the shop. He took a quick look at the barber, certain he had seen the man someplace before, and then he knew. He had been one of the riders with the marshal on that make-shift posse that had ridden into Opal Sprague's yard. He saw the man giving him a second appraisal, probably, like Larrabee, certain he had seen this customer before. Larrabee went across and climbed into the barber chair. "How much for a shave and a bath, and a place to change my clothes?" he asked.

The barber gave Larrabee a professional appraisal. "Hair trim and shave will be six bits," he said. "I get four bits for the bath, but you can use all the hot water you want."

"I'll take the works," Larrabee said. *A dollar and a quarter*, he thought. *Hell's bells, I'll have a buck seventy-five left. I might even drop by that Dolly Varden's saloon.*

CHAPTER FOUR

THE WOMAN WHO OWNED DOLLY VARDEN'S HOTEL, SALOON, AND café was past forty, but a knowledge of paint and powder that she had learned through the years, and a way of touching up her naturally auburn hair, served her well, and she was a handsome woman that any man would notice, and most men did.

She called herself Dolly Varden. That wasn't her name, but that was of little matter. She had put aside her family name a number of years ago because her early upbringing was not a happy memory. A hard-scrabble farm in the flinty hills of Kansas, never enough food, a father who expressed his frustration and wrath by taking it out on his children, and a mother who had died in childbirth, clutching a stillborn infant in her arms. At sixteen she had been pretty and voluptuous, and with the constant herds of cattle trailing up from Texas and the little town at the end of the track swarming with cowboys, she found a way to make a living.

She had drifted on, always west, and she had settled finally in this remote valley at the foot of the towering mountains. There was a gold strike on at the time. It had lasted but a short while, but she had still been young and she had heard men talk of the high valleys and the lakes and streams and of an illusive trout called the Dolly Varden. She had liked the sound of it, and she had given herself that name.

The Dolly Varden, men said, was a trout that was hard to

catch, but the right man could catch one, and that thought appealed to Dolly. The man who had the best chance of catching her sat across the table from her now. It was Will Baker, the deputy U.S. marshal. She had known him a long time; she understood the hurt that was in him that would never go away; she knew his every mood and went along with them all. She was hopelessly in love with him.

She looked at him now and said, "So Opal Sprague hired herself a hand. What's he like?"

"Like any other drifter," Will Baker said. "Six-day growth of beard . . . clothes you can smell a day before you see him. Ugly damn galoot."

"Can he ride a horse?" Dolly asked.

"He was on one," Baker said.

"Well, that's a step in the right direction," Dolly said. "Did you talk to Rupert Cunningham?"

"Yeah, I talked to him," Baker said, "and damn it, I see his side of it."

"In other words he's not going to give her the supplies she needs." It was a flat statement.

Will Baker was starting to get uncomfortable. "Damn it, Dolly," he said, "you're a businesswoman. How would you feel? Driving fifty mules across the mountains with only half the help she needs. Rupert would be taking a hell of a risk."

"So would she," she said.

"That's the point," Will Baker said. "I think she ought to call the whole thing off."

"And give up a government contract for fifty mules that could get her really started . . . get her established on her own? She could buy another good jack . . . a couple of good Morgan broodmares. . . . Would Frank Sprague have given up an opportunity like that?"

"That's different," Will Baker said. "Frank Sprague was a man everybody could depend on. He owned that land outright and he raised the best mules in the valley. . . ."

"She's got the same thing," Dolly said.

"But damn it, she's just a woman!" Will Baker said.

"So am I," Dolly said softly. "Or had you forgotten?"

Will Baker's voice softened. He put his hand out and covered hers. "You know I haven't, Dolly. I don't know what I would have done without you after Billy died." He was suddenly ill at ease, and he reached into his vest pocket and took out a gold watch. He snapped open the case and stared down at the face of it.

"I've always loved that watch," she said.

"Yeah," Baker said "It's a beauty. All engraved and all. It's real gold." He looked up and met her eyes. "It's all I've got left of my dad. I always figured when I cashed in I'd leave it to Billy." He snapped the watch closed. "Things don't always work out the way you planned."

"There were good memories, too, Will. You've told me."

He grinned. "You mean about my dad's headlight for his locomotive?" He chuckled. "When he finished a run he took that headlight off and brought it home with him. Wasn't no other engineer good enough to use that headlight." With the softness of memories his face was relaxed, even pleasant. "I can still see him sitting there at the kitchen table, polishing that lamp. Had a big brass eagle on top of it and brass leaves down the sides. He'd scrub away on that concave mirror until there wasn't a spot on it, and then he'd refill it with fresh carbide. When he'd get a call to go out on a run for a week, he'd take that lamp. I never once saw him kiss my mom goodbye, and I don't remember him ever touching me."

"A lot of men are like that."

"He was tough, Dolly. He made me toe the line every minute of my life. God, how I resented it. And then when Billy came along I decided he was going to have all the love and affection I'd never had . . ." There was moisture in Will Baker's eyes when he looked across at her and instinctively she took his hand. "I look back now and realize my daddy was right and I didn't learn from it. I made every goddamn mistake there was with Billy. . . ."

"Don't, Will," she said. "Life has to go on."

"And that's the hell of it, ain't it?" he said. "Thirty years I've been in this business. And what do I wind up with? Nursery maid to fifty mules and an outlaw brat who should have been shot on sight instead of going through all that damned legal mumbo jumbo." His features set. "It ain't like it used to be, Dolly," he said. "I was a lawman once. Me and Frank Sprague. And we were good ones. And how does he wind up? A guard, that's all, murdered by a bunch of scum that wasn't fit to polish his boots. And look at me. I'm a damned errand boy, nothing more."

She squeezed his hand tighter. "Why don't you quit?"

"I've thought about it," he said.

"Think harder," she said. "I could sell this place. I've had a dozen offers. We could get that little ranch we've always talked about. Get us a few head of cattle. . . ."

A rare grin crinkled the corners of Will Baker's eyes. "You're mighty persuasive, Dolly."

"You staying here at the hotel tonight?" she asked.

"Have to," he said. "Got to keep an eye on my prisoner."

"Good," she said. "Maybe I can be even more persuasive." She stood up. "I have to go see about things in the kitchen. Stick around, will you?"

"Try and get rid of me," he said.

The barber was a man who liked to talk. Being on Marshal Baker's makeshift posse in search of three escaped convicts was the biggest thing that had ever happened to him in his life, and he wasn't going to let it pass by.

The snip of his scissors was a lulling sound to Larrabee Lucas Stone and he might even have dozed, but the nasal whine of the barber precluded that. "Yes sir," the barber said. "Eight hours we was out there. Little off the side?"

"I reckon," Larrabee said.

"Barberin' sure does develop a memory," the barber said. "Minute you walked in that door I knowed I'd seen yuh. Come in over Nevada way, did you?"

"I was in Utah and Nevada was in the way between there and California," Larrabee said.

The barber cackled. "That's a good one," he said. "Nevada was in the way. Never had much use for Nevada."

"You from Nevada?"

"No sirree," the barber said. "Native Californian, I am. You know what they say. 'Miners came in forty-nine, whores in fifty-one, and when they got together they produced the native son.' Just a sayin'. Started toward Nevada once. Up north, it was. Seen some lava and a bunch of sagebrush and right then I knowed I wasn't gonna like it so I turned around and come back. No sir, this here's all right for me." He fluffed Larrabee's hair. "So you're going to work for Opal Sprague."

"She offered me a job," Larrabee said.

"Fine girl. Had to be for Frank Sprague to marry her. Salt of the earth, Frank Sprague." He stropped his razor. "Gonna help her drive those mules across the mountains?"

"If that's the job."

"Awful late in the year," the barber said. "You want to leave that mustache?"

"Take it off."

"Clean shave. You got it." He sloshed the brush around the lather cup. "Sure got a good guide. Criminal or not, that Lee Kirby knows those mountains. Course with Will Baker along, Lee Kirby ain't gonna cause no trouble. Hard man, Baker." The razor scraped against Larrabee's cheek. "Too bad about Baker's son. You knew about that, didn't you?"

"Can't say I did," Larrabee said.

"Went bad. They hanged him. Will Baker ain't never got over it. But nobody talks about that. When you talk to Will Baker don't you ever mention it."

"Hadn't planned on talking to him," Larrabee said. "I'm awful anxious to get into that hot water."

It didn't stop the barber. "I'm sure gonna earn my six bits," he said. "You got a heap of whiskers. Sort of wiry. Anybody ever tell you that?"

"Can't recall they did."

"Some barbers don't. Afraid they'll hurt the customer's feelings. Me, I speak out my mind." He made an elaborate show of stropping the razor again. "Guess you knew Opal Sprague and Lee Kirby was cousins, didn't you?"

"Nope."

"Yep, they sure are. All part of that Hoover clan. Fenton Hoover's one who escaped. They'll get him. We got a good sheriff. Soon's he gets here he'll form a real posse. Two of them convicts is killers, you know."

"Fenton Hoover one of them?"

"You foolin' me?" the barber said. "Hell, Fenton Hoover is a chicken thief. Been in and out of jail so many times, this time when they caught him they decided to give him a couple of years in the prison. Tell you one thing, though. With Fenton Hoover out of jail I wouldn't leave my horse tied on the street too long, know what I mean?"

"I'm settin' where I can see my horse," Larrabee said.

"Quite a tribe, those Hoovers," the barber said. "Livin' up there in those hills. They interbreed like a bunch of cats, way I hear it. Everybody's related to somebody else. Fenton Hoover's Opal Sprague's uncle, you know."

"You finished?" Larrabee asked.

"Sure am," the barber said, snapping his cloth. "Now like I said, you can have all the hot water you want."

"Appreciate it," Larrabee said.

It was a full hour later when Larrabee finally exited from the barbershop. Feeling expansive, he had tipped the barber a quarter, and the barber had immediately run next door to the gun shop to tell his fellow posseman everything he knew and a lot more about the drifter Opal Sprague had hired to work for her.

Larrabee had taken full advantage of the barber's offer of all the hot water he wanted. Clean-shaven, with his hair trimmed and clean clothes, he felt like a new man. The heat was still oppressive. There was no wind and a cloud cover was scudding across the sky. He glanced up at the mountains and saw the turbulent black clouds and a slash of lightning. It was raining up there, but down here in the valley there was only the oppression of increased humidity. A drink would go right good, he thought. He paused a moment to see that his horse, Snort, was all right, then went on to Dolly Varden's place.

Dolly had rejoined Will Baker at the table and when the swinging door swung wide she saw the sudden narrowing of Will Baker's eyes. "What is it?" she said.

"That's him," Will Baker said. "That's the drifter Opal Sprague hired."

Dolly Varden took a long, hard look. She saw a tall, lean man, and in any woman's eyes he would have been handsome. She liked the angular set of his jaw and the steely glint of his gray eyes and, as a woman, she sensed an inherent shyness in him, a certain aloofness that made him almost untouchable. She said to Will Baker, "That's him?"

"That's him, all right," Will Baker said.

"You're damn poor at describing people," she said. "Six-day growth of beard . . . clothes you can smell before you see him . . . ugly damn galoot . . . I'm telling you, if I were twenty years younger, that one would never get out of town until he had put his boots under my bed."

"Now, Dolly," Baker said. "I wish you wouldn't talk like that. You've been out of the business a long time."

Dolly Varden got up from the table. She pressed a forefinger against the tip of Will Baker's nose. "Who said anything about business?" she said. "I'm talking pure pleasure. That's one hell of a hunk of man."

Larrabee went up to the bar, feeling a deep sense of relaxation from the long, hot bath and was conscious of the fragrance of the toilet water the barber had provided so generously. "Whiskey," he said to the bartender.

The doors of the saloon burst open as a man was shoved violently into the room. He was followed quickly by another, fists cocked. Larrabee sized them up quickly . . . two young cowboys from one of the nearby ranches. There must be other saloons in town or these two had been here earlier because they were both beyond a little bit drunk. One said, "I hate a thief, but I hate a lyin' thief a whole bunch more."

The first cowboy had recovered his balance and he lunged forward, his fist swinging. It missed by a mile. It was doubtful he could even see his opponent. "That's too much," he said. "You finally pushed me too far."

"Then what are you gonna do about it?" the first one said.

"Gonna kill you first," the second one said, "then I'll decide."

They made a lunge toward each other and it was doubtful anyone saw Larrabee make the move, but he was there between them, one hand grasping the front of each man's shirt. He was thrusting them apart, holding them there.

"This is a private fight!" one cowboy sputtered. "You dealin' yourself in?"

"Not unless I'm invited," Larrabee said.

"Hey, Ace!" the other man said, "I smell froo-froo water. You smell it, Ace?"

"Yeah," Ace said. "I smell it. Either he just come from a whorehouse or he works in one."

Larrabee jerked the two men close. His voice was flat, hard. "There's a lady in the house," Larrabee said. "We don't need that kind of talk."

The one called Ace twisted away from Larrabee's grip. He was wearing a gun and he wasn't playing anymore. From the corner of his eye Larrabee saw Will Baker half rise from his chair. Ace's voice sounded sober. "You know something, Pony?" he said. "The froo-froo water man wants to deal himself in. Shall we invite him?"

"Let go of me, stranger," Pony said, "and we'll just have ourselves a little do-si-do."

Larrabee shrugged. "Suits me," he said, "but I think we'll lay down a few rules."

"Such as?" Ace said.

"Well," Larrabee said, "when I throw you across the room you're gonna land on some tables and chairs and bust 'em all up." He turned to Pony. "And when I toss you across the bar, maybe I'll throw you too far and you'll stick your head through that lookin' glass back there. Now them things cost money and somebody's gonna have to pay for 'em and it ain't gonna be me. This lady's got a mighty nice place here and I don't want to see it messed up, so let's the three of us just go outside where I'll have a lot more room to tromp you."

Ace and Pony looked at each other and they looked at Larrabee Lucas Stone. He was smiling, but he meant every word he said. They saw those gray eyes and the eyes weren't smiling at all. The two young cowboys had never seen such confidence in a man, and they didn't miss that well-worn cedar-butt gun on Larrabee's hip. "Hell with it," Ace said suddenly. "That wouldn't be no fun. Buy you a beer, Pony?"

"It's about time," Pony said. "You owe me three."

They went down to the far end of the bar, staying away from Larrabee Stone.

Dolly Varden stood there, looking down at Will Baker. "You didn't do much to help him," she said.

Will Baker grinned. "He didn't need any help."

Dolly moved across to the bar. "Thanks, stranger," she said. "Those two have caused me trouble before." She smiled. "Ever think of taking a job as a bouncer?"

"You offering me one?" Larrabee asked.

"The way I hear it, you've already got a job," she said.

"I don't recall saying so," he said.

"You don't have to," she said. "The walls in this town have ears. I'm Dolly Varden. I own the place. Drinks are on the house."

"Obliged," Larrabee said.

"She's a fine woman," Dolly said.

"Who?"

"Opal Sprague. I'm glad you signed on with her. She needs help bad."

From the corner of his eye Larrabee saw the blocky form of Will Baker get up from his chair and start toward the bar. Baker's chiseled features were set in hard lines. Larrabee was suddenly conscious of the holstered gun he wore, and he wished it weren't there. He hadn't done anything wrong, but in some towns a man wearing a gun stood out, and from what little he had seen of Will Baker he figured Baker was a man who could ask a lot of questions. Baker said, "What are you doing in town?"

"Came in for a bath and a shave and a haircut," Larrabee said. "Any law against that?"

"Don't push me, stranger," Will Baker said. "We got a prison break on our hands and a couple of killers loose. For all I know you might be in with 'em. I got a damn good idea to lock you up until this thing blows over."

Larrabee was a man who didn't like being pushed around. That's where Sheriff Harry Brockwell had made his mistake. He shouldn't have pushed Larrabee, and this Will Baker was doing the same thing. Larrabee was grinning, but there was a new hardness in his voice. "Seems to me that would be up to a county sheriff to decide," he said. "The way I hear it, deputy U.S. marshals just see that the prisoners get to where they're supposed to be and hand out court papers and things like that."

He couldn't have hurt Will Baker more if he had slapped him across the mouth. There had been a time when Will Baker had been a man hunter to be feared, but times had changed and he was becoming more and more an errand boy, and it was eating away at him. "I'm taking you in," Will Baker said.

"On what charge, Will?" Dolly Varden said softly. "He's got a job."

"Like hell he has," Will Baker said. "Opal's not going to drive those mules across the mountains. Rupert Cunningham's not going to give her the supplies."

"Seems I heard something about that," Larrabee said. "Mrs. Sprague told this Cunningham jigger she didn't need his damn supplies."

Larrabee couldn't quite figure Dolly Varden's part in all this, but she was certainly a lot more interested than she was in just preventing a head-on clash between these two men. She said, "What did Opal tell him?"

"Well," Larrabee drawled, "as I recall it, she told Mr. Cunningham what he could do with his supplies." He held up a hand quickly. "All ladylike, of course."

"What the hell's she gonna do?" Baker exploded.

"The way I get it, she's gonna kill a mule and make jerky out of him and get by on that," Larrabee said. He downed his drink and looked directly into Will Baker's eyes. "Now, me," he said, "I like mule jerky a whole bunch, so I'll do just fine. How about you, Marshal?"

Again he found it impossible to read the expression on Dolly Varden's face. He didn't know if she was going to laugh, cry, or just plain explode, but whichever it was, she had liked what Larrabee said. For a moment Will Baker's mouth hung slack but before he could say anything the doors of the saloon swung wide and a man stood there, stocky, wide, a black mustache slashing across his upper lip. He wore two guns and there was a star on his vest. Baker said, "Vern Ogden! By God, it's about time!"

"Got the word in Independence," Sheriff Ogden said. "Swore in a posse. We got 'em pinned down, Will. Where the creek comes into the river, right back of Opal Sprague's place."

"They got guns?" Baker snapped.

"They got a damn arsenal," Vern Ogden said. "Dan Snyder's got a knot on his head the size of a goose egg. He'll be all right, but they cleaned out his gun shop. Took every gun he had. It's gonna be a hell of a shootout, Will," the sheriff said. "I figured you'd want to be in on the kill."

"I wouldn't miss it," Will Baker said.

Larrabee thought he saw Dolly Varden's lips moving, almost as if in a prayer. She didn't utter a sound. She just stood there as Will Baker hurried after Sheriff Ogden into the gathering night. Larrabee Stone had been completely forgotten. He felt ill at ease and he said, "Sounds like they got 'em."

Dolly Varden looked at him a long time and then she said, "Did Opal Sprague really tell Rupert Cunningham what he could do with his supplies?"

"Well, ma'am," Larrabee said, "she seems like a real proper woman and she didn't say it in so many words, but I reckon Rupert Cunningham got the message all right."

Dolly Varden threw back her head and started to laugh. It was a deep down, throaty sound that seemed as if it had been wanting to come out for a long time. "God bless her heart," she said. "It's time somebody told that windbag off."

"Fact is," Larrabee said, "I really don't like mule jerky all that much."

The laugh died and a wash of concern crossed Dolly Varden's face. "You mean you're not taking the job?"

"I didn't say that," Larrabee said. "Fact is, I've been told twice if you don't have a job around here you'd wind up in jail, and I don't like being cooped up."

"Give him another drink, Gus," Dolly Varden said.

The bartender shoved the bottle down the bar. Larrabee looked at the bottle and he looked at Dolly. "Trying to get me drunk?"

"I've got a feeling it would take a lot more than that to get you drunk," she said. "Nobody's told me what you call yourself."

"Larrabee Lucas Stone," Larrabee said. "Since that's quite a mouthful, I answer to Tex real quick." He poured a drink.

Dolly watched him toy with the glass, saw him make three wet circles on the bar, then watched him down it. She said, "Tex, would you do me a favor?"

He gave her a sidelong glance, then stared down at his glass. "I've found out doing a lady a favor without knowing what it is first can get you in a whole bunch of trouble," he said.

"All I want you to do is deliver a message to Opal Sprague."

"You seem pretty sure I'm going back there."

"What you do after you deliver the message is none of my business," Dolly said.

Larrabee shrugged. "Guess it won't hurt me to listen."

"I want you to tell Opal Sprague that Rupert Cunningham changed his mind. You tell her Rupert said she can have all the supplies she needs with no strings attached. Make sure she knows there's no strings attached." She looked at him intently. "Will you do that for me, Tex?"

"Well," Larrabee said, "you bought me two drinks, so I guess I'm sort of obligated." He grinned. "Besides, I saw a lot of hay in her barn and I need a place to sleep." He touched the brim of his hat with the edge of his hand. "Appreciate your hospitality, ma'am." He turned and went outside.

It was growing dark and the black clouds obscured the moon and stars but in the half-light the mountains stood blue and ominous. A flash of lightning split the sky and for a brief second revealed those stark, granite cliffs. He swung into the saddle.

For a moment he hesitated. Why in hell didn't he just keep on riding? But he kept thinking of Opal Sprague, out there alone, and a gun battle shaping up in her backyard, and he thought of what Dolly Varden had said. He had seen Opal Sprague's face and he knew how much those supplies must mean to her. His hand was slack on the reins and the horse looked around as if asking him what he wanted to do.

"Now don't go getting any ideas, Snort," Larrabee said to the horse. "I'm just going to deliver a message and that's all."

The horse gave a startled snort at the unaccustomed dig of Larrabee's heels into its flanks. It lit out at an easy canter in the direction of Opal Sprague's ranch.

CHAPTER FIVE

IT WAS FULL DARK WHEN LARRABEE ARRIVED AT THE RANCH. High up in the peaks increasing slashes of lightning threw flares of brilliance across the blackening sky and a mumble of thunder rose intermittently above the sounds of his hoofbeats. There was a light in the window of Opal Sprague's cabin.

He dismounted and stood there a long time, telling himself he shouldn't get mixed up in this, knowing he would. He told himself he could deliver the message, get back on his horse, and ride out of there, but instead he led the horse to the barn and unsaddled.

He went across the yard then, back toward the cabin, and when he was near enough he could see the girl seated at the kitchen table. She had her face in her hands and she was leaning forward, and he saw her shoulders move, as if with silent sobs. She looked so damn small and alone and helpless. He raised his hand and knocked quietly on the door.

There was a long pause and then a voice that he remembered much more than he believed he did said, "Who is it?"

"Larrabee Lucas Stone, ma'am," he said. "The one you hired."

He waited for some time. Standing here by the door he couldn't see her movements, but in time the door opened a crack. The light from the lamp outlined half her face and the shadows made her eyes seem larger than he had remembered. He thought of spring skies and new grass and blankets of blossoms. She was staring at him, intently, as if she had never seen him before, and he remembered. He didn't look quite as he had the first time she had seen him. He managed a grin and he said, "I shaved and cleaned up a bit, but it's me, ma'am!"

The door opened wider, reluctantly, he thought, and now the light was full on her and he saw her face fully and he knew she had been crying. He said, "I was told to bring you a message."

"I didn't expect to see you again," she said. "What message?"

"Lady by the name of Dolly Varden. She said to tell you Rupert Cunningham changed his mind. He says you can have all the supplies you want, no strings attached."

She stood there staring at him, seeing a man she had never seen before in her life. He was smooth-shaven and a faint fragrance of toilet water touched her nostrils. He had kind eyes and they crinkled some now as he smiled at her. There was only the height and strength of him that seemed at all familiar. She said, "Come in. I have coffee on."

"I'd like that, ma'am," he said. She opened the door wider and he went inside, taking off his hat, feeling ill at ease. He towered over her.

She said, "Dolly Varden doesn't even know me."

"She knows you, ma'am," Larrabee said. "She said some mighty nice things about you."

"She said nice things?" She said it with the eagerness of a child seeing a gift-wrapped package, unable to believe it was for her. "What did she say?"

"That Rupert Cunningham said you can have the supplies, no strings attached."

"Yes," she said. "That." She sat down at the table, utterly confused. "I don't understand."

"Neither do I, ma'am," he said. "But she asked me to tell you."

"And you rode out here, all the way from town?"

"It wasn't nothing," he said, and he remembered how she had reacted when he had complimented her cooking.

She said, "Do you think it's true?"

"All I can do is tell you what she said."

She became even more flustered and she got up from her chair. "Sit down," she said. "I'll pour some coffee."

He sat down at the table and he saw her go to the stove and he thought again about how a woman can be beautiful just going about her ordinary household chores. She turned toward him, the coffee pot in her hand, and she was smiling. He realized he had never seen her smile before and it was like sunrise blazing across a meadow after a summer shower. "If that were true . . ." she said.

He shrugged and tried to be nonchalant but he didn't feel that way. "It's what she said, ma'am."

She came to the table and poured two cups of coffee and put the pot on the table, and then she sat down and she was suddenly a little girl, bubbling over. She said, "If I had the supplies, I know Will Baker would help me because he promised my husband he would look after me, and he was my husband's best friend, and Lee knows every pass in those mountains. . . ." She stopped, embarrassed and out of breath. "I'm sorry," she said.

"Don't be," he said. "There's been times when I wanted to do something real bad and it looked like everything was going wrong, and then, all of a sudden, things fall into place." He grinned. "It's a deep-down good feeling."

She regained her composure and with it she tried to put on a front of dignity. She was sitting here with a stranger, telling him innermost thoughts he had no right to know. "I really appreciate you telling me," she said. "I'll go into town in the morning to see if there's anything to it."

"I got a feeling there is," he said. "This Dolly Varden seemed mighty positive."

She fought herself to keep from asking what nice things Dolly Varden had said about her. She hadn't heard many nice things in her life. She said, "You want sugar or milk or anything?"

"I take it straight," he said.

"I figured you would," she said.

He didn't know why he tried to read more into that simple statement than was there, but he did. He looked across the rim of his cup and met her eyes and for a moment they held, and then she looked away. "Coffee's hot," she said.

"Yep, sure is," he said.

The discomfort between them was a swelling, pressing thing that kept growing to the point where it threatened to destroy them both, but the sharp crack of a rifle nearby broke the tension. There was an answering shot, and then another, and then a fusillade of crackling sound that rattled through the cabin. The girl was on her feet, her eyes wide, startled. He got up and stood in front of her and without knowing he was doing it he put his hands on her arms.

"The sheriff got a posse," he said. "I heard it in town. Said they got those escaped convicts surrounded. Out here back of your place."

"Oh my God!" she said, and she was suddenly near him, her face pressed tightly against his chest. He put his arm around her and held her close, trying to protect her from her thoughts.

"Maybe your uncle wasn't with the other two," he said. "He was alone when he came here. Maybe he got away."

She looked up at him and all the tension of the past few days spilled over and she was no longer trying to control her tears. She was crying, and the tears ran down her cheeks, and every thought that had been in her mind exploded at once. "I thought I was through with it," she said. "I tried. God how I tried."

"It's all right," he said.

He stroked her hair, and her face was buried against his chest and her voice was muffled. "Just because I'm a Hoover," she said. "I didn't choose the name. I haven't done anything, but I'm a Hoover. I thought if I got married and changed my name, but it's no good. Nobody will give me a chance. I've got a contract on those mules. If I could have delivered them . . ."

"We'll do it, ma'am," he said.

"I was crazy to even think about it."

She was warm and soft and he felt the sobs shaking her body. She had endured too much, and now she was there in his arms, her soul naked and raw and exposed. Another explosion of rifle fire echoed through the cabin and he felt her tense against him as if one of the bullets had ripped into her flesh. "I could have made it on my own," she said. "I know I could have."

"We can still do it," he said.

She seemed to have heard him for the first time, and she heard that pronoun "we." Until now, she had been entirely alone, and she still didn't believe what she heard. Only then did she realize he was holding her. Her sobs stopped and she pushed away from him and looked up at him, searching his face, trying to read his thoughts. She said, "You were in town. People talk. You must know about me."

"Yes, ma'am," he said. "I guess I do. You're too stubborn to sign away your ranch to get the supplies you need. You expect to drive fifty mules across those mountains with half the help you need. It's late in the season, and God knows what kind of weather you'll find." He started to grin. "Don't make much sense," he said, "but I guess I'm like you. I'm just bullheaded enough to think we can do it."

He saw those incredibly blue eyes, wet with tears, and her face was flooded with a hope she didn't dare believe. But there it was again. He had said "we." She said, "You mean you'd take the job?"

"Let's put it this way, ma'am," he said. "I'm dead set on going to Millerton. That's where you're delivering those mules. If I was to get paid for a trip I was going to make anyway . . ."

"I'll pay you," she said. "I'll pay you well as soon as I deliver the mules."

"I expect you to, ma'am," he said.

She was totally flustered, embarrassed by her outburst, and suddenly at a loss to know what to do with her hands. She started to fuss with her hair, decided against it, put her hands across her breasts, and then took them away quickly. A single rifle shot rang out. It seemed to smash through the cabin. He saw her catch her breath.

"I heard in town your uncle wasn't a killer. He strikes me as a loner. Probably ain't even with the other two."

"He was kind to me," she said. "Ever since I was a little girl. He said I wasn't like the others."

"I figure he was right, ma'am," Larrabee said.

She wasn't used to compliments and she didn't know how to handle them. "You have to believe me," she said. "I know he's been in lots of trouble, but he's a good man."

"I believe you," he said.

"The shooting's stopped," she said.

They stood there, the two of them, and now there was a wall between them, and there was no reason there should be except that he was a man and she was a woman. He said, "Will Baker knows you're here alone. Maybe he'll come by."

"No," she said. "He won't."

He fumbled for words and said, "Will you be all right?"

"Yes," she said.

"I'll sleep in the barn," he said.

She nodded.

He started toward the door and she said, "Mr. Stone?"

"Yes, ma'am?" he asked.

"Do you mind if I call you Larrabee?"

"It's my name. I answer to Tex if it's easier."

"I like the name Larrabee," she said. "Mine's Opal."

For a moment he stood there, looking at her, so alone, a totally desirable woman, so torn by emotion she was completely vulnerable. He put on his hat and nodded, not trusting himself to speak. Another time . . . another place.

Her voice was soft. "Good night, Larrabee," she said.

He smiled. "Good night, Opal." He went out into the night and he felt his heart beating high in his chest. He walked rapidly toward the barn. When he entered, his horse nickered quietly. He turned on the animal and his voice was harsh. "All right, goddamnit," he said. "So I lied to you. I took the job."

Dolly Varden poured herself a shot of whiskey and downed it. It was an unusual thing for her to do. The doors of the saloon opened and a deputy sheriff came in. He said, "They got 'em. One of 'em is shot all to hell but he'll live to hang, I reckon."

"Will all right?"

"Ten feet tall," the deputy said. "Ain't another man on earth likes running a lawbreaker down the way Will Baker does. He told me to stand guard outside Lee Kirby's room. Guess in the excitement he forgot all about Lee."

"He's up there," Dolly said. "If he had come out I would have seen him." She paused. "Did they get all three of them?"

"Only two," the deputy said. "Fenton Hoover wasn't with them." He crossed the room and went up the stairs.

On the far side of the valley where the land sloped up through sagebrush and tumbled boulders to meet the granite shoulder of the mountains, Fenton Hoover crouched in the night darkness of man-planted locus trees that surrounded the neat ranch house. There was a light in the window and he had watched it a long time, just as he had watched the four horses in the corral. There was a big sorrel he fancied above the others. In time the light went out and Fenton Hoover made his move.

High above him in the towering spires he knew so well, thunder muttered, and at times flashes of lightning gave him a second look at the horses in the corral. He had heard the distant crackle of sound from over near the river and he knew it for gunfire. He didn't care. The two convicts meant nothing to him. There had been much confusion over their escape; the prison gate was open and he had walked out. It had been as simple as that. He moved slowly toward the corral.

Long experience had given him a way with horses, and the owner of the ranch had thoughtfully left a saddle, a bridle, and a blanket on the corral fence. It was as if a providence Fenton didn't really believe in had stepped in to help. He spoke softly to the big sorrel that had caught his eye.

The window in the farmhouse was still dark, and he led the sorrel from the corral and saddled it carefully, smoothing the blanket with his hand. He swung into the saddle then and rode quietly away from the ranch. High in the peaks the thunder crackled and fat drops of warm rain splashed against his face. *Let's have more of it,* he said to himself. *Rain wipes out tracks real good.*

The slope of the land was gradual but steady, and when he looked back the lights of the town were below him. He grinned broadly as the rain pelted against his face. The sagebrush thinned and he came to the first clump of juniper. Another mile . . . two maybe, he would come to the first pines.

A moment of worry pinched the corners of his faded eyes. He thought of Opal and hoped she was all right. He wouldn't hurt Opal, even if it meant giving himself up. The land rose beneath the hooves of the big sorrel and the mouth of a canyon loomed ahead, starkly outlined by a flash of lightning. Opal would be all right, he told himself. She had to be all right.

He reached out and patted the neck of the stolen horse. He felt a great surge of inner peace. Fenton Hoover was going home.

For a long time after Larrabee had left the room, Opal Sprague stood there, a dozen emotions tearing through her. She hadn't even recognized Larrabee when he had come to the door. He was handsome, and there had been a tenderness in him that she had known only once before in her life, and that was a long time ago. She had been young, and Rance Overton had been so understanding, and she had so wanted someone to love her. . . . She had given herself to him willingly and then day by day she had had to face the fact that he was no different from the others. She fought the longing she had felt for him, but she knew if she were ever to escape from a life she hated she could not stay with him. And Frank Sprague had come along and it was a way out. . . . She had married him, but she had never forgotten Rance, and she knew she never would.

And now Larrabee Lucas Stone had come into her life, and for a moment she had felt that same surge of desire that had overwhelmed her when she was with Rance. She was confused and startled by the intensity of her emotions . . . emotions that had never been stirred by her husband. She hated herself for her thoughts, but she was young and vibrant and there had been so much denial in her life. . . .

She forced herself back to reality. Larrabee Stone had said he would help her. She tried to make herself believe she had heard right. Larrabee Stone had said Rupert Cunningham was going to give her credit for the needed supplies. He had said there were no strings attached. He had said that Dolly Varden had told him to say that.

She thought then of Dolly Varden. She knew who Dolly Varden was. Everyone in town talked of her and of her past, but she had never said one word to the woman. Her husband wouldn't have allowed her to. Why would Dolly Varden come to her rescue, if that's what it was?

She undressed slowly and went to bed. Could she believe Larrabee Stone? She didn't know. She had lived with deceit so much of her life. But he had seemed so sincere. But so had Rance Overton at one time. She buried her face in the pillow and she thought of Dolly Varden and, when she did, that first impression she had of Larrabee, standing there in the light of the half-opened door, kept creeping into her thoughts.

CHAPTER SIX

MORNING FOUND DOLLY VARDEN STANDING AT THE WINDOW OF her room, looking across the street to Rupert Cunningham's store. She hadn't slept that night, and that too was unusual, for Dolly Varden was a woman who knew herself well and rarely acted on impulse, but that is exactly what she had done. Perhaps it had been Will Baker's remark that Opal Sprague was "only a woman." Perhaps it was a lot more. She didn't know for sure, but on impulse she had told the drifter that Rupert Cunningham was going to give Opal Sprague the supplies she needed. She had asked him to deliver the message and she had a strong feeling the drifter had done exactly that. Now she had to back up her statement.

She went to the dresser and opened the top drawer and took out a photograph that was there and for a long time she stared down at it. It was the picture of a girl in her teens, dressed in a school uniform. Even in the photo the child's large eyes were luminous and there was a haunting loneliness in the high cheek-boned face. Her name was Theresa Shoshone, a name the sisters at a convent had given her when they took her in as a foundling when she was only a few weeks old. Shoshone, because her mother was a sixteen-year-old Indian of that tribe who had died in childbirth . . . a long time ago, Dolly thought. Now the daughter was older than the mother who had borne her.

She put the photograph away and she thought of the times

she had gone to see this girl, always dressing primly, always successful in hiding her own past from the sisters, and she thought of the letters through the years, the only contact with the outside world the child had ever known. Through the years she had told the child of the marvelous person her mother was. No, she did not know her father. But there Dolly Varden had lied. She knew who the father was, but she had kept her silence . . . a sort of unwritten code she had imposed upon herself. Today she might have to break that self-imposed code.

It seemed an eternity before the sun flooded the street and the buggy came into sight. It leaned heavily under Rupert Cunningham's weight and she saw that Rupert's wife was with him. She hadn't counted on that. The buggy pulled up in front of Rupert Cunningham's store and he got down laboriously and reached up to help his wife. She was a sparse woman with a pinched face and lips so thin they formed an indistinct slash across her face, almost like a scar. Dolly Varden took a deep breath. She had made an impulsive statement but she had made it, and Dolly Varden wasn't one to go back on her word. She went downstairs.

The brief downpour from the thunderstorm had left the fragrance of damp dust in the air, but she didn't take time to relish it. She went resolutely across the street to the store owned by the most influential man in the town. She said good morning to Rupert's wife and got no reply. She hadn't expected one. To a clerk she said, "Rupert in his office?" She saw Rupert Cunningham's wife wince at the intimacy Dolly had shown by using her husband's first name.

"Sure is, Miss Dolly," the clerk said, and she went directly to the office.

Rupert Cunningham sat at his desk, shuffling through a pile of papers. He looked up and smiled his Santa Claus smile. "You're out early," he said.

Regardless of what else she was, Dolly Varden was not one to waste time on preliminaries. She said, "Rupert, I want you to do me a favor."

She could read the man like a book and she knew those

words were absolute music to his ears. He loved having people ask him for a favor, because when he granted one they would go out and brag about how good Rupert had been to them. Pride would keep them from mentioning they had given Rupert ten times more than they had received. It was his entire code of life, and he had become rich and powerful by applying it. And then she saw a hint of worry in his eyes. He knew that Dolly Varden was not one to ask for favors. He leaned back in his chair, expansive, but on guard. He said, "If I can do it, I will. We've been friends a long time."

"Let's say we've *known* each other a long time," she said.

Again she saw that hint of caution in his eyes. "Money?" he asked.

"You know better," she said.

"What, then?"

"I want you to give Opal Sprague those supplies she ordered."

"Well if that's all it is," he said, "There's no problem. I fully intended to."

"Provided she signed over her ranch to you."

The Santa Claus mask was fading. She saw the tension growing in him and knew he was trying to figure out what she was getting at. "That's a damn lie," he said. "I asked her to give me some security, that's all."

"Horseshit," she said. "You're talking to Dolly, remember?"

Rupert Cunningham's face was starting to flush. "What's this sudden interest in Opal Sprague?" he said.

"I've seen a dozen like her, that's all," Dolly said. "Impossible home situations . . . they have to get away. A lot of them came to me because there was nothing else for them to do. Opal took a different way. She married a man old enough to be her grandfather. Maybe going to work for me would have been easier."

There was a bluster in Rupert's voice now, but it was a cover-up. He said, "Frank Sprague was one of the finest men who ever lived in this valley."

"He was a tightfisted, sanctimonious, miserable old son of a bitch," Dolly said.

Rupert glanced at the door. He could see his wife moving around inside the store. His voice was a bare whisper. "What the hell are you getting at?" he asked.

"I told you. I want you to give Opal Sprague those supplies with no strings attached."

"You're out of your mind!" he said. "She doesn't have enough help . . . it's late in the fall, and God knows what kind of weather she'll hit. . . ."

"Would you have given them to Frank Sprague?" she asked.

"Of course I would have," he said. "That's an entirely different thing."

"Because Frank Sprague was too smart to sign one of your agreements, or because she's a woman?"

Rupert Cunningham's forehead was showing fine beads of sweat. "Because I'm a businessman," he said.

"Then your answer is no?"

"You're damn right it is. You can't come in here telling me how to run my business." She could see the confidence returning.

"All right, Rupert," she said. "If that's your answer."

She saw the full confidence returning. He got up from his desk and came across and put a pudgy arm around her shoulder. "No hard feelings," he said. "You're in business, just like I am. You can see how it is."

"Of course," she said. She started toward the door. She hadn't wanted to play her trump card, but she knew now she would have to. She stopped, turned toward him, and said, "By the way, I had a letter from Theresa."

She saw the quick caution come back into his eyes. "So?" he said. "You've had other letters."

"She's eighteen years old," Dolly said. "She won't be Theresa Shoshone much longer. She'll be Sister Theresa."

She thought she detected a slight trembling in Rupert Cunningham's hands. He went back to his desk, a position that gave him a feeling of power. He started to shuffle through some papers. "It's what she wanted," he said.

"At eighteen," Dolly said, "I figure it's time she knows who her real father is."

Rupert's hands froze. He didn't look at her, but he stood up slowly. His lips didn't move when he spoke. "Are you trying to blackmail me?" he said.

"Is that what you call it?" she said. "I'm not much up on legal terms."

In spite of the puffiness of his features, his face had drawn into a tight mask of menace. "You can't bluff me, damn you," he said.

"I didn't expect to," Dolly said. "But if I explained it all to your wife, she's such a good Christian I know she would understand." She went to the door and said, "Mrs. Cunningham? May I see you a moment?"

Rupert Cunningham was out of his chair with the agility of a cat. He lunged across the room and slammed the door closed. He stood there, leaning against it. His face was red and perspiring and his breath was panting through his nose. "All right, damn it," he said. "I'll give her the supplies. But if you ever try to pull anything like this on me again . . ."

"I know," she said. "You'll kill me. It will make a fine headline for Jason down at the newspaper. VALLEY'S LEADING CITIZEN KILLS WHORE IN DISPUTE OVER HER FEES. Jason would love it. He can't run this prison break story forever."

The door opened and Mrs. Cunningham stood there. "Did I hear someone call me?" she asked.

"No. No, dear," Rupert said. "Miss Varden just asked to be remembered to you."

Dolly smiled at the tall, sparse woman with the pinched face and, still smiling, undulated her way through the door. Mrs. Cunningham's face looked as if she had just swallowed a lemon. Her teeth were clenched when she said, "I wish you didn't have to deal with that sort of scum."

"She's a customer, dear," Rupert said. "She pays her bills."

"With dirty money," Mrs. Cunningham said. "The blatant hussy." She elevated her nose and snorted as if to drive all disagreeable odors from the room. "But I suppose you're right. Business is business and you take the good with the bad."

"Exactly, dear," Rupert said. "The good with the bad."
He went over to his desk and sat down heavily.

"Don't forget," his wife said, "the church board of trust-
ees meets at two o'clock this afternoon. Don't you dare be
late."

"I won't, dear," Rupert said.

"Well see that you don't," she said. She was half muttering to herself when she said, "Gallivanting around all night
chasing criminals, dealing with women like that . . ." She
snorted again and left the room.

Outside, Rupert heard the approaching wagon, the sound of
casual greetings. He got up and went to his office window
which overlooked the street and he saw the spring wagon.
Opal Sprague was on the seat and a man was driving. He
looked vaguely familiar, and then Rupert knew who he was.
It was Larrabee Stone, the drifter who called himself Tex.

Damn it, Rupert thought to himself, *maybe I can still find a
way out.* He got up and went into the main part of the store.
Through the open front door he saw Dolly Varden, still
standing there on his porch. *So help me God, I'll kill that
woman,* he thought. He left the office and went out into the
store, the smile broad on his face. He was once again the
benevolent Santa Claus who had done favors for everyone in
this end of the valley.

Opal Sprague sat on the seat of the spring wagon, her
hands folded demurely. It had been one of the strangest
mornings of her life.

She had gotten up early, as she always did, and out of habit
she had gone to the window and looked out at the splendor of
the White Mountains. And then she had seen Larrabee,
mounted, riding through her pasture, looking over the mules
with the casual glance of an auctioneer. Big Blue, her pet
mule, was following along behind Larrabee like a dog.

She dressed hurriedly and went outside just as Larrabee
was riding into the yard, the blue mule still following him.
"Morning, ma'am," he said. "That's a right fine bunch of
mules you've got out there."

The big blue mule saw her and trotted over to her, nuzzling
her shoulder. She patted the animal's nose and to Larrabee
she said, "Seems you've made a friend."

"Big Blue?" he said. He grinned and she wished he
wouldn't do that. He was so damned handsome and she had
hoped she had put those thoughts out of her mind. She
thought of Rance Overton and of the first time she had seen
him and of how her entire insides had gone to jelly . . . *I was
just a kid,* she thought. *I'll never make a mistake like that
again.* She looked at the angular young man beside her on the
seat of the spring wagon, and she wasn't at all sure she
believed what she was thinking.

They had had breakfast together and the list of supplies she
needed so desperately was there on the table. She hadn't
bothered to put it away. She was amazed at how much it
pleased her to have him ask for a second helping.

There had been little conversation during the morning meal.
There were too many conflicting thoughts in her mind to let
her descend to small talk. She glanced at him covertly from
time to time, trying to read him, and she knew she couldn't.
She remembered last night and the confident way he had told
her Rupert Cunningham had decided to give her the supplies,
no strings attached. God, how she wanted to believe that, but
she knew she couldn't, and yet she couldn't just sit back and
ignore the whole thing . . .

"Some of those mules look like they've had packsaddles
on them," he said.

"There are rich people come over from San Francisco,"
she said. "My husband used to pack them back into the high
country for trout fishing. Leave them there a week and then
go back and get them when he had a day off from the
prison." She flipped a hotcake in the pan. "It paid well,"
she said.

"I looked around," he said. "Figured you'd need the
spring wagon to pick up those supplies. I cut out a couple of
mules that acted like they were broke to harness."

"There are at least a dozen work mules out there," she
said.

There was that grin again. Annoying and tantalizing. He said, "Big Blue said these were a couple of good ones."

She thought of how often she had spoken aloud to Big Blue. She always felt guilty about it but when you were alone . . . "That's silly," she said.

"Talking to animals?" he said. "Sometimes I get darned sight better answers than when I'm talking to humans."

If he only knew how close that came to her own feelings . . . She said, "Sorry, but this is the last of the hotcakes."

The rest of the meal had gone in silence. She stole a glance at him from time to time and she thought of how good it was to have someone near her own age sitting there at the table, and then the thoughts of Rance Overton came back and she tried her best to shove them aside, but she never could. She remembered the small vegetable garden she had in back of the house and of how she had gotten a much bigger thrill out of watching her turnips grow than she had ever had going to bed with her husband. She hated those thoughts. They were immoral and unnatural, but they were there. When Rance Overton had taken her in his arms she had wanted to give everything of herself she had to give and she had . . . Larrabee Stone said, "Ma'am, if you're worried about picking up those supplies, I thought maybe I could go along with you."

How did he know that she wanted to hear that more than anything else on earth? She said, "If you want."

She had loved the drive into town with the wide valley and its scatter of cottonwoods, and the murmur of the stream, and the magnificent splendor of the mountains, glacier-streaked and gray in the morning sun, looming there ahead of them. She hadn't gone to town often. Her husband had taken care of the shopping and the everyday affairs. It was a woman's job to cook and to sew and to be there when a man wanted her . . .

They came into the town and reined up in front of Rupert Cunningham's store, and she was surprised to see Dolly Varden standing there in the doorway.

She wasn't so innocent that she didn't know who Dolly

Varden was. She had seen her before, but she had always been with Frank, and Frank had told her that no decent woman would talk to Dolly Varden. When she had asked him why, he had said, "Because I said so."

Secretly, Dolly Varden fascinated her. She wished she could know the woman and talk to her, because for the past few years there had been very few women with whom she had any contact. She went into the store with Larrabee following her, and Dolly Varden smiled at her but she didn't speak, and Opal thought of what an open and friendly and warm smile it was. Rupert Cunningham was standing in the door of his office. It seemed to her he was not quite the beaming father figure she had come to know. She noticed then that Dolly Varden had followed them in. Cunningham said, "You got that list?"

"Right here," she said. She handed him the piece of paper and he scowled down at it, running his eyes back and forth.

"Enough here to feed an army," Cunningham said.

"The high country gives a man an appetite," she said.

He grunted and motioned to his two clerks. He handed them the paper and said, "Give her what she wants." She saw the faint smile on Dolly Varden's lips.

Cunningham stood there and she thought she saw beads of perspiration on his forehead. She felt she should say something, and she said the first thing that came to her mind. "I figured we'd kill a deer along the way and have some fresh meat."

"If they haven't all moved down already," Rupert said. "Could snow up there any day, you know." He sounded almost as if he wished it would.

She followed the clerks as they started accumulating the various items. The store was like any other general merchandise store. There were shelves of canned goods and racks of picks and axes, and bolts of cloth and the inevitable pickle barrel and tin-lined bins that pulled out from under the counter to release their faint fragrance of coffee beans and the imperceptible smell of flour and sugar. The pungency of oiled floors mixed with the acrid tang of new leather that seeped from the racks of harness and the saddles astride sawhorses. She saw Dolly Varden and Larrabee Stone standing near each other, and although the words weren't intended for her ears, she heard Dolly say, "I see you delivered the message."

"Did you think I wouldn't?" Larrabee said.

"It crossed my mind," Dolly said.

She was puzzled by the exchange, but one of the clerks had moved over to the harness wall and he was taking down a halter. He smiled at Opal and said, "That's a lot of halters. I'll have to get 'em out of the warehouse."

She heard Larrabee say, "About those halters, Mr. Cunningham. That's a pretty high price you're asking."

She turned and looked at him, his interruption so totally unexpected. She saw a new expression on the face of Rupert Cunningham. His features were hard and set. "Don't see where it's any of your business," Cunningham said. "This ain't Los Angeles or San Francisco, you know. I got to pay freight on what's brought in here."

"How many feet in that coil of cotton rope?" Larrabee asked.

"Two hundred and fifty," Cunningham said. It was an automatic answer.

"We'll take two coils," Larrabee said.

The rage that had been building in Rupert Cunningham ever since his encounter with Dolly Varden spilled over. There was nothing he could do to contain it. He wasn't a violent man, and the young, lean cowboy who stood in front of him was more than a match for him, but at this moment he didn't give a damn. The words exploded across his lips, "I don't take orders from no damn saddle tramp!" he said, and even that wasn't enough. He moved forward and shoved Larrabee hard. He had amazing strength for a man of his girth.

Larrabee, caught off guard, stumbled back a step. His heel caught on a case of harness parts and he went down, hard. He snapped to his feet like a coiled spring. It had all happened so fast there was no way to react. The two clerks froze and Opal stood there, staring at Larrabee. She had never seen such open hatred in a man's face in her life. She was almost sure Larrabee would reach for his gun, but he didn't. He moved forward with the same motion that had brought him to his feet, and his left hand shot out and gripped Rupert Cunningham by the shirt front. He twisted his hand and jerked the massive man close.

"I don't like being shoved, fat man," Larrabee said. Opal didn't even recognize his voice. He said, "Don't you ever put a hand on me again."

The naked rage in Larrabee's face was a frightening thing to see. She remembered his smile and the softness of his voice, and the way he had put his arm around her last night, and she thought *this man would kill.* . . . Larrabee shoved Rupert away. "And I'll need a bunch of harness rings and snaps, too," Larrabee said.

"You heard the man, Rupert," Dolly said softly.

Opal turned quickly and looked fully at Dolly Varden for the first time. She wasn't used to the powder and rouge and the tease of curls that fell provocatively over Dolly's forehead. She felt a moment of envy. Dolly Varden looked as a woman should look.

The clerks were at a total loss. The second of violence in Larrabee Stone hadn't been lost on them, but Rupert Cunningham was their boss. They looked at Rupert, the open question in their eyes. Rupert's bulging eyes were protruding even farther. He stared at Larrabee and physical fear honed the edge of his rage. He said, "Give them the whole goddamn store if that's what they want. What the hell do I care?" He turned and went into his office and slammed the door shut behind him.

It was only then that Opal recovered her voice. "What happened?"

"Forget it, dear," Dolly Varden said. "Rupert was up all night with that posse. He's just out of sorts, that's all." She turned to the clerks. "And six quarts of whiskey," she said.

Opal said, "I didn't order whiskey."

Dolly Varden came over and put a hand on her arm. "Now, honey," she said, "you have three grown men to watch out for. It gets cold up in the high country and after a long day men can get real fussy, just like Rupert did now. There's nothing makes a man feel better than squattin' down by a campfire at night with a little whip of whiskey in the bottom of his tin cup." She turned to Larrabee, "That right, Tex?"

"Sounds good to me," Larrabee said. He was as totally relaxed as if the ugly incident hadn't happened, but Opal could never forget the wash of savage rage she had seen in his face, the momentary terror she had felt. She didn't know this man at all, and she was letting him give orders. She felt as if she had suddenly been left out of things . . . as if Dolly and Larrabee had taken over . . .

The clerks, with the help of Larrabee, loaded the wagon, and Opal stood by, feeling useless. She felt Dolly Varden's hand on her arm. The hand was soft and warm and friendly and reassuring. Dolly said, "I thought you'd want to know. They caught two of the convicts last night. Your uncle wasn't with them."

Opal felt a surge of relief. She met Dolly's eyes and said, "Thank you."

Dolly squeezed her arm. "You're gonna do fine, honey," she said. "You listen to Tex. He's a good man."

Opal searched her face eagerly. "You knew him before?"

Dolly shook her head. "I've been around men most of my life," she said. "You get so you can spot the good ones from the bad ones." Opal watched as Dolly went through the door. She saw her say something to Larrabee and she saw Larrabee grin at her, and then Dolly went on across the street, back to the hotel. There was something almost regal about the way she walked. She could see Larrabee securing a tarp over the load, his hands nimble as he tied everything in place, a reassuring man who seemed to know exactly what he was doing. Rupert Cunningham came out of his office.

He glanced around the store and then said to Opal, "You just remember this bill is a lien against the money you get for those mules." He sounded like a man who was desperately trying to show he still had authority.

"My husband always paid his bills," Opal said. "I intend to do the same." She went out to the wagon, and Larrabee was standing there, that easy smile on his face.

"Anything more?" he asked. "Or do you want to head on back?"

"I want to go home," she said. She started to climb up into the wagon but he was there at her side, his strong hand under her elbow. She let him assist her up and felt the confidence of the man as he took his seat and unwrapped the lines from around the brake lever. He turned the wagon and headed up the street and she sat there beside him, staring straight ahead, more confused than she had ever been in her life.

Inside the office, Rupert Cunningham stood at the window and watched them go. He was trembling, and he kept seeing the face of the drifter, drawn with rage. He had the feeling he had been facing death, and the thought scared the devil out of him. He went back to his desk, a place of security. He sat down and lowered his face into his hands. It had been a miserable morning. Dolly . . . his wife . . . Opal Sprague . . . and an eighteen-year-old girl whose only known last name was Shoshone . . .

Eighteen years. He had gone to Dolly because she was the only woman in town he could talk to about a thing like that. She had handled it well and kept her mouth shut all of these years, and he had supposed she always would, but he knew better than to try to call her bluff.

Rupert Cunningham felt sick to his stomach. He wished his wife would come in and say something about that church trustee meeting this afternoon. He'd tell her to get the hell out of here and leave him alone, that's what he'd do. And he knew he wouldn't. It suddenly seemed to Rupert Cunningham that women were taking over the world and he didn't like it one damn bit.

CHAPTER SEVEN

LARRABEE LUCAS STONE WHISTLED A SOFT TUNE AS HE DROVE the wagon back toward Opal Sprague's ranch. If he was conscious of her sitting there beside him, her hands clenched in her lap, he didn't show it. In time he said, "Sorry I lost my temper there for a minute."

She glanced at him and at that moment he looked like a man who had never lost his temper in his life. She was at a loss for words, and she said, "You thought he was charging too much for those halters."

He looked fully at her and grinned. "We've got cotton rope, harness rings, snaps . . . shucks, I can make those halters for one tenth of what he wanted for his."

"I have some halters," she said.

"Twelve," he said. "I counted them this morning. Five or six of them are in pretty bad shape. No matter, though. I'll fix 'em up. There's plenty of rivets out there in the blacksmith shop."

He sounded as if he knew more about her place than she did.

"That cowhide hanging there in the barn," he said. "If you didn't have plans for it, I thought I could cut it up. I found a quart of neat's-foot oil. I could soak the hide and replace some of the straps on those kyacks. Some of them are pretty frayed."

She felt she was losing control . . . that this stranger had moved in and in one day had taken over completely. She felt a quick surge of rebellion. "And what other plans do you have?" she said.

"I was figuring on going along with yours," he said. "With all those halters, you must figure we can't just loose-herd those mules."

There was a smugness in this man that was totally irritating. "Four people with fifty mules? Any idiot would know you can't loose-herd them."

"Not at first, anyway," he said. "Mules are funny critters, though. We'll probably find that after a couple of days ten or twelve of them will just sort of trail-break themselves and with Big Blue leadin' 'em . . ." He squinted off into the distance. "I've seen that happen."

"You've driven mules before?"

"Yes, ma'am, I have," he said. "Couple of years back I helped drive fourteen hundred head from North Powder, Oregon, clean back to Cheyenne, Wyoming."

"Fourteen hundred!" she said. "How big a crew did you have?"

"Twelve wranglers and a troop of horse soldiers," he said. "And even then it wasn't too easy. Mules can get sort of unpredictable at times."

"I know," she said. He glanced at her and saw the worry coming back into her eyes. He looked ahead, avoiding those eyes. He didn't like seeing hurt in them.

He said, "This Will Baker . . . you can count on him going along?"

"He was my husband's best friend," she said. "When Will Baker gives you his word it's as good as his bond."

"And the other one?" he said. "The one you're helping out?"

She felt a sudden annoyance. "What makes you think I'm helping him out?"

Larrabee was watching the road ahead. He shrugged. "Man gets out of prison . . . you offer him a job . . . I'd say that's helping him out."

She disliked the way he anticipated her thoughts and yet

when he gave an answer it was always perfectly logical. She said, "Lee Kirby is my cousin. We've known each other since we were kids. As for me helping him out, that goes both ways. He knows mules and he knows those mountain passes better than anyone else."

"I see," he said. For a long time he was silent and then he turned, and perhaps it was the way the sun hit his face or perhaps it was his smile, but he was the same man who had put his arm around her and held her close when she had heard the rifle fire. She tried to reconcile the face she was seeing with the face she had seen in that instant when he had lunged at Rupert Cunningham, and she couldn't do it. He said, "You know something, Opal? Seems to me we've got a right fine crew. We're gonna deliver those mules for you, and I don't see where you got one thing to worry about."

He was so downright positive about it she felt a surge of assurance run through her. He was actually a total stranger to her but she believed him and she was glad he was here.

Larrabee slapped the lines against the backs of the mules. He glanced back at the mountains . . . tall spires of granite rising sheer from the floor of the valley. A thin wisp of clouds threw a veil across the uppermost peaks. "Not one thing to worry about," he said again. Deep inside he wished he could believe what he was saying.

The silence seemed endless. From time to time she glanced at him, totally aware of his nearness. She kept thinking of Dolly Varden and of how she and Larrabee had seemed so at ease around each other. She wished she would feel that way, but she couldn't. She thought of the whiskey and of what Dolly Varden had said, and of how quickly Larrabee had agreed. She said, "What's a whip of whiskey?"

He glanced at her quickly, his expression almost puzzled, and then his features relaxed and he stared at the road. "Well," he said, "depends a lot on a man's drinking habits. Could be anything between a dollop and three fingers in a washtub."

"Oh," she said. She didn't have the faintest idea of what he was talking about. She had a feeling that deep down inside he was laughing at her, and it made her mad. *Damn it,* she thought, *I wish I were a little more like Dolly Varden.*

She thought of the look that would have been on her late husband's face if he had suspected she could harbor such thoughts.

Will Baker awoke suddenly and turned his head to avoid the glare of brilliant sunshine that was pouring through the window. He looked at the other side of the bed, and Dolly wasn't there, but the faint fragrance of her lingered in the room, and her presence was in the frilly curtains at the window and the fancy coverlet on the bed. He got up slowly, feeling the stiffness in his joints, and he went over to where his vest hung neatly on the back of a chair and lifted out the heavy gold watch. He snapped it open and felt a surge of disgust with himself. It was almost noon.

He dressed, and saw that water had been poured for him in the huge china basin that sat on the marble-top commode. A white linen towel had been laid out carefully for him. He sloshed water on his face, dried it, and then stopped short, staring at himself in the mirror. He had forgotten about Lee Kirby.

A deputy had been assigned to guard the kid, but damn it, it was Will Baker's job and he had let fatigue and the pleasure of Dolly cloud his thinking. He went out into the hall and looked down toward Lee Kirby's room. There was an empty chair outside the door, but no deputy.

Feeling a quick surge of guilt, every inch the lawman now, he went to Lee Kirby's room. The door was open and the bed looked as if it hadn't been used. The coverlet was taut, folded precisely over the pillow. He looked across the room and saw the open window. It might have been opened for ventilation; it could have led to escape over the first-floor porch.

Something akin to panic gripped the pit of Will Baker's stomach. In his thirty years as a lawman he had never lost a prisoner. The fact that technically Lee wasn't a prisoner was lost on him. He hurried down the hall and went quickly down the stairs. There were perhaps a dozen men in the dining room bar. They all turned at once and looked at him, and he felt another discomfort. Everyone knew about his relationship with Dolly. It was just one more of Twin Pines' well-kept secrets but he felt the thoughts of every man at that bar. Dolly was seated alone at a table and he went directly to her.

"Where in hell is Lee Kirby?" he said.

"Don't get your blood pressure up," Dolly said calmly. "He's with Vern Ogden."

"What the hell's the sheriff doing with him?" Baker snapped.

"Trying to find out if Lee knows anything about where Fenton Hoover disappeared to, I imagine," Dolly said.

He felt embarrassed by the simplicity of the answer. "Yeah," he said, "I guess he would. Won't do no good."

Dolly made an almost imperceptible hand signal to the bartender. "Sit down, Will," she said. "Have a cup of coffee."

"I better get over to Vern Ogden's office," he said.

"The sheriff can handle things just fine," she said. "Sit down."

He was blowing this whole thing way out of proportion and he knew it. The bartender came across with a cup of steaming coffee, and Baker caught the warm fragrance of whiskey. He sat down. The bartender put the cup on the table and went back to his work. Baker looked across the table at Dolly, grinned faintly, and said, "I got to admit it does smell good."

"Kentucky bourbon," she said. "Your favorite." He sipped deeply of the scalding coffee and felt the warmth of it and the whiskey seep through his stomach. "I fixed Lee a big breakfast," she said. "He ate like a horse. First decent meal he's had in two years, I guess."

"More than he deserves," Baker grumbled.

"He's a good kid, Will," she said.

The remark angered him beyond reason. "They're all good kids," he said sharply. "That's what I kept telling myself about Billy. I kept telling everybody he was just a little wild . . . just being a boy. I even believed it myself. He wound up with a rope around his neck." He fought down the emotion and to cover it he reached into his vest pocket and took out the heavy gold watch and snapped it open and stared down at it.

Dolly's hand reached across the table and closed over his. Her voice was soft. "Your father must have thought as much of that watch as he did that locomotive headlight of his," she said. "When he left it to you, I think he was trying to tell you something."

"He should have told me when he was alive," Will Baker said. He gulped down the remainder of his whiskey-laced coffee and stood up abruptly. "I'm going over to Vern's office," he said. He turned and tramped heavily out of the saloon, and the men at the bar turned and glanced at his back, then went back to their drinking.

He stood on the sidewalk a moment, taking a deep breath. It was hot, and yet there was a feel of fall in the air, a certain indefinable quiet, a passing of summer, a lonely time. He angled across the street toward the sheriff's office.

As he approached the office, he heard a burst of youthful laughter and a pain shot through him. It sounded like the way Billy used to laugh. He opened the door and Sheriff Vern Ogden sat tilted back in his chair, his feet on his desk. Lee Kirby was sitting across the desk from him, and they both had cups of coffee in front of them. Vern Ogden looked up and said, "Will. Get some sleep?"

"He tell you anything about Fenton Hoover?" Baker said.

"Bill Lloyd was in this morning," Vern Ogden said. "He lost a horse and a saddle last night. Lee and I figure Fenton's headed for the high country."

"I could have told you that," Baker snorted. "That damn Fenton Hoover could steal the gold out of your teeth."

Lee Kirby was grinning. "Provided he didn't talk you out of it first," he said.

Baker turned on him savagely. "You're damn proud of him, ain't you? Him and all the rest of your thieving relatives. You're all alike, the whole damn bunch of you!"

There was a quick tension in Lee Kirby's young face. He stood up slowly and said, "I'm going out and get some air."

He went outside and stood there on the sidewalk, in full view of Will Baker and Vern Ogden.

"You taking the boy out to Opal's?" Ogden asked.

"It's what the damn papers say, ain't it?" Baker said.

"It was good of Opal to give him a job driving those mules across to Millerton," Vern Ogden said. "That went a long way toward getting him his parole."

"I'm not sure she's even gonna drive those mules across," Baker said. "Rupert hasn't decided to give her the supplies she's got to have."

"Rupert must have changed his mind," Ogden said. "She and her hired hand came in this morning and loaded up."

It was the first Will Baker had heard of it, and he tried to conceal his surprise. "Well," he said. "I talked to Rupert. Told him to bend a little if he could." He felt totally ill at ease. He said, "Her hired hand?"

"That drifter."

"And there's another thing," Will Baker said. "Who in hell is he? Might be on the run himself for all we know."

"If he is I haven't heard about it," Vern Ogden said.

"That don't mean a damn thing," Baker muttered. Ogden had taken his feet off the desk.

"I know Opal well enough to know she's going to try to deliver those mules," Ogden said.

"There's your key word right there," Baker said. "Try. You taken a look at your calendar lately? You see that thunderstorm that hit last night?"

"If anybody can get through those mountains, Lee Kirby can," Ogden said. He shuffled through some papers, then looked up. "I rented a horse for Lee over there at the livery. You can bring it in when you come back to town. County's paying for it." He grinned at Will Baker. "Lee's a good kid," he said.

He might as well have exploded a bomb under the feet of Will Baker. "What the hell's the matter with all of you?" he shouted. "You're treating that punk like he just graduated from high school or something! Goddamnit, he's a criminal!

Can't you get that through your heads? I give him three months and he'll be back inside those walls!''

"Maybe not, Will," Vern Ogden said patiently. "He's got a damn good job in a bank waiting for him once he gets to Millerton." He glanced down at his desk. "His papers say all you have to do is see he gets to Millerton."

"Papers!" Will Baker exploded. "That's the trouble with the law today. Everything's done on paper. Well, by God, it was different in my time, Vern. You and me come from a different school. The nicer you are to these bastards, the sooner they'll turn on you. You'll find that out, Vern. The hard way.''

He stalked outside and Lee Kirby was standing there on the sidewalk. Baker looked at him a long time and said, "It's all going your way, ain't it?"

"It's good to be outside, if that's what you mean," Lee Kirby said.

"A good bed to sleep in, a big breakfast, a horse to ride at county expense . . . What more do you want?"

"To get to Millerton and get settled down," Lee Kirby said.

"It's all so damn easy. Two years inside and then everybody treats you like a hero. They're a bunch of suckers. You get your belly full and get everybody to like you, and then when they least expect it, you turn on them."

"I don't plan on going back inside those walls, Mr. Baker," Lee Kirby said.

"You don't plan on it," Will Baker said. There was disgust in his voice. "How many times have I heard that?" He fought down a tearing rage that was inside him. "Go down to the livery and get your free horse," he said. "I'll meet you in front of the hotel. The papers say I got to take you out to Opal Sprague's."

For a long moment Lee Kirby looked at him, then he nodded and went off toward the livery stable down at the end of the street. Will Baker stood there and watched him walk away. He was a handsome kid, tall, a bit too lean from two years of prison food, pale from the lack of sunlight. He had a lot of muscle and there was a certain pride to the set of his shoulders.

If Billy Baker had lived, he would have been just about Lee Kirby's age.

CHAPTER EIGHT

LARRABEE LUCAS STONE SAT ON THE METAL SADDLE OF THE grindstone and worked his foot against the wooden pedal that carried the rod to the crank on the revolving wheel. The coffee can with the nail hole punched in the bottom dripped water onto the spinning stone, and the curved, metal knife Larrabee held against the abrasive took on a razor-sharp patina. The straps on the canvas kyacks were in worse shape than he had thought at first. He'd have to cut more strips of cowhide and soak them overnight in neat's-foot oil. He felt a strange contentment. So far he had made eight halters out of one of the coils of cotton rope. He glanced toward the cottonwood log cabin, but Opal was nowhere in sight. He had thought maybe he would tell her just how much he had accomplished. Just to make conversation.

He finished sharpening the knife, rolled back his sleeve, and put a few drops of the dripping water on his forearm. He tested the knife on his arm, and the hair came off as slick and clean as if it had been a razor. He left the grindstone, feeling a deep sense of satisfaction, and as he started back toward the barn he saw the two riders coming from the direction of the town of Twin Pines.

The one riding slightly in front of the other he didn't recognize. A young man, it seemed from here, but there was no mistaking the second rider. The blocky, determined shape of Will Baker, the set of his shoulders, was something that once seen you didn't forget. He thought he had better go to the cabin and tell Opal, but there was no need. The door of the cabin opened and she was standing there.

For a second he looked at her and he didn't know what it was that was different, but it seemed to him she had changed her hair somewhat. There was an elusive curl that dropped down over her forehead. She looked beautiful standing there in the afternoon sunlight. The shadows had already started to touch the east side of the Sierra. He said, "We got company."

He saw her face brighten and she said, "It's Lee and Will Baker." He noticed that she mentioned Lee's name before Will Baker's, and seeing the eagerness in her face, he felt a touch of fleeting envy. Lee Kirby was family. It had been a long time since Larrabee Stone had known family.

The two men rode into the yard and Opal went out to greet them. It was Lee Kirby who spoke first. He said, "Hello, cousin Opal. It's right good to see you."

"It's good to see you, Lee," she said.

There was a moment of awkwardness and Larrabee Stone stood aside, no part of this. Will Baker swung out of his saddle with an amazing agility for a man his age. He dropped his reins and ground-tied his horse and said, "There's more damn papers to sign, Opal. You got to look at your clock and tell what time I got him here, then you got to sign on the bottom and say how much you're gonna pay him . . ." He snorted. "So help me, if we had another earthquake like we had back in the seventies, nobody would notice. They'd be too busy signing papers."

"Come inside, Will," Opal said. "You can show me what I need to do."

There was a half grin on the young face of Lee Kirby. He said, "You sure you can trust me out here alone, Baker?"

Will Baker looked at him and there was a hard bitterness in his eyes. He shook his head. "No," he said. "I'm not sure at all. But if you make a run for it, I'll hunt you down, and don't you forget it." He turned and followed Opal inside the cabin.

Lee Kirby sat there on his horse, his hands folded on the

saddle horn. Larrabee wasn't sure whether Kirby had seen him standing there or not. He grinned up at the kid and said, "Might as well step down and rest your saddle."

Lee Kirby turned and looked at him fully for the first time. Twenty . . . twenty-two years old . . . Larrabee couldn't figure exactly. He had the muscular build and the certain hardness of a man much older, but the shy, awkward grin on his face was that of a man much younger. The first thing Larrabee noticed about him was his paleness, and he knew without being told that this was the kid who had just been let out of prison. Lee stepped down from the saddle.

"Name's Lee Kirby," he said.

"I figured as much," Larrabee said. He saw a change in Lee Kirby's expression, a sudden mask, like a guard between himself and the outside world. Larrabee said, "My handle is Larrabee Lucas Stone, but it saves a heap of time of you just call me Tex." Larrabee put out his hand. Lee made no move to take it. "Miz Sprague tells me you know quite a bit about mules," Larrabee said.

"Been away from them a couple of years," Lee said.

The self-consciousness of the statement made Larrabee uncomfortable, and he thought he might as well face it. "Look," he said, trying his best to make Lee Kirby feel comfortable. "I'm just a hired hand like you are. I told this lady I'd help her drive those mules across the mountains and I reckon you told her the same, so it looks to me as if we're both sleeping in the same bunk."

"You know about me?" Lee Kirby asked.

"Miz Sprague said you knew those mountains as well as any man alive."

"I been in prison," Lee Kirby said.

"A lot of men have," Larrabee said. "It's getting out that counts."

"Yeah," the kid said. Larrabee still had his hand extended. Lee Kirby wiped the palm of his hand across the front of his shirt. "There's some don't feel that way," he said.

"Your callin' name's Lee?"

"That's my name."

"Well, Lee," Larrabee said, "the only time I take pedigrees into consideration is with horses and mules. You don't look like neither one of those to me. I don't feel what I've done or where I've been is any of your damn business and I feel exactly the same way about you."

For a long moment Lee Kirby looked at him and then a slow grin started forming around his lips and grew and touched his eyes. The kid was downright handsome, and Larrabee felt a little twinge of remembering. He thought of himself five or six years back and he wondered how things might have been if he had taken a different turn someplace along the trail.

"Thanks, Mr. Stone," Lee Kirby said. "That sets fine by me."

"We're gonna be together for a spell," Larrabee said, "and I reckon it would save a lot of time if you just call me Tex."

The grin had left Lee Kirby's face, as if there was still some uncertainty in him, but now it flashed back again, full blown. This time it was Lee who stuck out his hand. Larrabee took it and shook it warmly.

"Ain't Opal got the best damn lookin' bunch of mules you ever saw in your life?" Lee Kirby said.

It was apropos of nothing, but it was his way of saying that he and Tex were going to get along just fine.

Larrabee said, "I got some cotton rope and some rings and snaps. I been making up some halters. You know how to make halters?"

The kid looked at him and grinned. It was the grin of a man who was able to find humor in his own misfortunes. He said, "I've made quite a few hair bridles in the past two years."

Larrabee said, "Any man who can make hair bridles can make a mighty fine halter. Want to take a whack at it?"

"I ain't against keeping busy," Lee Kirby said.

The two of them turned and walked toward the barn, and it seemed to Larrabee there was a new confidence in Lee Kirby's stride.

* * *

Inside the cabin Opal shuffled through the official-looking papers, read them carefully, signed in four places, folded them neatly, and handed them back to Will Baker.

Will Baker said, "Opal, I'm going to tell you this straight out. Frank Sprague was my closest friend and I won't let you down come hell or high water. I told you I'd help and I will, but I don't want you to try to make this drive."

"I have no choice, Will," Opal said.

"Damn it," Will Baker said desperately. "There's no telling what kind of weather we'll run into. We haven't got enough help. Put it off 'til spring. I'll get a decent crew."

"It's a government contract, Will," Opal said. "I had to put up a bond. It took the last cent I had! If I don't deliver on time I'll forfeit it." She met his gaze squarely."Everything Frank dreamed about depends on me delivering those mules."

"Then you won't back down," Baker said.

Opal Sprague stood up. She shook her head. "No, Will. I won't back down. Are you with me or not?"

"I told you, Opal," Will Baker said, "I'll stick with you. I think I'm being a damn fool and so are you, but I'll stick with you."

"Thanks, Will," she said.

There was nothing more to say. He looked at her, standing there, her back stiff and straight, a woman who was defiant and determined, but a woman who was worried too. He was glad he knew her.

He turned and went outside and Lee Kirby wasn't there. Thirty years of being a lawman gave him a wash of apprehension, and then he heard the ring of a hammer against rivets and anvil. He went over to the barn and through the open door he saw Larrabee Stone and Lee Kirby working side by side. There was a coil of cotton rope on the floor of the barn. He smelled the pungency of neat's-foot oil and saw Larrabee Stone take a long strip of cowhide. He had dragged a canvas kyack over to the anvil and now the hammer rose and fell as Larrabee riveted the leather onto the canvas. Will Baker could see the ripple of muscles in Larrabee's back as the hammer rose and fell. In time Lee Kirby turned and saw him standing there in the open door of the barn. Kirby held up a length of cotton rope. "Making some halters," he said.

"You're on your own, Kirby," Will Baker said. "For now. You're still my responsibility until you get to Millerton."

"I understand," Lee Kirby said.

"You make one false move, I got every right in the world to shoot you down."

"That's plain enough," Lee Kirby said.

"I don't like leaving you out here alone," Baker said, "and I want you to understand this. You move off this ranch and Opal's the one who'll be in deep trouble. It's gonna be right smack on your shoulders."

"I don't plan on leaving," Lee Kirby said.

"See that you don't."

It seemed to Larrabee the marshal was pushing the point way too far. He hadn't particularly liked the man the first time he saw him; he liked him less now. He said, "Marshal, if it will make you feel any more comfortable, maybe you could swear me in as a deputy . . . pin a badge on me. Then I could keep a gun on him until you got back."

Will Baker looked steadily at Larrabee Stone, and that hard, granite face was a face that had no pretense. He didn't like Larrabee any better than Larrabee liked him. Baker said, "It would be a cold day in hell before I'd swear you in as a deputy. How in hell do I know but what you ain't on the run from the law yourself?"

That slow grin crawled across Larrabee's face and crinkled the corners of his eyes. He shook his head slowly from side to side. "You don't know, Marshal," he said. "And I don't figure I'm gonna tell you."

For a long moment the two men stood there, measuring each other, each one trying to decide how far the other could be pushed. Not far either way, they both decided. Will Baker made an inarticulate, coughing sound in his throat. He turned and went across and picked up the reins of the rented horse Lee Kirby had ridden out from town. He swung into the saddle of his own horse, and, leading the livery horse, he headed back toward the town of Twin Pines.

It was coming on evening. The mountains had surrendered the granite grayness of full day to the encroaching blue of evening. Baker stared up at those towering peaks and in his mind he thought of the other side . . . the rolling foothills and the long, wide valley. Fifty, sixty miles away, no more as the crow flies. But a lifetime away if you had to wind your way through the many passes and over the sheer cliffs that defied a man to penetrate their vastness.

He rode steadily toward the little town. The late afternoon was as still as a grave, but an occasional leaf dropped from the cottonwoods, the beginning of defeat, the fight against the first frosts and the long winter ahead with its driving snow and its incessant winds. He thought of the task before him.

He thought of Opal Sprague, a child woman who had nothing more going for her than a bullheaded determination to find a life better than the one she had known. And he thought of Lee Kirby, a kid, really, no older than his own son would have been, a convict who, so far as Will Baker was concerned, should still be behind bars, and would be if it weren't for the changing laws that were moving too fast for a man set in his ways. And there was Larrabee Stone . . . a drifter with a hard set to his features and a steeliness in his gray eyes and a worn gun on his hip. A man Baker didn't trust.

A deep sigh swept through Will Baker's body. It was a hell of a poor crew to be attempting to drive fifty mules across some of the most rugged mountain country in the nation.

The sun dropped behind the peaks and clouds drifted in to obscure their jagged pinnacles. There could be snow up there. Any time.

Will Baker had a deep longing to see Dolly Varden. It was the one comfort he had left in life.

He rode on toward the town of Twin Pines.

CHAPTER NINE

DURING THE PAST TWO DAYS LARRABEE, TOO, HAD LOOKED AT those mountains and thought of the task ahead. He glanced down over the long, lush valley and the barrier of mountains at its rim, and he thought of the deserts that lay behind him and of the wandering he had done through the years, and suddenly he was more than a drifter who had picked up a job. It was like when he had driven cattle up from Texas. He hadn't owned one damn cow, but a man went through hell to get them to where they were going. He looked at those mules, out there in the pasture, and he saw the big blue roan. To himself he thought, *Big Blue, that little gal's depending on us. You do your part with those fifty mules and I'll do mine.*

In the days he had spent crossing the wastelands of Nevada, Larrabee Stone had grown used to looking at the sunsets. They had been like explosions where the sun had been bloated beyond belief, then dropped suddenly out of sight, and darkness and the cool breath of night had been almost immediate.

He stood there by the corral now, his foot on the bottom rail, his arms crossed on the top one, and he stared into the evening that was coming into the valley with such gradual ease a man barely noticed. The wall of granite that was the Sierra had become a cobalt blue of such magnitude that it spilled like paint from the rim of a bucket and splashed softly down into the floor of the valley where the yellowing leaves of the cottonwoods stood as silently as if they were holding their breath. There was a stillness, and sounds carried, and Larrabee Stone, a man who had been alone most of his life, suddenly felt a twinge of loneliness. He had never been in a place quite like this before.

The kid, Lee Kirby, who had just been paroled from prison, stood at the corner of the barn as if undecided about what he should do next. Larrabee had tried hard to become friendly with this boy as they had checked out the herd of mules, making sure they were properly shod. Lee Kirby, Larrabee had decided, was probably no more than twenty years old. *It's a hell of a thing,* Larrabee thought. *Twenty years old and two years of it behind bars.* A sensitive young man, raised up in those mountains without much contact with the outside world, and when he had finally found that outside world it had slammed an iron door behind him.

Larrabee stood at the fence a while, thinking perhaps Lee would come over to join him, but when he saw that wasn't going to happen he walked back toward the barn, as casually as he could make it. "Mules sure look in good shape," he said.

"Everything Frank Sprague touched was in good shape," Lee Kirby said.

Larrabee thought of the straight fence lines and the precise arrangement of the chairs in the cabin and of the way the stones of the semidesert area seemed placed in their proper position. "I sort of gathered that," he said. "You knew him?"

"Yeah," the kid said. "I knew him. He was head guard at the prison."

"A tough one, I take it?"

"He had rules he lived by," Lee Kirby said. "It was best if you kept to them."

The approaching darkness was marked by a deepening of the shadowy blues that were spilling down the sides of the mountains, and now the crickets had set up for their evening concert, and whereas the day had been pleasantly warm, a man was suddenly glad that the sleeves of his shirt were long, and the thought of a cook fire winking through the cracks of a stove door gave a man an inside warmth.

During these last two days he had felt a growing uneasiness when he was around Opal Sprague. He couldn't quite put his finger on the trouble, and he blamed it on the fact that she and Lee Kirby seemed so close. They had so much in common and sometimes, when they sat down to a meal, he felt himself completely out of the conversation.

He had grown familiar with names that cropped up often . . . Fenton Hoover, the escaped convict who had been hiding in the barn. He saw a tender warmth in the two of them which he envied each time they mentioned Fenton Hoover's name. The man had meant a lot to both of them. And there had been an almost guarded reference to someone by the name of Shug Purcell, and there was a girl, Lorella by name, and whenever that name came up, a soft longing crossed the young features of Lee Kirby, and sometimes Opal had reached out and put her hand over his, and once she had said, "It's going to work out, Lee. She's a wonderful girl. She'll be waiting for you. You know she will."

"Waiting for you . . ." Larrabee Stone once more felt that twinge of apartness. There was no one waiting for him. There never had been.

And then there were the infrequent references to Rance Overton . . . references so casual, so brushed away, it was obvious it was a name both of them wanted to avoid.

Both nights Larrabee had gotten up from the supper table and gone outside. These two had things to talk about that weren't intended for his ears. It was family talk, and Larrabee Stone was not a part of that family and he never would be.

He felt the languid laziness in the air this night, the reluctance of the valley to let loose of summer. It was like the timidity of a child gingerly putting a toe into a pool of water to test its coldness. The old feel of autumn . . . The summer dreaded facing the winter that lay ahead, for winter here, he sensed, could be a savage thing that swept down from the peaks of the Sierra and sometimes sent swirls of blinding snow across the valley. He imagined the mountains standing there all winter, guarding their whiteness like wolves baring their teeth with a warning that any attack would be repulsed. The rolling hills that shielded the blazing death of the desert on the east side of the valley were ominous threats in the summertime, but now they were soft and blue, a friendly beacon to come on back to places he knew far better than this. But there was no turning back. A man moved on ahead.

It was early yet, not even full dark, but he went into the barn and arranged his blankets on the soft, sweet-smelling meadow hay. There was nothing else to do. Opal and Lee Kirby would talk far into the evening, but Larrabee wouldn't be part of it.

Much later he heard Lee Kirby come into the barn and settle down in his own blankets. Larrabee's horse, Snort, nickered a soft good-night and Larrabee felt sleep creeping up on him. He had spent two days of damn hard work. He had checked out every mule in that pasture. He had put new straps on the canvas kyacks, and he and Lee Kirby, working side by side, had made halters enough for all fifty of the mules Big Blue would soon lead into the challenge of the mountains. He dozed off, and his last thoughts were of Opal Sprague . . . a young girl, so soft and vulnerable, and yet as tough as nails in her determination to deliver those mules in the face of near impossible odds. He had never known anyone exactly like her. He suddenly realized that she was in his mind a great deal of the time.

He could hear Lee rustling around, settling himself in his blankets. The smell of the barn and the fragrance of the new hay was a pleasant thing. There was a long silence and then Lee Kirby said, "Tex? You awake?"

"Yeah," Larrabee said.

"Opal and me been talking."

"Kinfolks have lots to talk about."

"I mean about the mules. She wants to know how soon we can hit the trail." Larrabee was quiet a long time. "I said I thought one more day you and me would be ready. I said I thought we could start out early day after tomorrow morning."

"What'd she say?" Larrabee asked.

"She said she wanted to know what you thought."

He didn't know why that simple statement gave him a sudden wash of warmth. "No reason we can't do it," he said.

"She wants to know how many pack mules you think we need."

"What'd you tell her?"

"I said three. She wants to know what you think."

"Makes sense," Larrabee said. "We can pack one with stuff we'll need every day. Some of the stuff we'll only need at times we can pack on the other two."

"Yeah," Lee Kirby said. "That's the way I see it."

"Then it's set?"

"If you say so." Larrabee heard the rustle of Lee's body against the straw. There was a long silence and Larrabee supposed the boy had gone to sleep. Lee said, "Tex?"

"Yeah, Lee?"

"Opal's counting strong on you. She puts a great store in what you think."

Larrabee Stone stared up into the darkness above him. He thought of Opal and he remembered the feel of her warm body when he had held her briefly. "Good night, Lee," he said.

"Good night, Tex," Lee Kirby said.

It was daybreak, the time Opal Sprague loved the most. The sun came out red from the desert and threw its first kiss against the granite spires that were the Sierra. There was a feeling of warmth and life in the sweet scent of the night's dew on the sagebrush-studded edge of the valley, and the fragrance that wafted up from the cottonwoods that clustered along the banks of the river.

She went to the long, ornate mirror and looked at herself, and then she dressed in the man's shirt and the heavy jeans. Glancing back at herself, she unbuttoned the top button of the shirt, showing an unabashed swell of her womanhood. She touched her short-cropped hair and started to push a vagrant strand back from her forehead, then she curled it down with her finger and let it lie there as if it were an unintentional piece of carelessness. It was the sort of thing Dolly Varden would do, she thought.

She went outside and into the morning, and the rising sun had now painted the towering cliffs of the Sierra a splendid gold with tints of blood red on the high peaks, and in the somber crevasses where the glacial snows never melted. There was a cool, clean crispness in the air, and she drew it into her lungs and felt the life of it. She saw Larrabee and Lee over by the corral fence, talking to each other. They seemed to be getting along fine and she was glad of that. She walked over to them and said, "You men want some breakfast?"

Lee Kirby looked at her and grinned his open, boyish smile. "My backbone just rubbed a hole through the front of my shirt," he said.

The breakfast was elegant, with thick slices of home-cured bacon and fluffy biscuits that soaked up gravy as sweet as a spring morning. And Opal, too, looked fresh and buoyant, and Larrabee saw the slight flush of her cheeks from the heat of the stove and he was aware of the deep blue of her eyes. He noticed that the top button of her shirt was open.

Lee Kirby ate ravenously, a man starved for home cooking, and through a mouthful of food he said, "Tex and I talked it over. He sees no reason we can't start the drive first thing in the morning. That right, Tex?"

He met Opal's eyes and saw the grateful hope there. "Soon as you're ready, ma'am," he said.

He was calling her "ma'am" again and she wished he wouldn't. She said, "I've been ready for a month."

"Then there ain't nothing stopping us," Larrabee said.

She said, "I'll drive into town this afternoon and tell Will Baker."

She refilled Larrabee's plate, spilling a bit of the gravy which she wiped up with the hem of her apron, and then she hurried out of the room and into the smaller room with the double bed where she had lain with her husband. He had been a good man. She knew that. Everyone said so. And now he was gone, and sometimes, in the deep of the night, she felt a gnawing guilt that she felt no great sense of loss.

From the day she was born she had lived within sight of those mountains and they were a challenge, and they were challenging her now. But regardless of the challenge, a person had to survive, and her survival rested on delivering those mules across those mountains.

She looked at herself in the mirror and an unbidden thought came to her mind. It was not self-pity; it was facing facts. She was twenty-four years old, a widow, and there were years ahead. She thought about Larrabee Stone. He's a dependable man, she thought, and she tried to put any other speculation about him out of her mind, but she couldn't help but wonder how a man who seemed to have such a soft tenderness about him at times had become a drifter. *I guess I don't know much about men*, she thought. *My husband said black was black and white was white and fence posts always stood in straight lines, and that was what life was all about.* Deep down inside she knew there had to be more to life than that.

Later, when the men had finished their meal and gone outside and she had cleared the dishes from the table, she went to the door and stood there, just wanting to drink in the majesty of the morning. She was surprised to find Larrabee standing there, looking off at the mountains. He glanced at her and looked away and he said, "I don't think I've ever seen anything as pretty as the way the sun hits those mountains when it first comes up."

For one brief second she wanted to tell him how she felt about the beauty of this land. She wanted to paint the pictures as she felt them in her mind, but then there was that sharp line of demarcation that could not be crossed. She had always felt it with her husband. She was a woman and he was a man. She had learned that so well from the two years she had been married to Frank Sprague. A woman had her place; a man had his.

She was confused by the turmoil that rose inside her each time she was around this man she barely knew. She was relieved when he said, "How long since those mules been shod?"

"Two weeks ago," she said. "There's a Basque comes through here spring and fall. He's expensive, but they say he's the best there is. Took the last of my money to have them shod, but I wanted it right." She wasn't complaining; she was making a simple statement of fact.

He said, "You got your money's worth. Lee and I have checked them all out. There's a barrel of mule shoes out there in the shed. We'll take some extras along."

He walked off to join Lee, who was stroking the nose of Big Blue. She was conscious of Larrabee's height and the broadness of his shoulders, and she felt a surge of confidence from the small fact that he had shown concern about the mules' feet. She went back inside the house. She had dishes to do and clothes to get ready. The enormity of the task that lay ahead was like lead in her stomach, but she felt comfort in the fact that Larrabee Stone had come along when he did.

She fixed a noon meal for the men and decided it was time to go into Twin Pines to find Will Baker. Sometime later, when she went outside, she found the buggy hitched up and ready. She saw that Lee and Larrabee had laid out three sawbuck packsaddles and the canvas kyacks were spread and ready for the supplies that the men were now unloading and laying out in neat lines in order of the use they expected them to be needed.

She was keenly conscious of the bottles of whiskey standing there on the ground, and Lee Kirby made it worse by grinning at her and saying, "Didn't realize you'd taken to drink, Cousin Opal."

She drew herself erect and said, "It gets cold up there in the high country. By the end of the day you three men will probably all be at each other's throats. There's nothing like a whip of whiskey in a cup of coffee to straighten out a man's disposition."

She didn't dare look at Larrabee Stone. She knew she would see that devilish grin that so often softened his features. She moved over to the buggy and Larrabee was there, and he put a hand under her elbow as she stepped up into the rig. Again she didn't dare look at him. She slapped the lines lightly against the back of the buggy mule and drove off toward the town of Twin Pines.

She found Will Baker in Sheriff Vern Ogden's office, and after a short greeting she said, "We'll be ready to leave first thing in the morning, Will."

The marshal looked at her a long time, searching her face. He said, "You sure you know what you're doing, Opal?"

"I'm sure," she said.

"All right," he said. "My bedroll is over at the hotel. I'll meet you out in front. Reckon you'll want to get up before daybreak, so I might as well go on out with you this evening."

She spent her time walking slowly back and forth on the short walks of the town, peering into the store windows. There was a dress shop and she stood there a long time, looking into the window at a handsome gown with lace at the collar. She had never owned anything like that. Maybe some day she would.

In time she saw Will Baker come out of the hotel. His saddled horse was at the hitch rail and he was carrying a bulky bedroll. Dolly Varden came out and stood there on the boardwalk, watching Will. Opal went across to join them. Baker tossed the heavy bedroll up behind the saddle. He started tying it down with the saddle strings, and still Dolly Varden stood there, watching.

When Baker had finished the task he turned toward Dolly, and Opal heard him say, "See you later then."

Opal saw the two of them looking deep into each other's eyes and then Dolly Varden stood on tiptoe and put her arms around Will Baker's neck, and she kissed him full on the lips. Across the street Mrs. Cunningham had just turned to go into the general merchandise store. Opal saw her staring at Dolly and Will Baker. She saw Mrs. Cunningham's back stiffen, her chin go up in the air. Her snort of disgust was audible enough to be heard even where Opal was standing.

Dolly had pushed herself away and she was still looking up into Will Baker's rugged face, only it wasn't rugged anymore. It was soft. Opal heard Dolly whisper, "Come back, Will."

"I always do, Dolly," Will Baker said, and even his voice had changed. He turned toward Opal and now he was the same man she had always known . . . that rigid, blocky face, that harshness in his voice. "I'm ready," he said.

She got into the buggy and headed back toward the cabin where Larrabee Stone and Lee Kirby were cutting out the fifty mules for the drive. She thought of Will Baker and the momentary softness she had seen in him, and she thought of Dolly Varden and envied her . . . a woman who had the courage to openly show her affection for a man. Opal had never been able to do that with Frank Sprague. Perhaps, she thought guiltily, she had never wanted to.

CHAPTER TEN

THE MORNING WAS EERIE. THE MIST THAT OFTEN LAY ALONG THE course of the Owens River was more than that. It was a ground-hugging fog that spread in scattered patches across the floor of the valley. The men and the mules seemed to be shuffling their way through muted clouds of smoke as they moved around in the thin gray light of predawn.

There was a soft chill, and the warmth of the cookstove in Opal Sprague's cabin had been welcome, but breakfast, by the light of a coal oil lamp, had been a silent affair as if the three men and the girl had suddenly realized the enormity of their undertaking.

Will Baker had said not a word as he bedded down in the straw of the barn last night with Lee Kirby and Larrabee Stone. He said nothing now.

In the dusk of the previous evening, Opal had cut out four saddle mules . . . one for herself to ride, one for Lee Kirby, and two for spares. She gathered up some of Frank Sprague's winter clothes for Lee to wear. The rest of the work she had left to the men, and they had done it well.

They were mounted now, all four of them, and as they moved out through the fog into the dawn, Opal felt a moment of terror as the separate herd of fifty mules, haltered, tied together by slack loops of the cotton rope, streamed out of the yard. The string of them seemed endless as they went past her. She saw Larrabee Stone, riding back and forth, pushing them into line, and it was hard to distinguish the man from his horse, they were so much a part of each other, both doing work they knew how to do.

Last night she and Lee had sat together, huddled over a map, laying out the route they would follow. She knew the lower stretches of this side of the mountains well; Lee Kirby knew the rest of it.

Big Blue, the pet lead mule, a small bell around her neck, walked confidently out in front of them all. She, too, knew her job. Those fifty mules behind her were her responsibility.

High on the rim of the escarpment, the prison looked down on them, remembering one who had escaped, two who had been brought back, and the one who had gotten out legally. It stood there with its adobe walls squatted against the earth, solid and sure of itself, and it seemed to say, "Make one slip, Lee Kirby, and I'll be here to take you back." Larrabee glanced at the prison and he glanced at Will Baker, and the man's face was flat and seamed and rugged and set, and it looked not unlike those prison walls, and his eyes, riveted on Lee Kirby's back, held the same message the prison held.

The sun came up and touched the granite face of the mountains and bathed it with an instant of softness, and the fog retreated before its onslaught. It was eight o'clock high when the tinkle of Big Blue's bell announced the arrival of the mule train in Twin Pines. A few people were stirring about, and merchants were out, opening their stores for the day. They all stopped and stared as the long string of mules, driven by Opal Sprague, Lee Kirby, Will Baker, and Larrabee Stone, headed down the middle of the main street of the town. They looked at a girl who they all knew had been married for two years and widowed for one, a child woman, but the woman in charge. And they saw Lee Kirby, a handsome young man with the prison paleness in his cheeks. They knew of the parole in his pocket and they could see the hurt of remembrance in his blue eyes. And there was Will Baker . . . thick-set, tough, relentless, a man who wouldn't let the past be the past. They all wondered about the drifter, Larrabee Stone, who sat so easily in his saddle, his lantern-jawed face expressionless, his eyes squinted ahead to the vastness of those towering, seemingly impenetrable peaks; and they all thought to themselves, *They're damn fools, the bunch of them. They haven't got a chance.*

From the window of her room in the hotel, Dolly Varden, a silk robe with a feather-frilled collar pulled loosely around her shoulders, looked down on the sreet as the mules came into sight. Across the street she saw Rupert Cunningham getting ready to open up his store, but he didn't open it. He, too, turned and looked at the mules.

Dolly thought first of Opal Sprague, and she wondered if she had done the girl a favor by getting her those supplies. But she had thought of a girl alone in the world, desperately knowing there was a better life someplace. She thought of a girl who had given two years of her life to a man old enough to be her grandfather . . . a miserable man, so far as Dolly was concerned . . . and she thought of how those two years must have been hell for a girl that young.

She remembered the first two years of her own life alone . . . in the tiny town of Kansas . . . the end of the rails . . . and the endless stream of cattle and the roisterous cowboys. Those years had been hell too, but she had gone on, and she had made a life for herself. Opal Sprague deserved the same chance.

She looked at the tall, lean drifter who was so much a part of this now, and she wondered if this might be the man who would be the one who would help Opal realize her dream. There had been men like this in Dolly Varden's life. Perhaps she had made a mistake in letting some of them go.

And then her gaze fell on Will Baker . . . blocky, erect, a piece of granite staring straight ahead, and she thought of the tenderness that was inside the man and the hurt that would never go away. Like a million parents before him and a million that would follow, he blamed himself for the failure of a son who had wound up at the end of a rope. And he covered the hurt inside him with a wall of gruffness and a blunt arrogance that had nothing to do with the realness of the

man. Dolly Varden knew. She knew the tenderness and vul-
nerability that was inside him.

She had no intention of going down there and telling him
goodbye once more. She had said her goodbyes. She had said
them many times before.

A sickening wave of apprehension swept through her. She
had a feeling she was looking at that stiff, broad-shouldered
back for the last time.

Across the street, Rupert Cunningham inserted the key in
the lock of his store door, then removed it as the mules came
into town. He ignored the people completely and saw only the
three pack animals, the kyacks bulging with supplies. His
supplies. His money. His loss. He never expected to see any
of them again.

He glanced across toward the hotel and thought of Dolly
Varden who held a club over his head, and would for the rest
of his life. He thought of a half-breed bastard child who
would soon be a nun. And he thought of that little spread of
meadow along the creek that had been so jealously guarded
by the late Frank Sprague. Rupert had been so sure he'd have
it, and now it was gone. And why in hell did Opal Sprague
ever have to get into this in the first place?

He twisted the key savagely in the lock and went inside the
store and to his office and he sat down at the desk, his only
sanctuary. A vision of his own wife flashed across his mind
. . . a woman with a hawk face and lips so thin they looked
like a scar. He had never liked her, but her father had had the
money that had put Rupert in business.

He buried his pudgy face in his hands. *God damn all
women*, he thought to himself.

Floyd, the barber, watched the mules go by with the deep-
down eagerness of a ghoul. By God, if they made it there'd
be talk enough to last for a lifetime. But suppose they didn't?
Floyd, the barber, savored the thought.

He could tell of the lanky drifter he had shaved, right here
in this chair, and let bathe there in the back room. He could

tell of those steely gray eyes that held a promise of death. He could talk of the lost mule train and he could tell of the marshal whose only son had died at the end of a hangman's rope, and no one would dare speak of that, he would say, even to this day. And of the girl who had been married to the toughest head guard ever known . . . the man who had been killed in a prison riot. And of a convict who had been paroled, and he would shake his head sagely and say, "It was just as well. He come from bad stock, that one. He would have been right back in there anyway. That Hoover clan was a bad bunch. They was bad all the way through."

The west side of the valley that snuggled against the foothills was much lusher than the east side, with its carpet of sage and occasional sand dunes where, sometime in the past, the river, swollen with snow melt, had overflowed its banks and wandered at will through the flatness of the valley. There were trees here on the west side and a scatter of homes and gardens well tended. And ahead were a few patches of small ranches. They went by the one where Fenton Hoover had helped himself to a horse. It meant nothing to Larrabee, but the other three knew that this was the small spread of Bill Lloyd, and they knew of Fenton Hoover's theft. There were no secrets in the town of Twin Pines.

The land lifted slowly, through piles of boulders and great clumps of stunted sage and brown bunches of cured grass. Big Blue, the bell on her neck a soft tinkle, unhaltered and untied, followed alongside Opal Sprague, as if ready to do whatever the girl asked of her. Lee Kirby rode in the lead, gripping the rope that looped the long string of mules together halter to halter. Will Baker rode at the side of the line, about halfway back, and Larrabee Stone brought up the rear, riding Snort, ready to move from one side to another if any of the mules balked or tried to pull out of line. He squinted ahead to the vastness of those granite peaks and he thought to himself, as others had, that it was a hell of a crew to be pushing fifty mules into that devil-mass of snow-streaked granite whose upper reaches were so full of death they couldn't even support vegetation.

He thought some of reining his horse and just riding south, down the long valley along the rocky foothills to a place he had heard of called Walker Pass. It was a low and easy way across to the valley beyond. John C. Fremont had discovered it long ago. He thought of doing that, but he looked at the fifty mules and at the girl who had guts enough to try this impossible task, and he knew he was going to go along with her.

The wind came up . . . a few puffs at first, and then a steady movement of air that held the breath of the desert. It sucked through the valley until it built up speed and lifted the sand and drove it against their faces.

They paused briefly, and still in their saddles, backs turned to the wind, they shared the cold lunch that Opal had prepared, and it was then Larrabee realized that Will Baker had decided to make the most of this.

Stuffing the sandwich in his mouth, hunched against the stinging, wind-driven sand particles, Baker rode up and made a careful check of the pack mules. He rode back, reined up, and said to Larrabee, "I see you like a diamond hitch. Loads like these, a box hitch would be a hell of a lot better."

Larrabee shrugged. "Matter of opinion," he said. "That argument's been going on for years."

"Damn wind," Will Baker said.

"You call this wind?" Larrabee said. "Back in west Texas we used to hang a log chain from a fence post. When it stood straight out, then we said the wind was blowing."

Baker turned on him, almost savagely. "I never met a Texan yet that didn't tell that story," he said. "I don't like Texans. The biggest . . . the best . . . the greatest . . . If it's so goddamn great, how come so many of you are out here in California? Why don't you stay where you were born?"

"Where were you born?" Larrabee said casually.

"Ah, go to hell," Will Baker said.

It was a pattern that was to continue, Larrabee was soon to learn.

They had left the dirt road that led to the scatter of hard-scrabble ranches, and now they were following a trail. They came to a fork and Larrabee saw Lee Kirby motion Opal back. They conferred briefly, then Opal nodded and she headed Big Blue up the trail to the left. The wind lashed at them with a merciless relentlessness.

In a short time Larrabee saw the wisdom of the strategy of Opal and Lee. They rounded a jagged upthrust of land that was nothing more than a gigantic pile of house-size boulders that looked as if they had been tossed in a heap by some ancient god who had gone mad. There was not one blade of grass . . . not one indication of life. But the wind was cut off as suddenly as if it had been sliced through with a knife. Behind them they could still hear its howl as it roared through the long valley.

The rise of the slope had been almost imperceptible, but the last time Larrabee had looked back he had seen the lush greenery and the scattered roof of the town of Twin Pines, and it looked small and startlingly far below them. He wondered dully if he would ever see it again.

The trail grew rocky and steeper, but it was a definite trail, and then below, on the floor of the canyon, he saw the line of willows and over the ring of shod hooves on stone he could hear the far-off burble of a stream.

The sun had dropped behind the towering peaks of the Sierra, and shadows were crawling up the eastern face of the sheer escarpment, painting it with varying shades of blue that thinned to a deathly gray in the fast gathering evening.

Opal Sprague and Big Blue, followed by Lee Kirby, holding the lead rope, turned down an abrupt slope and they came to a narrow meadow that hugged the stream. The first of the Jeffery pines were there, and the pinon and sage was a thousand feet below them. This was where they would camp that first night.

They didn't talk much as they unsaddled the pack mules and crowded the others into the cramped quarters of the narrow valley. Will Baker did his part while Opal looked through the well-packed kyack to find the supplies they'd need for supper. Suddenly Will Baker said, "Where's that Lee Kirby?"

"Over yonder, looking for deadwood for the fire," Larrabee said.

"I don't want him out of my sight one minute," Baker said.

"I ain't seen him make no move to run," Larrabee said.

"I wish he would," Will Baker said. "I just wish he would."

Opal was busying herself around the fire and the smell of fresh coffee was already in the air which had grown crisp with the first touch of evening. Larrabee had finished unsaddling. The mules were still tied together, but he had loosened the lead rope to where they were free to graze on the meager grass of the narrow valley. He said to Opal, "Mules ain't settled down as yet. Close to home as we are, I guess we better set up a watch on them. What do you say, Baker? Draw straws to see which one of the three of us takes the first four hours?"

Opal Sprague was laying strips of bacon in the huge frying pan. Smoke was swirling around her face. She didn't look up when she said, "There's four of us. We'll stand three hours each."

"No real need of you standing watch, ma'am," Larrabee said.

"I said I'd take my turn." Her voice said clearly that she expected no favors and wanted none.

"Three hours . . . four hours. Don't make no difference," Baker said. "If you think I'm gonna leave that kid out there alone in the night . . ."

"Then it looks to me like you got a six-hour shift," Larrabee said. "Three hours of your own and three hours of your marshal work."

Larrabee thought he saw a faint grin on the lips of Lee Kirby.

During the next two days the four riders and the mules had fallen into a pattern as they moved steadily upward. Some twenty of the mules had trail-broken themselves, knowing all they had to do was follow the tinkling bell of Big Blue. Some of those, Lee and Larrabee had decided, could be unsnapped from the lead rope. The entire operation was becoming more compact, more efficient, easier to handle.

The stream they followed was dwindling as they moved closer to its glacier-fed source. There were only scatters of willow here and a few stunted and wind-twisted groves of aspen, already deserted by most of their leaves, for the nights here were cold.

It seemed like a world of granite, and the mules' hooves clanged against the talus and slipped under patches of glacier scree, boulders that had been ground to near powder by the forces of many avalanches. They saw vistas of great beauty where it seemed they could see for miles, and the deep, comforting green of the forest was below them and over it all were the ever-present afternoon thunderheads . . . towering feather beds of misshapen white cumulus standing silent and unmoving, their gigantic heights dwarfing even the majesty of the mountains. And ahead of them were always more rising peaks . . . more desolation.

They had now established the fact that a noon stop of an hour or more was, in the long run, a timesaving thing. It gave the mules a chance to settle down and catch a breather, and it gave the humans a chance to adjust to the increasing altitude. They would loosen the cinches of their saddle mounts and enjoy a leisurely meal. It was good for all of them.

In the chill, gray dawn of the third day they moved away from the stream and Lee indicated an invisible trail that cut up through a tumble of boulders.

Larrabee glanced at Will Baker. The man had aged in the last few days. He slumped in his saddle, and his sharp barbs toward Lee Kirby had been tempered some. The man was older than Larrabee had suspected at first. He was tough and he was rugged, but he was older, and the altitude was beginning to tell on him. The times they dismounted, Will Baker would move to a rock and sit there, his head bowed forward, staring down at the ground. Opal sat as erect in the saddle as ever, a determined person who had one goal in mind, and that was to deliver these mules.

It hadn't been easy for her, Larrabee realized. Even the small, necessary moments of privacy had been difficult for all of them. The men had formed a habit of reining up together and looking back over the long trail and they would continue to stare back down the line until they heard Opal's now-familiar call of "Let's move 'em out!" And then they would push on, higher up the trail, always higher.

The weather had remained cooperative, revealing only the afternoon display of the magnificent thunderheads, gentle reminders that nature was always in charge in this country. It was hot in the exposed areas, but the quick chill of altitude was there when they moved into patches of shade. At times, small cloud groups, thousands of feet below the thunderheads, moved languidly across the sky, throwing black, passing shadows across the face of the mountains. There had been no rain.

Lee Kirby reined up and waited until Larrabee, still riding the end of the line, caught up with him. The sun was ten o'clock high. "Got a place for a noon stop in mind?" Larrabee asked.

Lee nodded. "There's a meadow with a stream, hour or so ahead," he said. "It's beyond that I'm worried about."

"Worse than this?"

"A lot," Lee said. "We won't make many miles tomorrow. But if we can get across that shortcut trail I know, we'll drop down into some pretty fine country."

"I won't mind seeing it," Larrabee said.

A slow grin spread across Lee's face. "Neither will I," he said.

Larrabee, his skin long exposed to sun and wind, had felt no particular effect from the thin air and the beating sun. But Lee Kirby's prison pallor had turned to a deep red and his nose was peeling. It made him look even more kiddish than he was. But his spirits had seemed to rise with every foot forward they took. The grin stayed on his lips and there was a faraway look in his eyes. "A couple of more days," he said to Larrabee, "and then it's all downhill to Millerton."

Larrabee saw the look on Lee Kirby's face, and to himself he thought, *I got a hunch there's more waiting for you in Millerton than just a job.*

A four-prong buck bolted across their path and went down the slope and into the thickets below, bounding high in the air with each jump. They had spotted deer several times along the way, always moving down the slope, instinct telling them that winter was never far behind autumn. They hadn't taken time to try for a shot at one yet, but when Larrabee saw that buck bounding down the slope the juices in his stomach started churning as he mentally calculated how long it had been since he had wrapped himself around a good venison steak. And then he saw the meadow.

It came up on them with a startling abruptness. They moved out of the scree and the talus, and dropped down swiftly, and there it was below them, a small valley with a tiny jewel of a lake and grass still green, even at this time of year. That's where the buck had been headed. Larrabee rode up alongside Lee Kirby and said, "This where we'll noon?"

"Maybe longer," Lee Kirby said. He jerked a thumb in the direction of Will Baker. Baker was slumped in his saddle. "Tomorrow's gonna be a damn hard day," Lee Kirby said. "Figure we better cut this one short and get outselves some rest. The mules are starting to breathe pretty heavy. They can use it too. I've talked to Opal and she agrees."

"Makes sense," Larrabee said. He couldn't help but think about that buck that had bounded into the thicket beyond the tiny lake.

CHAPTER ELEVEN

THEY CAMPED THERE IN THE LITTLE VALLEY, AND THE MULES, COMpletely trail-broken by now, had been unsnapped from the long lead rope, and they grazed contentedly and drank deeply from the tiny sliver of lake.

Opal fixed a fat lunch, but Baker ate sparingly. He wasn't hungry, he said. His face was drawn and gray. Larrabee said to Lee, "Reckon that buck we saw on the way down is right over there in that thicket lookin' us over right now."

"Reckon he could be," Lee said.

Larrabee looked across at Opal and said, "How'd you like some fresh venison?"

"It would be a mighty fine change," she said.

"Come on, Lee," Larrabee said. "Let's go get us a buck."

Larrabee didn't miss the quick glance that passed between Lee Kirby and Opal Sprague. Lee shook his head. "You go ahead," he said.

"No fun hunting alone," Larrabee said. "Nobody to brag to."

Will Baker raised his head and now his face was craggy again, his eyes steady, and his voice was harsh. "You think I'm gonna let that kid go out there alone in these mountains with a rifle in his hands, you're plum crazy, Tex."

Larrabee saw the quick anger rising in Lee Kirby. The kid had taken about all the riding he could stand. "I don't need any damn rifle," he said, "but if I want to go hunting with Tex, by God I'll go!"

The sudden tension in Lee Kirby was a tangible thing, and Larrabee wanted to do what he could to relieve it. He went over to his horse and drew his rifle from the saddle scabbard. Opal, too, wanted to get Lee's mind off Baker, Larrabee figured, for she came across and looked at the rifle. It was a .44/.40 carbine. She said, "I always figured a .44 was sort of big for deer. I like a .30/.30."

Larrabee patted the rifle affectionately. "Old Betsy and me been together a long time," he said. "Besides, it uses the same shells my six-shooter uses. Saves me lots of money and there's been times when money's been somewhat hard to come by."

"We going or not?" Lee said. He was still seething.

"Something I got to do first," Larrabee said. He reached into his saddlebag and took out a box of cartridges. Almost as if it were a ceremony, he carefully removed three of the stubby shells. He laid them in the palm of his hand, jiggled his hand until they were aligned the way he wanted them, then he tossed them into the air. As they fell, he scooped them up with a downsweep of his hand.

Opal was staring at him in complete puzzlement. "What was that all about?"

"Well," Larrabee said, "my Norwegian mother taught me that. Said her granddaddy and her own daddy . . . that's my granddaddy . . . whenever they went hunting back there in Norway they always went through that rigmarole first and they never once in their life failed to come back with a deer. So I started trying it, and it ain't never failed me yet."

She was looking at him, a half smile on her lips. She was shaking her head from side to side as if she thought he had taken leave of his senses. Larrabee suddenly felt a little foolish. "Well," he said sheepishly, "some folks are scared to have a black cat walk in front of them, ain't they?" He dropped the three cartridges into the pocket of his sheepskin-lined coat.

There was a gruffness in Lee's voice. He said, "You stand here talking long enough, that buck will be so old he'll be too tough to chew. You want me to flush him out for you or don't you?"

"Let's go get him," Larrabee said. Again he saw Opal looking at Lee, her expression worried, anxious, almost as if she were afraid. He wondered what it meant.

Larrabee and Lee moved on foot as silently as Indians, through the willow thickets along the shore of the small lake. Their eyes were fixed on a stunted grove of aspen, just up the slope across from them. They saw a flash of white, a flash of tan. The deer was still there. Larrabee levered a shell into his rifle and they saw a quick movement in the aspen grove in response to the sound. He looked at Lee and grinned and nodded his head. Lee's lips were drawn tight. He made no response. Larrabee inched his way up a sloping rock. Lee was about six feet below him.

Suddenly the buck came out of the aspen grove. Larrabee threw the rifle to his shoulder, but as he did the buck turned and disappeared back into the aspen. "He's coming out your side," Larrabee hissed. "Here!" He tossed the rifle down to Lee. "You'll get a clean shot!"

He had called it right. The four-prong buck came out of the aspen, momentarily bewildered. He stood there, stiff-legged, snorting with alarm. Lee had the rifle and it was as clean a shot as a man would ever get in his life, but Lee didn't raise the gun. He just stood there and he started to tremble all over, and then he threw the gun down as if it had suddenly become hot in his hands. The clang of the gun against the ground was all the buck needed. He had spotted them.

He took off through the willows in stiff-legged bounds. No one could get him now. He went out of sight behind the brush, then bounded into the air, and as he did a rifle cracked and the buck crumpled in a heap, neck shot in midleap.

Larrabee's mouth fell open in startled surprise. He turned and Opal was standing there, the smoking rifle in her hands. Larrabee said, "That was some shooting."

"I was raised with guns," Opal said.

"I believe it," Larrabee said. A grin came to his eyes and spread across his face. He looked across to where Lee Kirby was standing, his arms wrapped around the trunk of a tree. He was making deep, retching sounds. The kid was violently sick. There was a low chuckle in Larrabee's throat. "I've seen a lot of cases of buck fever," he said, "but I've never seen one like that."

There was a fixed harshness in Opal's face that he had never seen before, and her eyes bored steadily into his. "It's more than buck fever," she said. "He had a hunting accident once. He was fourteen years old. He hasn't gotten over it."

The grin was totally gone from Larrabee's face. He felt a little foolish. He fumbled for words. "It must have been quite an accident," he said.

"It was," Opal said. "He shot the back off his stepfather's head."

Larrabee felt something akin to sickness rising inside him. He said, "My God, Opal. I didn't know."

"No way you could have," she said.

"I'll talk to him . . . ."

"Leave him alone," she said. There was a whip in her voice. He was seeing a side of her he had never seen before. Her voice softened. "Besides," she said, "we've got a buck to skin out."

They worked together, side by side, the two of them. Opal had slashed the buck's throat, unmindful of the blood that spurted over her hands, and she didn't wince as they ripped open the belly and the hot, wild smell of the entrails thickened the air. Larrabee kept glancing at her. Her face was set, and she was as hard as nails as the knife sliced with the practiced expertness of a squaw. She stood up and there was blood on her hands and a few splatters on her face. "Can you pack him?" she said.

"Sure," Larrabee said. "Can you give me a hand heisting him up?"

He knelt down and together they worked the dead deer around his shoulders and he knew the blood was seeping into his coat. His legs straightened and he stood up, packing the deer. They started back toward camp, and it wasn't until then that either of them realized the sky had grown black. A flash of lightning illuminated the granite peaks and a rumble of thunder rattled through the narrow valley.

Above them the black-bellied clouds were tumbling to smash themselves against the mountains. The lightning blended with the crashes of thunder, now so intense it seemed to jar the very granite cliffs around them, and the first fat drops of rain fell on their faces. They were in for a gully-washing high mountain storm.

The storm increased in fury and the thunder, trapped in the sound box of the granite cliffs, was of ear-splitting intensity. It was dark, but it was just midafternoon. The jagged forks of lightning that licked down against the peaks illuminated the meadow with a blue-green light.

Larrabee, staggering under the weight of the deer, and Opal, running alongside him, were so thoroughly soaked with the incessant downpour, it became funny and they were both laughing, almost hysterically, when they came into the camp. Larrabee shrugged out from under the weight of the deer. "Meat for supper," he said.

A crashing blast of thunder made speech impossible and then as it rattled away he heard Will Baker say, "Supper, hell. How you gonna build a fire?"

Both Will and Lee had put on their yellow slickers and Larrabee went to his saddle roll and untied his. He put it on from old habit, but he was so wet by now he didn't know why he even bothered to make the gesture.

"It'll pass," Lee Kirby said. "It always does." Lee seemed almost elated by the fury of the elements. And then the hail came, sudden, pea-size and bigger, driven by a gust of wind that whipped down from the mountains above them and drove the hail in a slant of stinging pellets. It rattled against their slickers as they turned their backs to it, and Larrabee saw Opal, hunched against its sting. He threw his slicker around her and felt her body close to him, and the hail bounced off their backs like the rattle of buckshot against the protective feathers of a high-flying goose.

And then it was gone, as quickly as it had come, and the four of them stood there and watched the gray seeps of rain move down the canyons and pause in the valleys, and the thunder retreated with it. The lightning flashes continued, savage pronged fingers of destruction, but the caged-in roar of the thunder was no longer here in the tiny valley. It rumbled and grumbled and muttered its way out toward the long valley of the Owens River.

The startled mules had set up a braying that was almost as bad as the thunder, and the three men shrugged out of their slickers and went out to try to reassure the animals. The air was suddenly fresh and sweet, and Lee Kirby sucked the thin air deep into his lungs. "It's pretty when it does that, ain't it?" he said.

Will Baker said, "You got one hell of a funny sense of beauty."

They got the mules quieted down and went back to the camp. Opal was standing there, her soaked hair plastered to her head, her saturated clothes clinging to every curve and crevice of her body. She and Larrabee looked at each other and they both started to laugh again, the laughter of people who were bone tired, who had shared moments together, who had both felt fear. It was the laughter that is the release from tension.

"You look just like a wet chicken," Larrabee said.

"Take a look at yourself," Opal said. "You ever seen a drowned rat?"

They both started to laugh again and Will Baker said, "And you two have got a damn weird sense of humor."

Finding dry wood for the fire was not all that difficult. It was surface wet, nothing more, and Larrabee took out his pocketknife and shaved off some slivers of pitch pine. He struck a match, and tendrils of black, scented smoke curled upward. Then he added twigs, and when the flame had turned orange and was five or six inches high he carefully laid on the dampened pieces of windfall pine. They dried instantly and caught, and within a matter of minutes a fire was burning brightly.

"I have to get out of these clothes," Opal said.

"Sure," Larrabee said. He bent over the fire and then suddenly realized she was a woman with three men, and she was embarrassed and confused. She didn't want to strip down naked right there in front of them.

Larrabee went over to the packsaddles and removed two of the pretective cover tarps. He selected three aspen, close together but out from the others, and he rigged up a makeshift dressing room. He turned and saw Opal watching him. He grinned and gestured toward the enclosure. "All yours, nice and private," he said.

"Thank you," she said simply.

She went to the pack that carried the extra clothing and rummaged out a change. She clutched the clothes under her arm, for the first time feeling a twinge of self-consciousness, then she went behind the canvas enclosure and stripped. She looked down at the smoothness of her naked body and she thought of Larrabee and how they had laughed together. A quick sense of guilt swept through her as her thoughts started to stray further. She dressed hurriedly.

Larrabee, too, was feeling a twinge of consciousness as he and Lee curried down the backs of the three pack mules and turned them loose to roll and shake the sweat from their hides and then join the others to start grazing contentedly. They gathered instinctively around Big Blue and the saddle animals, animals who knew and trusted one another. Lee had rigged a makeshift line between a couple of aspens and Larrabee draped the saddle blankets over it, giving them a chance to air. Without glancing at Lee, he said, "Tough climb tomorrow, you say?"

"Yeah," Lee said. "A tough one and a narrow trail, but if we can make it, it will cut at least three days off our time."

"Any doubt about making it?" Larrabee said.

"Nothing's sure, is it?" Lee said.

Larrabee turned then, and he figured he might as well face up to it. It had been preying heavily on his mind. "Lee," he said, "I'm sorry about the deer hunt."

"My own fault, in a way," Lee said. "I should have refused to go, but the marshal keeps ridin' me and it just felt like I had to do something to show him he didn't own me."

"Yeah," Larrabee said. "I know the feeling." It had been like that when he busted the hole in the side of the jail back there in Gillette, Wyoming.

"He's so damn sure I can't go straight," Lee said.

"And you're just as sure you can?" Larrabee asked.

Lee turned to him, and for the first time his emotions were all there in his face . . . open, clear-cut, completely honest. "The devil in hell himself couldn't stop me from getting to Millerton," Lee Kirby said.

"Is there more than just a job waiting for you there?" Larrabee asked.

"Yeah," Lee said. "There's a hell of a lot more. My freedom . . . future . . . a house of my own . . . someday kids . . ."

"What's her name, Lee?" Larrabee said.

The smile on the kid's face was as totally sincere as his emotions had been. He grinned and once more he looked like a country kid with the skin peeling from his nose. He didn't try to dodge the question. He didn't seem surprised that Larrabee had asked. He acted almost as if he had hoped someone would ask him.

The words gushed out. "Her name's Lorella," he said. "We've known each other ever since we were kids. There never has been anybody else for either one of us. She told me she'd wait for me, and I know she will. She's over in Millerton right now." He stopped suddenly, quickly embarrassed, realizing his outburst. Larrabee watched the discomfort growing. Lee shrugged and said, "Well, that's beside the point."

Larrabee shook his head. "No it ain't, Lee," he said. "It's the whole point."

Larrabee saw more warmth in Lee's face than he had seen

since he had met him. Lee said softly, "How come you're so anxious to get to Millerton, Tex?"

"Because I've never been there," Larrabee said, and he felt the total emptiness of that answer.

CHAPTER TWELVE

OPAL WAS FRYING UP THE HEART AND THE LIVER OF THE DEER. SHE had peeled some potatoes and cut up some onions, and the tantalizing smell of the frying food floated through the thin mountain air. She looked at the men, wet, tired, and sniping at one another, and she decided it was time to break out the whiskey.

After the brief thunderstorm, a quick chill had come into the gathering night. She went to the packsaddles and got a bottle. She was self-conscious about it, Larrabee saw, not even sure of what she was doing. "If I may, ma'am," Larrabee said.

He took the bottle from her hand and opened it with the ease of old habit, and he poured a small dollop in one of the tin cups. He extended it toward her. She shook her head.

Lee Kirby was standing next to him, and he half turned and handed the cup to the kid.

"Wait a minute," Will Baker said sharply. "I don't want my prisoner getting drunk."

Opal Sprague's voice was as soft as ever, but it held a whip of authority. "He's done a day's work like the rest of you, Will," she said. "The rain got him as wet as it did anybody else. If he wants a drink he'll have it."

Larrabee was surprised at the way Will Baker backed down, but he heard him mutter under his breath, "That's the trouble with the world today. Treat prisoners like they're human."

"Reckon I'll put some coffee in mine," Lee Kirby said.

"Now that sounds like a right smart idea," Larrabee said. "Baker?"

"I'll pour my own whiskey," Will Baker said.

They hunkered down by the fire in the gathering twilight and sipped their coffee laced with whiskey, and by the time they had finished their meal the night turned cold and the black silence of the pines was around them. There was a faint lapping sound from the shores of the tiny lake. The mules grazed contentedly on the lush grass of the Alpine meadow and the tinkling of the bell on the neck of Big Blue was the only intrusion of sound in this cold, granite-rimmed world.

Bellies full, and suffused with the warm, relaxing glow of the whiskey, they bedded down early. Lee Kirby and Larrabee Stone, Will Baker off to one side—he was a man who preferred to be alone—and Opal, observing the long protocol that dated back to Eve, off by herself, the eternal separation of woman and man.

For a long time Larrabee lay there, his hands laced behind his head, looking up at the brilliance of the stars. In time he said, "You awake, Lee?"

"Yeah," Lee Kirby said. "I'm awake."

"You want to talk about tomorrow?" Larrabee said.

He knew the kid did. He had watched his expression while they ate, and he had seen the worry there. "It's a tough trail," Lee Kirby said. "Narrow . . . cuts right across the face of a cliff. If we can make it that way we'll save three . . . maybe even four days."

"Sounds to me like it's worth a try, then," Larrabee said.

There was a long silence and then Lee Kirby's voice floated across to him. "I didn't mean to bust out like I did about Lorella."

"Don't see no reason you shouldn't have," Larrabee said.

"I hope you get to meet her, Tex," Lee said.

"I hope so."

"If it was only for her, I'd make it," Lee said. "But then there's this man who promised me a job. He was on the jury. You know that?"

"I didn't know."

"He didn't figure I was guilty of that store holdup. He kept holding out, right to the last minute, and even at the end he told me he didn't think I was guilty." There was a long pause and then he said, "And neither did Lorella. She knew better."

"Were you?" Larrabee said.

"What?"

"Guilty?"

"I served two years in prison, didn't I?" Lee Kirby said. "Let's leave it at that."

The morning broke gray and cold and the men had to put on their sheepskin-lined coats again. Frank Sprague's coat didn't fit the lean frame of Lee Kirby too well, but it covered him and it was warm. The light was thin when they saddled the pack mules, and Larrabee took one last look at the tiny valley where Opal had shot the deer. He had quartered the animal and wrapped the meat in gunnysacks. It was cold enough so it would keep for a few days until they could use most of it up. One of the pack mules snorted and shied as it caught the scent of the wild game.

They moved out of the valley and up a talus slope, the pines and the other vegetation left behind them now, and they wound in and out through boulders until they came to a level spot where it seemed there was no place to go. A sheer granite cliff rose in front of them. There was a straight wall of granite to their left, and to their right a seemingly endless expanse of torn rock, tossed wildly by a violent upheaval in some ancient time. It was sheer desolation.

"Now what?" Will Baker said.

"There's a trail angles across the face of that cliff," Lee said, staring intently at the barrier facing them.

"Damned if I see it," Will Baker said.

"It's there," Lee Kirby said. "An old Indian trail. Legends say they used it for years, the Paiutes and the Shoshones. It's a known fact prospectors brought packtrains across there."

"And outlaws used it too. Is that right, Kirby?" Will Baker said.

Lee Kirby turned on him quickly and Larrabee didn't miss the anger in the kid's eyes. "Yeah," Lee said."That's how the famous Hoover gang used to get across to do their raiding and killing in the Owens Valley. Is that what you wanted me to say, Marshal?"

The two men's gazes locked. "I just wanted you to admit you've got us damn well lost," Will Baker said. "I say we turn around and head back." He turned to Opal and his voice softened. "Admit it, Opal. It's no use."

Opal didn't back down. She said, "If Lee says the trail's there, it's there."

"How about it, Lee?" Larrabee asked.

He had seen the concentrated worry in Lee's face as he kept staring hard toward that sheer granite cliff. Without turning his head, Lee said, "Sometimes I forget I've been away for two years. There's something different up there. I can't put my finger on it. There's a slash down the side of the cliff I don't remember seeing."

"Avalanche, maybe?" Larrabee suggested.

"Yeah," Lee said. "Could be that." He looked at Opal then and said, "On up a few hundred yards there's a level spot of soft ground surrounded by boulders. There's enough room there to hold the mules so we don't have to keep them strung out like this. Hear tell it's a place where the Indians camped after crossing the cliff trail."

"You want to move on up there?" Opal asked.

"It would be best," Lee said."Then I'll scout on up the trail and take a close look at what that avalanche done. I'd like to take Big Blue with me, Opal. If she can make it across, so can the rest of the mules."

"And if she can't make it across?" Will Baker asked.

"I'll turn around and bring her back and then we'll figure out something else," Lee said.

"I've already got it figured out," Will Baker said. "We're gonna turn back."

"We'll do what you say, Lee," Opal Sprague said.

*   *   *

The open space of ground was there, exactly as Lee had described it. It was crowded quarters for the fifty mules and the pack animals and the riding stock, but by one of them guarding the trail that had brought them here, the herd was boxed into a natural enclosure. There was no grass and there was no water. It wasn't a place where you'd spend much time.

There were no words exchanged as Lee snapped a ten-foot lead rope onto Big Blue's halter, and leading the animal behind him he went out through the rocks and out of sight.

"I don't like him going out alone like that," Will Baker said. "With a mule to ride, how do you know he won't get on and just keep riding?"

"Why don't you leave him alone, Baker?" Larrabee said. Opal heard that same flatness in Larrabee's voice she had heard back in the store when he had faced up to Rupert Cunningham.

"Why don't I leave him alone?" Baker said. "Because he's an outlaw, that's why, and I hate outlaws. He comes from bad seed, that one. The Kirbys . . . the Purcells . . . the Hoovers. They been raiding and stealing clear back to gold rush days, and when a posse gets on their trail they head for the high country and they disappear and then when things cool down here they come again. The whole damn bunch of them are intermarried; the Kirbys, the Purcells, the Hoovers. And the damn Hoovers are the worst ones of the bunch."

Opal's face had gone white and her lips were drawn against her teeth. "My name was Hoover before I married Frank Sprague," she said.

Will Baker caught himself. He tried to cover his embarrassment. "You're different, Opal," he said. "You were a good wife to Frank. Everybody knows that. You're different."

"Am I?" Opal said. "Then maybe Lee is different, too."

"Don't see why you should worry much about it, Baker," Larrabee said, and his voice was back to normal. "Look yonder."

Lee and Big Blue had come out of the boulders and were in full sight. They were moving along easily, as if they had found a good solid trail, but from here it looked as if they were moving straight across the face of an unbroken cliff. "Why don't you level a shell in your rifle, Marshal?" Larrabee said. "He makes a move you don't like, you could pick him off the face of that rock easy."

Baker was trying to avoid Opal's steady gaze. He was sick about his outburst and his dragging her into it. His voice didn't sound natural when he said, "The kid was right. There's a trail across there."

They stood there together, the three of them, and they watched Lee leading Big Blue, moving slowly up the trail. Big Blue followed along behind him with the long confidence of an animal who had learned to trust man. The figure of the man and the mule grew small as they moved higher up the trail, but they were in full view, and Opal and Baker and Larrabee kept their eyes glued to them. They had now reached that peculiar gray streak that had bothered Lee so, and the three saw them stop, and Lee apparently dropped the lead rope of the mule and moved on alone.

He tentatively tested the footing. They saw him place one foot, leaning his weight against it, then moving the other. He moved on, and once he seemed to slip and stumble to his knees, but he was up immediately and he went on farther, head down, as if examining each inch of the ground.

In time, apparently satisfied, he turned and went back. They saw him pat Big Blue's neck, and Opal thought she saw him put his arm around the animal's neck and give her a hug, and then he picked up the lead rope and he moved back, leading the faithful animal forward. They seemed suspended, there on the side of the cliff, with a sheer wall towering above them and a straight, unbroken drop into eternity below them.

Big Blue stepped gingerly now, testing. Lee never once tugged on her rope. He waited until Big Blue was sure of herself and then the animal moved forward, with almost mincing, dainty steps. Larrabee saw the hope in Opal's eyes. "It looks like it's open," Opal said. "It looks like we can make it that way."

"Yeah," Larrabee said "If there's too much loose stuff up there, we've got those short-handled shovels. We can move some of it out of the way."

For just those brief seconds Opal and Larrabee had been looking at each other instead of at the trail, and then they heard Baker's hissed warning. "Look out!" The words were pushed through his teeth, as if he thought Lee Kirby could hear him.

They saw Big Blue stumble and go down on one knee. She regained her footing and by instinct lunged forward to avoid further danger, and now both forelegs were out from under her. She braced her back legs, pushing and shoving against the sliding debris that had now been jarred loose and was rattling down the sheer face of the cliff. They stood there helplessly as they saw the mule's back legs go out from under her, and she slid over the side of the cliff. They could hear only the distant, wild tingling death knell of her bell as the big mule's body tumbled over and over, down the sheer granite, to land on the jagged rocks five hundred feet below.

There was a second of stunned silence, and then a great racking sob that shook her body came out of Opal, and she threw herself against Larrabee and buried her face against his chest. "Oh my God!" she sobbed.

He held her close, tight against his body, and one hand reached up and stroked her hair. There wasn't anything to say. Not right now. He kept his eyes riveted to that trail on the cliff. There was only a big swirl of dust. Had Lee gone over with the mule?

And then he saw Lee standing there, standing a long time, looking down, perhaps at the broken body of the mule. Larrabee had no way of knowing. He knew only that in some way he wanted to help Opal. He said, "Lee's all right, honey. He's coming on back down the trail."

Only then did she move out of his embrace. He looked down into her tear-streaked face, and then she seemed to realize where she was and she pushed away from him. "Thank God Lee's safe," she said.

Will Baker was standing there, rubbing a hand back and

forth across his vest, not knowing what else to do. He said, "Opal, I'm sorry. I'm sorry about the mule. I'm sorry about what I said. I lost my head, Opal. I'm sorry."

She didn't answer. They watched Lee come back down the trail and disappear out of sight, and in time he came through the boulders and stood there in front of them. His face was ashen and he was trembling. "Opal," he said, "maybe I should never have taken Big Blue up there."

"You did what you thought was right, Lee," Opal said.

"There's no use trying the trail," he said. "We can't make it. Not with the mules."

"Opal," Will Baker said. His voice was soft, even paternal. "You tried," he said. "You tried hard, but there comes a time when you got to face facts. Let's turn around. Go back down to the valley where we camped last night. All of us will get some rest and then we'll head back home."

Opal's voice was brittle. "Back home?" she said. "To what? The only thing in the world I've got is these mules. I didn't sign any paper, but Rupert Cunningham would find a way to yank that ranch out from under me. I've got nothing but these fifty mules and the name of Sprague, and I got that name because I was sick of people like you throwing it in my face that my name was Hoover."

"Opal, I'm trying to help," Will Baker said.

Opal ignored him. She turned to Lee Kirby and said, "Is there another way to go?"

"Yeah," Lee said. "There's another way. We can follow along the high ridge here. Five or six miles, maybe. It won't be easy. But then we can drop down and that's no problem, and there's a valley down there that's full of timber and there's a lake and there should be grass." He paused and looked off into the distance, a man reliving a moment of his life, and then he turned to Opal and said, "You remember the valley, Cousin Opal. Me and Lorella and you and Rance came over from the hot springs and camped out there once. The valley was full of flowers and the lake was full of trout."

"Yes, Lee," Opal said. "I remember the place."

Larrabee felt completely left out. This was suddenly a

private conversation between two people who had known each other a long time.

Opal thought back to that valley and that camping trip. Rance Overton had hated Lee Kirby even then. Everyone knew it. But in those three days in the valley Rance had forgotten his hatred, and Rance Overton and Lee Kirby had become the stepbrothers they should have been all along. She remembered the valley.

It was there in the valley that Rance Overton had come to her in the middle of the night, the most handsome man she had ever known or ever would know, and he had told her he loved her. She had stroked his cheeks and seen the burning desire in those black, impenetrable eyes, and she kept hearing those words, "I love you." She had wanted to be a full woman. She had wanted to please him. She had wanted to give herself to him, and she had. Yes, Opal remembered the valley. She fought to bring herself back to the present, and she said, "And after that, Lee?"

Lee was trying his best to make it sound easy. "Over the pass and that's the last one," he said. "There's a good trail around the side of the mountain and then we start down. There's good forage . . . there's water. With luck, four . . . five days, we should be in Millerton."

"Suppose we can't make the pass, Lee?" Opal said.

Again Larrabee felt this was a conversation in which he had no part. He sensed that Lee was trying to be casual and offhanded. "We'd take the old trail down through the hot springs."

Larrabee saw the frozen tension in Opal Sprague. "I won't go back there, Lee," she said. "Suppose they're there?"

"Not likely," Lee said. "Not this time of year."

"If they'd made a raid," Opal said. "If a posse was on their trail. You know they'd hole up there."

"We'll make the pass," Lee said.

"I won't go back to that valley, Lee," Opal said. "I got out of there once. I married an old man I didn't love, just so I could change my name. I gave two years of my life, Lee."

"So did I, Cousin Opal," Lee Kirby said. "If you want to turn back, it's all right with me."

Larrabee sensed the tearing indecision in Opal. She turned then and looked fully at Will Baker. She and Lee had just told this lawman of the secret hideout of the Hoover gang. Will Baker was no fool. He had figured it out from what they had said. Baker said, "Don't do it, Opal. Turn back."

Opal said, "You've got a good horse under you, Will. I'll give you plenty of supplies to make it on back to Twin Pines. You go on back there. That's where you belong. Lee and I are going on." She turned then and looked at Larrabee. "And you, Mr. Stone?" she said.

Larrabee forced a grin. "I hired on to deliver a bunch of mules to Millerton," he said. "I never walked away from a trail drive in my life. I don't want to start now."

Opal said, "Tell me what you want, Will. I'll give you whatever supplies you need."

Will Baker said, "Frank Sprague was the closest friend I ever had. I told him I'd look out for you. I've got a badge that says I'm supposed to stay with this kid until I get him to Millerton. I've given thirty years of my life honoring that badge. I'm not going to turn my back on it. I'm going with you."

Opal said, "Lee, you know the best way. You ride out in front. You take the place of Big Blue. Will and I will ride flank. Mr. Stone," she said, "if you don't mind riding drag . . ."

"I'm just a hired hand," Larrabee said. "I'll do it your way, boss."

They started rounding up the mules and led them out through a tangled mass of stone where one rock seemed no different from the other. They put the three pack animals in the lead, and Will Baker did his part, as efficiently as if nothing had ever happened. The mules moved out of the earthen enclosure and now Larrabee and Opal, both mounted, were the last ones through. Opal reined up and looked across at Larrabee. She said, "I made a fool of myself. I shouldn't have broken down that way. It was only a mule."

Larrabee looked at her and shook his head. "No, honey,"

he said softly, "Big Blue was more than a mule. She was your friend."

Opal felt the tears welling in her eyes and she rode forward quickly so this tall stranger, a man she didn't know, wouldn't see them. She thought of Big Blue and how much a person could come to think of an animal, but she thought of Larrabee too, and she remembered that twice he had called her "honey." It was just a word. He had meant nothing by it. But in all her life she had heard so few words of affection, and the few she had heard were from an outlaw uncle by the name of Fenton Hoover and from a man she had loved too well . . . a man who had gone all bad.

She rode on, doing her part to keep the mules in line, and somehow, hanging in her mind, was a simple five-letter word. Honey. It was a good word. It had a soft sweetness about it.

The next few hours were a living hell of endless boulders as big as houses and the ground had turned to solid granite. The mules' shod hooves clanged against the unyielding stone, and now they were picking their way through treacherous talus and slipping and sliding on patches of scree, but they kept moving forward.

Noon came, and the humans felt hunger gnawing at their bellies and the mules felt thirsty, but there was no place for a noon stop and there was no water. Larrabee ran a practiced eye along the mules and he reined out around a boulder and he rode up alongside Lee Kirby. Larrabee said, "We got four or five of them going lame, Lee. There's two mule shoes laying alongside the trail back there."

Lee nodded. "When we get down to the valley we'll lay over a day or so." He looked at Larrabee and tried to force a grin. "You know how to cold-shoe a mule, Tex?"

Larrabee returned the grin. "I got a dollar says I can shoe a mule faster than you can, day or night."

"If you'll wait until payday until I've got a dollar, you've got yourself a bet."

They left the ridge finally and started down a long, gentle

slope. The going was easy, and there below them they saw the first of the timber, thick and lush, long canyons of it, and they entered the pines and the cedars and wound their way through, always descending. It was near dark when they came to the mouth of the valley. They came out of the timber and the valley spread out before them, long and wide. The mules caught the scent of the water in the lake that held the last reflection of the peaks around it.

They came to a grassy meadow and Lee said, "We'll make camp here." To Larrabee he said, "You and me have got a little chore to take care of, then we'll make camp and settle down."

"Whatever," Larrabee said.

Lee rode on across the meadow and down the shores of the lake, and Larrabee rode beside him. They came to the end of the valley and it seemed like a sheer cliff, but there was a ten-foot wide cleft in it, and the stream that fed the lake tumbled through that open break in the rock wall.

Lee dismounted. He said, "Figured we'd gather up some windfalls and pile them across that opening there. With us camped back at the entrance of the valley and this only way out fenced off, we got ourselves as fine a natural corral as you ever saw. We can turn the mules loose and let 'em roll and drink and graze."

"Sounds good," Larrabee said. "Those mules have got a rest coming after today."

They gathered brush and small-sized logs and they piled them across the only exit from this valley. As they worked, their nostrils caught a faint scent of campfire smoke. At the opposite end of the valley, Opal had already started setting up camp.

CHAPTER THIRTEEN

As Larrabee and Lee rode back from their fence-building task, they saw Opal busy there at the campfire. She was bone weary, Larrabee knew, for he, too, felt the strain of the long day, but Opal was trying not to show it.

Will Baker had sliced thick steaks from the hind quarters of the venison and Opal had floured them and dropped them in the pan, and the tantalizing fragrance of the frying meat floated through the thin air of the high valley. Larrabee was suddenly aware that none of them had eaten a bite since breakfast. He saw Will Baker standing there, one of the bottles of whiskey in his hand, and as they dismounted Baker offered them the bottle.

The coffee was boiling lustily, and Larrabee thought of how many times he had smelled coffee boiling over a campfire on the long trips he had made on so many trails. He had always remembered that fragrance, but with Opal standing there by the fire it seemed that coffee had never smelled as good as it did this night.

Baker had already unsaddled the pack mules. There was a lot to dislike about the man, but he was trying to do his part.

There were few words passed among them as they ate there in the gathering darkness of the night with only the glow of the campfire to shed any light. The flames threw shadows across their faces, and at times illuminated their tense expressions. It was Opal who poured the coffee and passed around the bottle, and the three men laced their brew deeply and then they saw Opal pause, and Larrabee suppressed a chuckle as he saw the "what the hell?" look on her face, and she poured a hefty dollop of whiskey in her own cup.

She had never tasted whiskey before in her life, and it was amazingly good. She felt the warmth of it seeping through her body, and she caught herself thinking of those two years with Frank Sprague and of how, whenever she had tried to be the least bit frivolous, he had looked at her sternly and said, "It ain't seemingly." She wondered what her dead husband would think now, seeing her here with three men, around a camp-fire, drinking whiskey. He would most certainly say, "It ain't seemingly." The whiskey stirred warmly in her stomach and she thought to herself, *Frank Sprague, I don't give a damn.*

They were all exhausted, and they crawled into their blankets early, unworried about the mules. The chance of preda-tors here in the high country this time of year was remote. Bears were seldom found above the eight-thousand-foot level, and the deer, who might chew up a halter or even a shirt to get to the sweat salt, had moved on down to lower elevations. They hadn't seen one deer since Opal had killed that one in the valley. They slept deeply through the night.

It was broad daylight when Opal awoke, and she was startled by the fact that she had slept that long. Fully clothed, she got out of her blankets quickly and she saw that the fire had been built and the coffee pot was sitting at the edge of the coals, keeping hot. Will Baker was off to one edge of the clearing, smoothing his blankets. She heard the long delayed ring of a hammer in the thin air, and looking up toward the end of the valley, she saw Lee and Larrabee.

They had five mules in a rope enclosure and they were working at shoeing the animals. Will Baker moved over and said, "You got any more of that whiskey?"

Opal was surprised at the question. She said, "Sure." She went over to the pack and rummaged around and handed him the half-empty bottle. He uncorked it, tipped it to his lips, and drank deeply. He let out a sigh. "Was a time," he said, "when I could sleep on a pile of rocks and think nothing about it. I'm getting old, Opal. When I wake up in the morning, there's an ache in my bones. I'm right glad you thought of that whiskey."

"I didn't think of it," Opal said. "It was Dolly Varden's idea."

She saw a quick change come over Will Baker. His eyes went soft and even the muscles of his face relaxed so his expression didn't appear so rocky and stern anymore. He looked at the bottle he held in his hand. He said, "I might have known. Dolly would think of something like that." He looked up and grinned. "My favorite brand, too."

Opal looked at him and said finally, "Will, why did Dolly Varden help me get those supplies?"

Will Baker looked at her and shrugged. "Don't try to figure it out, Opal," he said. "It's Dolly's way."

"She's a wonderful woman, isn't she, Will?" Opal said.

"She's more," Will Baker said. The gruffness returned to his voice. He went over and picked up an ax. "I'll find some windfall and cut some more wood for the fire," he said. "Looks like we're gonna spend the day here."

Up in the rope enclosure Larrabee, stripped to the waist, struggled with the back leg of a mule gripped between his knees. He held the hoof tightly and worked with a rasp, then, reaching down and picking up a new shoe, he put it in place, started the nails with light taps, then drove them home and clenched them against the mule's hoof. He dropped the mule's foot, slapped the animal on the rump, turned, and Lee was standing there, grinning at him. Lee said, "I finished mine five minutes ago. You owe me a dollar."

"You picked a tame one," Larrabee said. "That son of a bitch there tried to kick the guts out of me."

Lee chuckled. "Mules have been known to do that," he said. "I'll take my dollar."

"Two dollars on the next one?" Larrabee said.

"Whooee," Lee said. "I'm on my way to my first million

dollars. All I got to do is find myself enough mules and a sucker to bet with.''

"As long as you pick gentle ones and shoe the front foot, you might make it,'' Larrabee said. "I'd advise you to leave the rough ones to the experts.''

"Two dollars it is,'' Lee said.

They worked together, side by side, two men good at what they were doing, feeling a deep-down pride in being aware of it. The muscles rippled in Larrabee's naked back.

In time they finished with the mules, slapped them on their rumps, and hazed them back toward the grazing herd. Lee Kirby looked at Larrabee and said, "You satisfied? You owe me two dollars.''

Larrabee reached up and scratched his tousled hair. He squinted across at Lee Kirby. "Let's take a two-sided look at this,'' he said. "Suppose I'd a got all the gentle, front-foot ones and you had got the mean ones and it wound up with you owing me two dollars. Would you have paid me right now?''

"I told you,'' Lee said. "I'd pay you when I get paid.''

"I meant to tell you exactly the same thing,'' Larrabee said.

Lee shoved Larrabee playfully. "You're not only a rotten mule shoer,'' Lee said, "you make new rules as you go along.''

Larrabee went over and took his shirt from the limb where he had hung it. He put it on and tucked it into his pants. "Why don't we go on back to camp and see if Opal will feed us something?'' Larrabee said. "It might improve your disposition.''

"I hope it preserves your memory to the point where you won't forget you owe me two dollars,'' Lee said.

Larrabee clapped an affectionate arm around Lee's shoulder. "Son,'' he said, "when you're dealing with an upright, honest man, you don't have a thing to worry about.''

Lee nudged him in the ribs with his elbow. "I'll decide that when I get my two dollars,'' he said.

They went back toward the campsite, totally satisfied with their morning's work.

*   *   *

The noon meal was sumptuous with thick deer steaks, and the gravy that Opal had made from flour and pan drippings cried to be sopped up by the fluffy biscuits she lifted from the heavy iron Dutch oven nestled deep in the coals of the fire. She felt the joy of being a good cook as she saw the three men relaxing there, sated with food, and Will Baker said, "As long as we're taking a day off to relax, I plan to relax."

He went over into a small grove of trees and spread his blankets. Tugging his saddle into place, he placed his head against it, and Opal and Larrabee and Lee exchanged winks as, within what seemed like seconds, they heard Baker's heavy snoring.

"Think I'll saddle up and take a little ride for myself," Lee said. "I'd just like to look over this valley once more. It's kinda special to me."

Opal said, "You know what I'd like to do most of all?"

"Whatever it is," Larrabee drawled, "I'd go ahead and do it."

"I'd like to take a bath," she said.

"There's a lot of water out there just waiting," Larrabee said. He reached over and took a couple of leftover biscuits.

She looked at him and said, "You still hungry?"

"I'm going to take myself a walk," he said. "I saw some jaybirds and a couple of chipmunks up there when we were shoeing the mules. Thought maybe I'd feed them." He ducked his head. "I sort of like watching birds and little critters," he said.

She looked at him and thought, *you're a strange man, Larrabee Stone. You knew exactly how I felt about Big Blue and you like to feed squirrels and birds.* He grinned at her and said, "Besides, you'll want some privacy for your bath."

Both men moved off, and Lee saddled up one of the mules, and she saw Larrabee strolling down toward the shore of the lake, picking up pebbles, throwing them out into the water. He hadn't shaved since they had left Twin Pines and he was beginning to look more like the drifter who had ridden into her yard that day when Fenton Hoover had hidden in her barn. But the stubble of beard and the well-used clothes were different now. She had seen the man beneath them.

She took a bar of soap and a towel and walked down to the edge of the lake, and an old inherent modesty made her seek out a clump of willows, although she felt confident none of the three men would be watching her.

She stripped naked and she stood there and remembered the valley and that night with Rance Overton. She had assumed they would be married. She had been so young and inexperienced. And when they went back to the valley of the hot springs she couldn't wait to tell Uncle Fenton, the one man she knew she could trust. And then Rance Overton had left the valley and one month passed, and then another and another. And Fenton Hoover had brought her a poster. There was a fair likeness of Rance Overton on that poster and the reward was one thousand dollars. He was wanted for armed robbery and rape. That ugly word had glared up at her and burned itself into her brain. Rape.

She was desperate, and the old man with a pack mule had wandered down into the valley. An old man alone, seeking solitude in a fishing trip. In her desperation she had thrown herself at him; she realized that now. He was kind, and he told her of how he lived alone, down there in the Owens Valley, and of how he was looking for a housekeeper to hire.

That had been all she needed, and when she left the valley the old man was beaming and she had announced to one and all that she was to be married. She would never forget the lingering hurt in the eyes of her uncle Fenton Hoover.

It seemed so long ago now it was totally unreal. She tested the water of the lake with her toe.

It was brutally cold, but she stepped out into it and felt it creep up to her knees, chilling. She reached down and splashed the water over her body and soaped herself. She couldn't bring herself to dip completely under, but she furiously splashed water over herself and over her face and her hair, and when she rubbed herself down with the towel her entire body was tingling. She slipped into her clothes and felt the comforting warmth of them, and then she decided to take a brisk walk to restore her circulation.

Larrabee sat with his back against a rock, the full sun on his face. In patches of shadow the air was chill, but here in the sunlight there was a filtered warmth. He looked out at the valley and the glistening lake, a place where summer had but a brief stay, pausing apologetically to give way to the nudge of autumn, knowing that winter was close behind. A chipmunk came out of a pile of rocks. It stopped tentatively, one paw raised, and stared across at the quiet form of the human.

Moving slowly, Larrabee reached into his pocket, drew out one of the biscuits, broke it, and tossed a piece out a few feet in front of him. The chipmunk's nose twitched and its inquisitive bright eyes saw the morsel on the ground. It could not resist the temptation. It moved forward, snatched up the piece of bread, then it raised on its haunches and, turning the bread over and over in its front paws as if to examine it, bit into it and liked what it found and gobbled it down greedily. Larrabee grinned and tossed out another piece of biscuit.

The chipmunk grabbed it eagerly, but this time he ran back into the security of the rocks. "That's right," Larrabee said aloud. "Go hide. I'm the world's most famous chipmunk killer." He tossed out another piece of bread, hoping to entice the little animal out of the rocks.

A stellar jay swooped down from a pine bough, snatched up the morsel, flew back, and gulped it down hungrily. Larrabee's voice rose in simulated anger. He said, "You stupid jaybird! That was for the chipmunk! You miserable thief, why don't you wait your turn?"

The black-crested blue jay let out a stream of raucous bird obscenity intended to scorch Larrabee's ears. Larrabee's voice rose in response to the screeching abuse. "All right, you dirty blue-back buzzard," he said. "Come on down here and fight like a man! I'll poke your bloody beak down your throat!"

Larrabee heard the suppressed giggle, and then the giggle could not be held back any longer. It broke out into a full-throated laugh. He turned, and Opal was standing there, looking down at him. She was laughing hilariously and she dropped down on the grass beside him.

"That's the funniest thing I ever saw," she said. "A grown man arguing with a jaybird."

Larrabee felt like a fool. "Well, damn it," he said, "that bird's a thief."

Instinctively Opal reached out and gripped his arm and leaned her head against it. "You're crazy," she said.

He turned and looked down at her and he said, "You ought to laugh more often, Opal. You're beautiful when you laugh."

She released his arm. "I am?" she said.

Her face was tilted toward him and the top two buttons of her shirt were open, and her hair was wet and her face was scrubbed, and she smelled of soap. He leaned down and kissed her solidly on the lips.

He felt that second of resistance and then her arms were around his neck and she pulled him close to her. Her lips parted and they were as soft as velvet as they pressed against his. She clung to him as if never wanting to let him go. He pushed her away and stood up abruptly. "I best go look after the mules," he said.

He walked away and she sat there on the grass, her heart beating high in her chest, frightened by the emotion she had felt in that instant. She got up then and walked slowly back to the camp.

As she prepared supper that evening, she made it a point to avoid Larrabee's eyes, and she knew he was doing the same. They ate quietly and she brought out another bottle of whiskey and poured them all a drink and then, on impulse, she poured one for herself.

Lee said, "I rode on up through the opening there. Trail's fine up ahead. If the weather holds good when we make camp tomorrow night, we'll be on the west side of the mountains. We ought to line out as soon as there's light to work by."

Will Baker sipped his whiskey and stared deep into the embers of the campfire. Larrabee and Lee together took the tin plates down to the lake and scrubbed them clean with sand

and rinsed them off, and as if by mutual agreement, they laid out their bedrolls, Opal's close to the still glowing fire.

Deep silence came with the descending darkness, and the stars came out brilliant and larger than life. Opal slipped off her jeans and crawled into her blankets, wearing only the man's checkered shirt. It came almost to her knees. She stared up into the starlit night, remembering this valley and a night that seemed so long ago.

Her hand moved down and caressed the smoothness of her belly, and then it moved lower and found the moist warmth of her desire. The stars reeled crazily overhead, spinning in eccentric circles, and she saw the face of Rance Overton, dark, handsome, and those piercing black eyes, demanding, demanding . . . And, oh God, how she had wanted to answer his demand.

And then that vision was gone and there was the slow smile of Larrabee Stone, and she felt his lips pressing against hers and she remembered throwing her arms around his neck and the wild desire that had swept through her in that instant. A shudder ran through her body and she clenched her teeth to stifle a low moan. The stars came back into focus. She felt a moment of deep guilt at her uncontrolled self-indulgence, and then she turned on her side and went swiftly to sleep.

Larrabee Stone stood there by the dying fire. Unbeknownst to any of them, he had made one final check on Opal each night on this trip.

He looked down on her, sleeping so peacefully, her lips parted slightly in a soft smile. The dying fire threw shadows and lights across her features. She was, he thought, the most beautiful thing he had ever seen.

Damnit to hell, he thought to himself, *I'm falling in love with her. That's the last thing on earth I wanted.* He tried to shut the thought out. He was a drifter with no intentions of settling down. He was silly to feel this way. A passing fancy, just because they were alone and had been thrown together this way.

He went over and crawled into his blankets and propped his

head against his saddle, and he looked up at the stars . . . great silver patches pasted flatly against a velvet night.

He had to put her out of his mind, he knew. But just as surely he knew he would always remember that kiss. He thought of Lee Kirby's words, "If the weather holds . . ." He drifted off into a fitful sleep.

It was two o'clock in the morning when the weather changed.

CHAPTER FOURTEEN

THERE WAS NO DISTANT SPECTACLE OF LIGHTNING, NO RUMBLE OF thunder coming closer and closer. There was only deep silence as the leaden clouds moved slowly across the sky, blotting the stars one by one. The temperature dropped with their advance.

The four awoke to a world that was ominously gray and, after the warming sun of the day before, the biting chill was even more noticeable. Larrabee built up the fire and they all shrugged into their sheepskin-lined coats and warmed their hands over the welcome heat. Will Baker's teeth were chattering against the unexpected cold. He went to the packsaddle and took out a bottle of whiskey and drank deeply, shuddering against the bite of the drink. He looked at the others with a touch of embarrassment. "Cold," he said needlessly.

There were no bird twitters this morning in the predawn chill. Larrabee's horse blew through its nostrils and the sound cracked through the valley. The quiet lapping of water against the pebbles of the lake shore was like the crashing of waves. All sounds were magnified ten times in this cold, gray world that had closed around them.

They relished the hot coffee and found comfort in the smell of frying bacon and in the reassuring aroma of the woodsmoke. Both Larrabee and Lee pulled on gloves before going out to round up the mules and line them up for the day's trek across the final pass. Opal cleaned up the camp and Will Baker, saying nothing to anyone, saw to loading the pack animals.

The mules were fractious after their day of freedom, and Larrabee and Lee spent precious time rounding them up. They strung them together again, the cotton rope slackly looped and snapped, halter to halter. Even the pack mules were tied together, for the passage ahead was a narrow one and there was no way to go but single file. There was thin daylight but no hint of sun when they finally lined out the mules. Larrabee and Lee had ridden ahead and removed the makeshift barrier from across the mouth of the narrow opening in the granite cliff. They rode back and by prearrangement Lee took the lead rope of the three pack mules and rode ahead. Will Baker held the lead rope attached to twenty mules; Opal followed, leading ten; and Larrabee was the last to string out, tugging the remaining twenty into a reluctant movement.

They came to the opening in the cliff and Will Baker said, "You expect us to go through there?"

Lee said, "Why not? The stream got through there, didn't it?"

Lee rode on ahead, tugging the three pack mules behind him. They pushed through the narrow passage, so tight in spots that the canvas kyacks grated against the granite walls. Opal, confident, took her string of ten mules into the opening and they reluctantly followed the pack animals. And then Baker, seeing no way out of it, rode into the opening. They followed the tiny stream, the mules' hooves splashing through the water, and they stuck to the stream that through the centuries had cut its way down through the monoliths of mountains.

In time the canyon opened out into a barren, rock-strewn valley that looked as if it might have been left over from some explosion on the moon. They all bunched up together and Lee Kirby said, "There's a good trail from here on up to the pass. If the weather ain't too bad, we can top it by noon."

Will Baker said, "And if the weather gets worse?"

"Then we'll figure another way," Lee Kirby said.

The clouds were a leaden mass on the hidden peaks now, pressing down as if they would crush the mountains themselves. They found the trail, through the thinning, stunted timber, and they wound upward, always upward. When they came to a wide spot, Will Baker held back momentarily and Larrabee rode close enough to him to hear him say, "It's too damn cold to snow."

It was an old saying, oft repeated, and within a half hour it proved to be the lie it was. The first fat flakes of snow drifted lazily down in the still air. The iron-shod hooves of the mules clanged against the ancient lava, the only indication that there had ever been life in this growing desolation that allowed no living thing to survive. They saw the last of the stunted, wind-twisted pines, and the forest dropped off behind and below them.

They came to a broad flat and paused for a rest. The snow was increasing in intensity, but there was all the confidence in the world in Lee's voice when he said, "It's not even sticking to the ground. As soon as we get over the pass, we drop down fast. Weather's always a lot better on the west side of the mountains."

They rose steadily upward, along the well-defined trail, and then they heard the low, moaning sound rising from below them. Looking back, Larrabee saw the vast forest and was surprised that it would seem this way. When they had been there, the trees were scattered, but from this distance the forest looked like a solid green mass, and he could see the treetops tossing and twisting. The wind had come up, down there in the valley. The snow started coming thicker.

They crossed a ridge and dropped down momentarily into a swale that shut out the sound of the moaning wind, and then they started their final climb and as they wound their way around the shoulder of a jagged peak, a new wind, coming, it seemed, from a totally different direction, hit them fully in the face.

Along with the wind, the snow increased in intensity and now, instead of drifting idly down, it was slanting against them and it swirled around them until they were engulfed in it, a tiny island in the center of the growing storm. And this was just the beginning . . . a warning. Another hour and that wind would suck breath from a man's lungs and freeze the moisture in his eyes.

A huge downdraft of air caught the white smother and threw it in swirls against the broken granite. Below them the forest sent up its wailing. The band of mules lowered their collective heads and the wind whipped at the cropped tails and the roached manes. Larrabee saw the growing concern in Opal's face and he wished there were something he could do or say, but mere man was a puny uselessness in the face of an angry nature. He saw her bow her head against the stinging cut of the wind and the increasing splatter of the snow against her face.

They came to a level spot and Lee held up his hand for them to halt. They bunched the mules and the four of them were there together. Conversation was not easy for the wind snatched the words from their lips. "Too much for us up there in the pass," Lee said. He had to shout the words.

"I say turn back," Will Baker said. "Go back to the valley where we were last night. There'll be some protection there."

"There's a shorter way," Lee said. "A hundred yards or so ahead the trail forks. It's a short run down into a valley."

Baker stared intently at the young parolee. "Back home. Is that it, Kirby?"

There was something close to terror in Opal's face. "There must be another way, Lee," she said. She was pleading.

Lee shook his head. "You know better," he said.

She said, "Suppose they're down there?"

"They're kinfolk," Lee Kirby said. "They'll help us out."

Will Baker was looking first at Lee and then at Opal. "So it's just like you planned it, right from the first, ain't it, Kirby? I wondered how long it would take you to turn. I didn't expect it this soon."

Larrabee saw the tension building in Lee's face. He was fighting to control himself. Lee said, "You don't have to go anyplace you don't want to, Baker. You can go back or stay here and freeze to death if you want, but, by God, I'm getting

Opal and these mules out of here." He looked at Larrabee.
"How about you, Tex?"

"I'm with you, Lee," Larrabee said.

"Sure you're with him," the marshal said. "You're part of
it. I knew from the minute I saw you you were no damn
good."

"Have it your way, Baker," Larrabee said.

Will Baker said, "There's one thing I want you to remember. As far as I'm concerned these are government mules.
You touch these mules and it's my business. It's a big thing,
stealing government mules."

"I'll try hard to remember that, Baker," Larrabee said.

They moved on upward, into the teeth of the storm, and
then they saw Lee's signal and he veered off sharply to his
left, leading the pack mules. They fell in behind him and now
the wind was quartering against their backs. They dropped
down swiftly and came back into timber, and now the biting
cold of the wind was gone and there was only the moaning
complaint of the trees and it was warm here in comparison to
the breath of ice they had found on the barren slopes at their
back. It was still cold enough to freeze a man's marrow.

The altitude was taking a toll on all of them, including the
mules. The animals were panting heavily and Larrabee said,
"What do you think, Kirby? Can we stop and give them a
breather?"

"I figure we got to," Lee said.

Larrabee nodded and swung down from the saddle. Opal
rode up to him and he saw the worried expression on her
face. "It's gonna be all right," he said. "We best let the
mules blow and as long as they're doing that, wouldn't be
nothing wrong with having a bite to eat. At least maybe a cup
of coffee."

"If you think so," she said.

There was no moisture in the snow, and there was enough
wood around that Larrabee soon had a small fire going. They
had packed well this morning, and Lee Kirby had put the
coffee and the pot on top where it was easy to reach, and
there was jerky.

They all drank deeply of the steaming brew and chewed the nutritious juices from the dried beef. "There's some hot springs below," Lee said. "Always seems to be grass. We could hold up a day or so until the storm passes."

"Who in hell says it's gonna pass?" Will Baker said.

"Pretty early in the fall," Lee Kirby said. "They pass."

Will Baker said, "It all sounds too damn pat to me."

Larrabee Stone said, "You got a better idea, Baker?"

Will Baker had been squatting down, back hunched. He stood up slowly with the movement of an older man. The sheepskin coat gave him a blocky, massive look. He said, "Why don't the three of you lay it out plain for me? You think I can't see what's going on?" He shook his head. "I been a lawman too long. I know a skunk when I smell it."

"You know so damn much, why don't you tell us about it?" Larrabee said.

"You, Opal," Baker said. "You and Lee Kirby. First cousins. And Uncle Fenton Hoover. I say Hoover came by your place and you gave him supplies and let him go. He came straight here to tell the rest of your thieving relatives you were on the way with fifty fat mules."

Larrabee clenched his gloved hands tightly. He had to fight himself to keep from smashing Baker's face. His voice was flat and hard when he said, "Where do I fit in?"

"You came along at a mighty convenient time," Baker said. "And you, Kirby. Strange to me you got out of prison the same day."

Lee Kirby seemed suddenly old and tired. "Why argue with you, Baker?" he said. "You made up your mind about me before I ever got out." He ignored Baker completely. To Opal and Larrabee he said, "We best get moving."

Larrabee looked at Opal and he saw her biting her lips and there were tears welling in her eyes. He didn't dare look at Baker. He believed at this moment that if he looked at the marshal he'd kill the man. They swung into their saddles and moved downslope, and Will Baker came along with them, leading his string of mules.

The wind died, and the clouds spread out and the snow

came in wet, fat flakes that turned to water as soon as they hit. The flanks of the mules began to steam and by comparison it seemed suddenly hot.

They came to a small stream, and Lee Kirby dismounted, broke the ice scum with his bootheel, and let his saddle mule drink.

Baker said, "What's wrong with camping here, Kirby? Or maybe you got arrangements with your relatives."

Anyone could have seen the folly of camping here, Larrabee reasoned. It was near the mouth of a canyon and the storm, when it got under way, would funnel into this place and pile the drifts fifteen feet high. He looked at Lee Kirby and saw that the kid's gloved hands were made into fists, but his arms were straight down at his sides, and he held them there as if it were an effort.

Baker was mad. He was mad because that was a natural condition with him. It was easier to do your job when you were mad. He was mad because he had been pulled in on this mule drive. He was madder still because Fenton Hoover had escaped him and he had been given an ex-convict for a guide. "A loyal, true-blue jasper," Baker said. "Wouldn't tell on his pals. Kirby had a bunch of pals in that holdup, Tex. Did you know that? Nice playmates, but he wouldn't tell on them."

Lee Kirby stood up. His lips were tight. "Take off that badge," he said.

Larrabee didn't look up from stirring the fire. His gray eyes were flat and unsmiling. He said, "You talk too much, Baker."

Baker said, "Maybe there was a wench. Sometimes there is. That always helps. You talk and your pals will start playing around with your wench . . ."

Lee Kirby lunged across the fire and his fist smashed against Baker's jaw. It barely shook the marshal. Baker started walking forward slowly and Larrabee Stone stepped in front of him. "Keep your head, damn you," he said.

"It's all right, Tex," Baker said. "I won't cancel his parole. I'll just beat in his face."

Larrabee shoved Baker backward. "You want to play rough, you come through me first," he said. "Right now I don't give a damn for either of you. Kill yourselves off if you want, but not until we've got this weather behind us. I'm from a warm state. I don't like freezing."

"I'd like to know just what the hell part you got in this," Will Baker said.

"I'll tell you what my part is," Larrabee said. "I took a job. I expect to finish it because when I finish it I get paid. There's no more than that."

He looked at the girl and thought, *I'm lying to myself.* But the anger kept building until it was tight in his throat. "You've got to prove things, Baker," he said. "You've got to prove that a man who's made a mistake can't go straight. I don't like it, Baker. I get damn sick of listening to it."

The three men stood there and the fat, moist flakes began to drive, and now they were hard flakes that stung a man's cheeks. The wind had been low and broken by the trees. It started to wail. Half the mules drank at the stream; the others pawed the thin blanket of snow.

The wind blew the snow off the ground, and the pine needles were bare and brown and strangely dry. Lee Kirby said, "We're an hour ahead of it, maybe. We can make the valley."

They crossed a ridge and when they were on higher ground the snow stung their faces and puffed around the hooves of the mules. Lee Kirby motioned toward a nearly invisible trail and they went on down. Down through the scrub timber, along the forgotten trail, down and out of the storm. It was late enough for sundown when they came to the valley.

The valley was long and green, marked here and there with islands of timber. The mountains stood all around it, hunching their massive backs against the storm, shutting out the wind and the weather. The air was strangely warm and still, and the cloud mass above them was like a protective blanket. There was a small stream that was not frozen over, and here and there across the valley there were puffs of steam. The valley was laced with hot springs and there were patches of grass, as if the ground itself were warm.

Larrabee didn't know this country, but as he looked around he realized this place would make a fine hideout for a band of outlaws. He turned to Kirby and said, "It's a good spot, kid. You've got a good eye."

He was making conversation and the kid knew it. Kirby said, "You don't have to play word games with me, Tex. There's no other place to go, that's all."

"Then we're lucky you knew about it," Larrabee said.

"I knew about it because I was raised here," Kirby said.

Larrabee looked across at Will Baker and again he realized the man was old. He hadn't dismounted. He was hunched there in his saddle, feeling the cold more than the rest of them felt it, a man who was tired. But even more than that, a man who had devoted his entire life to running down criminals, and now, Larrabee knew, as surely as if Will Baker had told him, this "convict," as Will Baker had insisted on calling him, this young kid on parole, looking forward only to a job and being reunited with a girl he loved . . . this kid had led them into an outlaw hideout. It was all too plain.

Larrabee said, "All right, kid. So it's home ground. Do I give a damn?"

"There's fifty mules and there's Opal and there's you, too," Lee Kirby said. "There might be people still here in this valley. If there are, you're gonna meet 'em. I figure maybe I can talk to them. I sure as hell can't talk to a blizzard up there in the pass."

A shift in the wind brought the unmistakable smell of woodsmoke to Larrabee's nostrils. They weren't alone in this valley.

Opal, too, had noticed the distinctive smell of smoke. She looked at Lee desperately and Larrabee heard her say, "They're here."

"Maybe not," Lee said. "Maybe it's only Uncle Fenton. This is where he would head. There's always supplies in the cabins."

There was a faint hope in Opal's expression. "Or maybe it's Lorella and her dad."

Lee Kirby's voice was like a pistol shot. "No," he said, "Lorella and her dad left here two years ago."

For a long moment Opal looked at her cousin and there was a note of sudden realization in her voice when she said, "That was your deal, wasn't it? You pleaded guilty to that robbery and covered up for the others so Shug would let Lorella and her dad go."

"If I did," Lee said, "it was worth it."

"How do you know you could trust Shug?" Opal said.

"Because he knows I'd talk," Lee said. "I've got enough on him to hang him twelve times, and if that didn't work I told him I'd come back. I told him I'd see to it he'd be just as dead as those eight or ten others he's killed."

"I knew you weren't guilty, Lee," Opal said softly. "I've always known."

Larrabee saw Will Baker staring intently at the kid, and he thought of what the barber had told him back there in Twin Pines, and he wondered if maybe right now Will Baker wasn't thinking of that son of his who had gone bad.

Baker said, "I'm cold plum through. I want a drink of that whiskey."

"It's on the first pack mule," Larrabee said. "Right on top."

Baker moved stiffly to the mule. He lifted the tarp and brought out the bottle. He looked briefly at the others and then he uncorked the bottle, tilted it to his lips, and drank deeply. There was a note of embarrassment in his voice. "Warms a man," he said. He shoved the cork back in the bottle and replaced it in the pack.

"I want you to take that badge off and throw it away, Baker," Lee said.

"You planning to come at me again?" Baker asked.

"I'm planning to keep you from getting killed if I can," Lee said. "Like I said. Let me do the talking if it comes to that."

"Do what he says, Baker," Larrabee said quietly.

Baker unpinned the badge from his vest, but he didn't throw it away. He looked down at it, remembering the years, and he dropped it into the pocket of his vest.

"We best move on," Lee Kirby said.

"I don't want to go down to the cabins, Lee," Opal said. "Not just yet. Can't we camp here?"

"We have to face up to it sooner or later," Lee said.

"Then let's make it later," Opal said.

Lee looked at her, understanding completely. "Downstream a ways," he said. "There's some willow thickets and a stand of pine."

Larrabee saw Will Baker watching every expression on Lee Kirby's face. The marshal was beginning to wonder if maybe he had been wrong about the kid, Larrabee figured. They drove the mules down the warm stream to the flat Lee had chosen, and they started to make camp. Larrabee watched Baker.

The older man did twice his share of the work, building the rope corral, cutting boughs for a lean-to. He was a strange man, this Baker, a bitter, relentless man, part bulldog and part bloodhound, a highly trained tracker who knew nothing but human game, just as a springer knows nothing but birds. A man whose business was hating.

They started building the camp in the thicket near the edge of the stream. Larrabee was blowing a fire into life when he heard the command: "Stand up, man. Let's take a look at your teeth."

Larrabee stood up slowly, keeping his hand away from his gun. A massive man was there; a brute of a man with a full red beard. He stood there in the thicket, a rifle in his hand. The hammer of the gun was back and the gun was pointed at Larrabee's chest.

Fifty yards away Larrabee saw Will Baker come out of the willow thicket, his hands above his head. He was being pushed along by a rifle held in the hands of a tall, thin man with a slack jaw and a vacant grin. Two more heavily dressed men came out of the pines.

Lee Kirby and Opal Sprague had gone into one of the

timber patches to cut fir boughs. They came out into the open now. Their hands were at their sides, and an older man had his arm thrown affectionately around the two younger people. The older man said, "Look who's here, Shug." Larrabee recognized the man and the voice. It was Fenton Hoover, the man who had been hiding out in Opal's barn.

CHAPTER FIFTEEN

THE BEARDED GIANT LOWERED HIS RIFLE, AND THE SLACK-JAWED man turned his vacant gaze to Fenton Hoover, Opal, and Lee. The man with the red beard said, "Opal and Lee. My kids," he said, and his voice was soft. "By God, my kids have come back home." The rifle came up sharply and pointed directly at Larrabee's chest. "Who are you?" the big man said.

"Name of Larrabee Lucas Stone," Larrabee said. "My Norwegian mama, she always run my two names together, like Larrabeelucas, but that was such a mouthful folks started calling me Tex."

"He's all right, Shug," Fenton Hoover said. "I was hiding out in Opal's barn when a posse rode in. Tex, there, Could have turned me in, but he didn't do it."

Shug Purcell looked at Larrabee with new interest. "We've got a saying in our family," Shug Purcell said. "A man does you a favor you owe him one back. If you're a friend of Fenton's and Opal's and Lee's, you're a friend of mine. I make you welcome." He turned then and stared hard at Will Baker. He glanced at Fenton Hoover and said, "This one?"

Larrabee felt his heart beating high in his chest. He knew as sure as he was standing here that Will Baker's life depended on Fenton Hoover's answer. He thought he saw Fenton's arm tighten around Opal's waist. Fenton Hoover gave Will Baker a long appraisal. He had seen him before, on more than one occasion. He knew the marshal well. Fenton Hoover shook his head. "Never saw him before in my life," Fenton Hoover said.

Larrabee saw the relief flood Opal's face. Fenton Hoover was a magnificent liar. There wasn't anyone in the world who wouldn't have believed what he said.

Lee Kirby stepped into the breach. "We call him Smith," Lee said. "Don't know any more name than that. Just a drifter Opal hired on to help drive the mules."

"Smith, huh?" Shug Purcell said. "Handy name to have."

Larrabee let his gaze drift down the valley. The snow had slacked off and perhaps a mile away he could see a pine log cabin with smoke trailing from a natural stone chimney. He thought, but he wasn't sure, that on beyond was another cabin, and to one side was a building, low and squat with a tin stovepipe wired in place. There was smoke coming from that pipe, too. He heard Shug Purcell's voice. "What you lookin' at, Tex?"

Larrabee looked directly at the red-bearded man. "This setup here," he said. "It sure is a good one. If I'd a had a place like this back in Wyoming it would have saved me a lot of riding."

Shug Purcell was studying Larrabee's face closely. The slack-jawed man with the vacant stare in his eyes held his rifle steadily on Larrabee's chest. Shug Purcell said, "You on the run, Tex?"

From the corner of his eye Larrabee saw Opal's face, almost pleading, waiting for his answer. Larrabee managed to grin. He said, "Well, let's just say there's a sheriff back in Gillette, Wyoming, I'd just as soon not see anymore." He saw the quick disappointment in Opal's eyes.

Shug Purcell was grinning down at him now. He said, "Yeah, Tex. I know that feeling well." He relaxed noticeably and became almost affable. "Enough of that," he said. "You two are friends of Opal and Lee, that's good enough for me."

The slack-jawed man with the vacant eyes looked as if he wasn't mentally right, and when he started to speak, Larrabee knew that was so. The dim-witted one said, "There something you want me to do, Shug?"

"Yeah, Hubie," Shug said. "You take those three pack mules over to the cabin and unload them. Then you curry down their backs. I always take good care of my animals. Ain't that right, Opal?"

"Sure, Shug," Opal said. "You always were good to animals."

"I'll do what you say, Shug," the man named Hubie said. "I'll do just like you say. I always do just like you say, don't I, Shug?"

Shug Purcell shifted the rifle to his right arm. He put his left arm around the man named Hubie. "Yeah, Hubie," Shug said. "You always do exactly what I tell you to. That's what I like about you." He turned to the other two men. He said, "Take these mules up by the hot springs at the upper end of the valley. There's always some grass there. Besides, the snow ain't that deep and if I know mules, what grass ain't around the springs they'll paw down through the snow and get it."

He looked at Opal. "Fine-looking mules, Opal."

"They're sold to the government," Opal said. "I have to get them delivered on time."

"You sure done well by yourself," Shug Purcell said. "I'm right proud of you." The harshness came back into his voice and he swung the rifle. "Tex—Smith—you, too, Lee. Push back your coats and take off those gun belts you're wearing. Don't you worry. I'll take care of your guns. I take care of guns just like I take care of animals. But we're gonna go down to the cabin and have ourselves a family reunion."

Larrabee heard the sound of a rider. A mounted man came out of the pines. He reined up sharply and looked at the tableau there in front of him. He was a tall man, beautifully muscled. He wore a padded coat, but it was not bulky like the coats of the others. It clung to his broad shoulders and tucked in around his narrow waist as if it had been tailor-made for him. His complexion was dark.

The rider had the age-old advantage of a man on a horse

looking down at a man on the ground, but there was more to his presence than that. It was in his eyes, and Larrabee knew he'd never forget those eyes. They were black. They were not deep brown. They were black. Those eyes were staring intently at Opal. The man on the horse said, "Hello, Opal."

Opal was returning the man's gaze as if unable to turn away from it. "Hello, Rance," she said.

"Has it been three years?" the man on the horse said.

"It's been four," Opal said.

Rance Overton said, "When I heard you were married I sort of couldn't figure it." He smiled, and Larrabee couldn't believe it, but there was a softness in those piercing, black eyes. The man had eyelashes a woman would envy. "I hadn't forgotten you," he said.

Larrabee kept looking at the man on horseback and he felt a stab of jealousy such as he had never known before in his life. These two not only knew each other, it was obvious they had known each other too well.

The softness went out of Rance Overton's eyes as quickly as it had come to them, and he turned and now he was looking straight at Lee Kirby. He said, "Hello, little stepbrother."

"Good to see you, Rance," Lee Kirby said. He didn't mean it.

"Is it?" Rance Overton said. A smile with no warmth in it lifted a corner of his mouth. "So they let you out."

"Yeah, Rance," Lee said. "I got a parole. There's a job waiting for me over in Millerton."

"That's real nice," Rance Overton said. "Things always did go your way, didn't they, little stepbrother?"

Shug Purcell's voice was a sharp bark. He was a man used to giving commands. He said, "Forget it, Rance."

Rance Overton's gaze never left Lee Kirby's face. "Forget what? Forget Lee Kirby killed my daddy?"

"Damn it, Rance," Shug Purcell said, and his voice cracked like a whip. "It was six years ago. It was an accident. Everybody knows it was an accident."

Rance Overton was still staring intently at Lee Kirby and,

looking at Lee, Larrabee remembered how Lee had looked that day on the deer hunt. The smile was still on Rance Overton's lips. He shook his head slowly from side to side. "No, Shug," he said, without looking at the big man. "Not everybody knows it was an accident. I don't." He turned back to Opal and his eyes went soft and his voice matched his eyes. He said, "Opal, I can't tell you how good it is to see you again."

Shug Purcell was looking around the camp Opal and the others had started to build for themselves. It had started to snow again. "Can't imagine why you'd want to camp out when there's cabins nearby," he said. "I got the old cabin fixed up. You remember the old cabin, Lee?"

Lee Kirby was staring straight at Shug Purcell. He said, "I figured after Lorella and her daddy left you'd move into their cabin. It's a lot bigger."

"Yeah," Shug said. "I thought about that. But we come back here awful sudden and unexpected. Folks down there around Visalia were sort of upset about a missing payroll and they got downright unfriendly, so we moved back up here a little quicker than we thought we would."

"I figured you'd take Lorella's cabin," Lee said again. He was trying to find something out, Larrabee knew.

"We might just do that," Shug said. "But let's don't stand around freezing to death. Let's go on down to the cabin. Big fire going in the fireplace. We're gonna have ourselves a real family reunion."

The man named Hubie was standing there, staring vacantly at the other two outlaws. Larrabee heard him say, "I'm gonna take the pack mules down to the cabin. That's what Shug told me to do. I always do what Shug tells me. Shug likes me, you know that?"

Larrabee saw the two outlaws shake their heads and then they moved off toward the herd of mules. They unsnapped the lead ropes and coiled them, then they went to their horses and mounted up. Together they started hazing the mules up the valley to where the steam rose steadily into the thin air.

Shug said, "Don't worry about those mules, Opal. The

boys will look after them. Now mount up and let's move out. You and me and Rance and Fenton and Lee are gonna have ourselves a fine visit. Just like old times." His left eye squeezed shut. "Fifty mules is worth a lot of money."

Mounted, hunched in his sheepskin-lined coat, the gun belts of Baker, Larrabee, and Lee looped around his saddle horn, Shug Purcell became almost a caricature of a man. He was big beyond belief, broad and thick and paunchy with tremendous arms and gigantic shoulders. He was ugly to the point of being fascinating. There were a thousand seams and wrinkles above his red beard and some of them might have been knife scars. His face was mobile, full of expression, sometimes rocky and hard, sometimes flabby and even affectionate. His voice was like his face. He said, "Just like old times."

They rode down the valley, following Hubie and the three pack mules. Rance Overton hadn't asked where to ride. He took his place alongside Opal. They were followed by Lee and Fenton and when Larrabee and Baker moved up to join them, Shug said, "Why don't you two stay back here with me, Tex? I sort of like your company."

Larrabee glanced across at Shug. It was obvious the man was going to keep an eye on him. He rode just slightly back of Larrabee, the reins in his left hand, his rifle gripped in his right, alert, suspicious, watching their every move.

The snow was fitful, momentarily intense and then showing intentions of stopping altogether. The sheer cliffs that surrounded the valley kept the wind that still howled in the pass away from this small oasis in the middle of desolation. Larrabee's eyes searched the valley ahead.

Through a sudden rift in the weather, he got a closer look at the tiny settlement there ahead of them. There was a pole corral, empty of horses now, standing in front of the cabin which was stuffed back into the protection of one of the tiny pockets of the valley. It was an old cabin, with sagging log walls. The shakes on the roof were thick with moss. There was a fragrant trickle of woodsmoke from the natural stone chimney. There was a shed near the cabin . . . a makeshift barn, probably, and an outhouse off to one side. Some one hundred yards away was another log cabin, but it was long and built low to the ground, and again he noticed the wired-up iron stovepipe with its trickle of smoke. It looked as if it had been built for a bunkhouse. A half mile or so down the valley was another cabin, larger and more substantial, but it seemed abandoned. As they approached their destination, Larrabee heard Shug say, "Don't it make you feel good to come home, Opal?" He grinned. "Bet you thought a lot about Lorella, too, didn't you, Lee?"

The riders were all bunched close together now and in spite of the cold Larrabee could have sworn he saw perspiration forming on Lee Kirby's face. Lee's voice came through his teeth as he said, "I kept my end of the deal. I served two years."

"Sure you did, Lee," Shug said. "You was a real man about it. That's why I took such care of Lorella."

Larrabee saw Lee's hands tighten against the pommel of his saddle. His knuckles were bone white. "She better be all right," Lee said.

Shug was grinning broadly. "Last time I saw her she was fine as frog's hair," he said.

They came to the cabin and the pole corral and Hubie was already starting to unpack the mules. Hubie said, "When I get 'em unpacked, I'll curry 'em down good like you said, Shug."

"Sure, Hubie," Shug said. "I know you will. We're going to turn these saddle horses into the corral. You get some nose bags and give 'em a good bait of oats."

There was confusion on Hubie's face. "But you said to take care of the pack mules."

"You do that first, Hubie," Shug said patiently. "Then you get the nose bags and put oats in them and you put them on the horses in the corral."

Hubie's face lighted up. "I take off the pack saddles first."

"That's right, Hubie," Shug said.

They all dismounted and Larrabee moved forward to help Opal with her horse, but Rance Overton was closer to her.

Rance said, "You go on in the cabin and get yourself warm, Opal. I'll take care of your horse."

Opal looked at him and there was gratitude in her eyes. She said, "Thanks, Rance."

Larrabee tugged at his cinch strap with unaccustomed impatience. Lee had moved up close to him. With his face still against the side of his horse, Larrabee said, "I don't like your stepbrother a whole bunch"

Lee managed a faint grin. "You got lots of company," he said.

When they had unsaddled and turned the horses into the corral, they went into the cabin. It was larger than Larrabee had expected. There were four bunks built into the walls of the main room. A table and four chairs stood at the far end. Off to one side was a door that he assumed led to a lean-to kitchen, and a door in the back opened into the privacy of the single bedroom. Rance Overton's voice was soft, caressing. He put his arm around Opal's waist. "Look familiar, does it?" he said. Opal didn't answer. She just nodded her head and Larrabee saw the faraway look in her eyes that seemed to him to be more pain than it was memory.

"Fenton," Shug said, "go on out and help Hubie. Looked to me like there was some deer meat tied on one of those packs. Been a long time since we've had any good venison around here." He looked at Opal and grinned. "Been a lot longer since we had a decent cook."

Fenton Hoover went outside and he was almost immediately back. He was grinning. "There's four bottles of damn good whiskey in one of those packs," he said. Rance Overton said, "Well, what do you know about that? It's been almost as long since we've had any decent whiskey around here."

"Go ahead and bring it in, Fenton," Shug said.

"I could use a drink," Will Baker said. It was the first word he had uttered.

"Sure, Smith," Shug Purcell said. "This is gonna be a real family party."

* * *

In spite of her bone weariness and the obvious tension she was under, Opal Sprague lived up to her reputation as a cook. There were thick venison steaks and biscuits and gravy and fried potatoes. The men sat around the table, Shug at the head, Fenton Hoover on one side of him, Hubie on the other. There hadn't been enough chairs for all of them but Fenton had gone outside and come back with a bench. Lee, Larrabee, and Baker sat on the bench.

The men ate ravenously and Larrabee noticed that in addition to the three drinks he had had before the meal Rance Overton was having a glass of whiskey with his food. He noticed also that each time Hubie raised a heaping forkful of food toward his mouth he would hesitate and look at Shug. Shug would give him a silent nod and then Hubie would wolf down the food, chewing noisily. *The poor devil won't make a move without Shug's approval,* Larrabee thought.

Rance Overton, without his coat and his hat, was even more handsome than he had first appeared. He got up quickly and pulled out a chair when Opal finally sat down to eat. He was as graceful and as gallant as if the two of them were alone in a high-class restaurant. He said, "Opal, there's never been anyone can cook a meal like you can."

Opal smiled up at him. "Thank you, Rance," she said softly.

Once more Larrabee felt that deep stab of jealousy. There was a stirring anger in him as he thought, *Rance Overton's as phony as a three-dollar bill. What the hell's the matter with women that they can't see things like that?*

Shug Purcell said. "You ain't had much to say, Smith."

Lee Kirby said, "He don't talk much."

They finished the meal and Rance hastened to help Opal clear off the table. Larrabee felt they stayed in the kitchen a lot longer than they needed to. Shug sank into a chair and belched loudly. "Now that was a meal," he said. "Good whiskey . . . fire in the fireplace . . . snowin' outside . . . makes a man drowsy."

"I was thinking that," Larrabee said. "If there's hay out there in that shed, I can unroll my sugans there."

"Now just a damn minute," Shug said expansively. "You and Smith are guests of mine. There's bunks enough here for you two and for Rance and me. Lee and Fenton can go on over to the bunkhouse with Hubie. There's only Garth and Jay Dee over there." His voice became dreamy. "Was a time I had fifteen men in that bunkhouse. Damn good men, too." He came back to the present. "Plenty of room. And, Opal, you're gonna get the best. You're gonna have that back room there all to yourself. I know how it is with a woman. They like some privacy." He was suddenly in the past again. "That's the way it was with my wife. Ten years we was married, but she still liked her privacy." He got up and clapped an arm affectionately around Opal's shoulder. "Nothing but the best for you, Opal."

Opal said, "I am tired."

"Of course you are, Opal," Rance Overton said. "Is there anything I can get for you out of the packsaddles?"

"No," Opal said. "I'm fine." Larrabee saw the growing nervousness in her. She gave Rance a fleeting smile. "But thank you anyway." She started for the bedroom, then changed her mind. She sat down in one of the chairs. The strain was showing in every line of her face.

There was a long silence around the table. Rance Overton poured himself another drink. "I could use one of those," Will Baker said. Overton pushed the bottle across toward Baker. "Help yourself," he said.

There had been a tension building in Lee Kirby too, all through the meal. Larrabee had watched it, wondering when it would explode. Lee Kirby couldn't hold it in any longer. He said, "I want you to know something, Shug, and I want you to know it straight. Those mules belong to Opal, and I mean to see to it it stays that way."

Shug Purcell gave Lee a long, steady look. He said, "What's got into you, boy? You've changed. You ain't friendly like you used to be."

Larrabee said, "Maybe you don't understand how it is to spend two years in a prison cell. Seems like everything tightens in around you."

Shug said, "You know how that is, do you, Tex?"

"He knows," Fenton Hoover said. "That's how it is."

Larrabee realized Opal's eyes were searching his face and he thought there was a hurt disappointment there. He wished he could explain to her what he was trying to do.

Shug said, "You talk pretty straight, Tex. You been there?"

Larrabee felt Opal watching him intently. He couldn't back down now. He said, "I've been there. I couldn't take it. That's why I broke out."

He saw the hurt in Opal's eyes. She got up quickly. She didn't look at Larrabee. She went into the bedroom and she closed the door behind her.

Larrabee saw Will Baker looking at him, and he knew the thoughts that were going through Will Baker's mind. *I spotted you for an outlaw the minute I saw you.* That's what Will Baker was thinking. He was a lawman among outlaws and he was beginning to realize there was no way out of it for him. He had dealt with a hundred men like these and he knew if they found out who he was, that would be the end of him.

Lee Kirby said, "Maybe you didn't hear me, Shug. Those mules belong to Opal. I mean to see they get delivered. I got a job in Millerton and I mean to take that too."

Shug said, "I wish you'd calm down, boy. I ain't giving you no argument, am I? I don't mind you going in for yourself. I ain't against that at all." He leaned back in his chair. "But I don't want you to forget you got blood relatives and you just can't let relatives down." He shook his head. "Things have been mighty slow with us, Lee."

Larrabee saw the old trap starting to close around the kid, and he knew Baker saw it too. Shug was beginning to put the squeeze on him. He glanced at Will Baker and Baker had a sardonic smile on his lips. It was an old story to Baker.

Shug waved his hand. "We didn't come here to talk business, Lee. Just visit. Now why don't you and Hubie and Fenton go on over to the bunkhouse and get yourselves a night's sleep? We'll talk about it in the morning."

"Come on, Lee," Fenton Hoover said. "This don't do no good."

"I'll go get some sleep, Shug," Hubie said, "I always do just what you tell me."

For a long moment Lee stood there staring at Shug, wanting to say more, knowing, as his uncle had said, it would do no good. He turned and followed the other two outside. Shug Purcell shook his head. He reached out and got the bottle and poured himself a drink, then offered it to Larrabee and Baker. "You look kinda sick, Smith," Shug said.

Larrabee had a drink with the rest of them. He had long ago learned to hold his liquor when there was a need for it. He saw how it was going to be. Lee Kirby and Opal Sprague had a fight on their hands if they expected to get out of here with the mules. If he could play along, maybe he could get himself and Opal out of here and once he did he'd be willing to forget he had ever seen this valley. Baker, on the other hand, would have other ideas. If he ever got out of here he would want to come back and make a wholesale roundup of what was left of the Purcell-Kirby-Hoover gang.

Larrabee said, "We've had a hard day. I reckon I'll turn in."

"Sure, Tex," Shug said. "You do that. Take off your boots and stretch out comfortable. A man sleeps a sight better with his boots off." He lifted his hand from under the table and it was holding a gun. He laid the gun on the table. "I hope you boys understand about your guns," Shug said. "I never did hold to having too many guns around camp." He looked steadily at Baker. "You're gonna sleep a lot better without your boots too, Smith."

Larrabee glanced at Baker and nodded shortly. The two men sat down on the edges of their bunks and removed their boots. Shug, still grinning, the gun in his hand, walked across and got the boots. He said, "I'll tuck these under my bunk where they'll be safe from rats." His seamed face looked almost affable. "I hope you two sleep good," he said. He went back to the table and sat down. Larrabee and Baker heard him drop the boots heavily on the floor.

Larrabee and Baker crawled under the covers. The blankets were good and the heat from the fireplace was in the room. It would be hard to stay awake for long, Larrabee knew. Overton moved his chair closer to Shug's and the two men started talking in low voices. Listening to the droning monotone, Larrabee's eyes grew heavy. He could hear Baker's heavy breathing and he knew that the combination of bone-deep fatigue plus a full stomach and the whiskey he had drunk had been too much for the older man. He was sound asleep already.

Larrabee fought off sleep as long as he could, but it was a losing battle. He thought of Baker and was sure Shug didn't trust him. Will Baker, Larrabee decided, was a dead man. The thought made him sick to his stomach. Sleep took over.

CHAPTER SIXTEEN

Opal sat on the edge of the bed and looked around the Spartan room. There was a lighted kerosene lamp and she turned it up. The thin, yellow light revealed a battered dresser, a single chair, and nothing more. The straw mattress whispered beneath her weight. She had been able to hear through the thin wall and she knew Larrabee and Baker had gone to bed and now there was only the low drone of voices . . . Shug's and Rance's.

She was startled by the memory of the feelings that had swept her when she had seen Rance. She had never pretended that she had forgotten him, but she had never believed he could rekindle those old memories. But there was another memory that outweighed all the others. It was when Uncle Fenton had shown her that poster with the likeness of Rance on it, and the bold type that had seared itself on her brain: WANTED FOR ARMED ROBBERY AND ATTEMPTED RAPE. It was those last two words that haunted her.

At that moment, the desperation of growing up with a band of outlaws, knowing what they were, knowing they would never change, had risen up to strangle her. She had had to get away from it, and she had thrown herself at the first man who came along. An old man. But what difference did it make?

She was ashamed of it now, but it was a fact and she would have to live with it. If only Rance had been different. She had given herself to him willingly, and she would have given her life to him . . .

There had been three men in her life, and all of them had been wrong. Rance Overton. Frank Sprague, who had given her little more than a roof over her head and a new name. And then there was Larrabee Stone. She remembered how he had put his arm around her there in the cabin when she was terrified and the crackle of rifle fire was just outside her window. And she remembered the death of Big Blue and of his tender understanding. But most of all she rememberod his kiss, soft and yearning, and she thought of all the welling, lonely desire that had swept through her, unbidden.

Yes, Larrabee. Perhaps . . . but he was an escaped convict, on the run from the law. She had heard it from his own lips. He was no better than the others.

She was bone tired and there was a bed there, and she would be a fool not to use it. She undressed completely, and then put the man's flannel shirt back on. It would be the warmest thing she had. She turned down the blankets and then trimmed the lamp until it was only a soft glow. She crawled into the bed and pulled the covers around her. Sleep claimed her almost immediately. Her sheer exhaustion outweighed her thoughts.

She had no idea how long she had slept, but she awoke with a start. There was someone in the room. She reached out to turn up the lamp and she heard Rance whisper, "It's all right, Opal."

Her whisper matched his. "What are you doing here?"

"I had to say good-night," he said. He was moving over toward the bed. "I tried to forget you, Opal. I thought I had, but when I saw you again . . ." He sat down on the edge of the bed.

"You shouldn't be here, Rance," she said. She could smell the strong reek of whiskey on his breath.

"I should never have been anyplace else but beside you," he whispered.

"Please, Rance," she said. "We can talk tomorrow."

"There have been too many tomorrows for me," he said.

"I want you now." He leaned down and pressed his cheek against hers and again, unbidden, those memories rushed through her. She shoved against him.

"Leave me alone, Rance," she said.

"Do you really want me to?" he said. She saw his face coming closer and now his lips were against hers. She tried to turn her head. "I want you, Opal," he said. "I need you."

She realized he was unbuckling his belt, pushing down his trousers. Panic seized her, and then his body was pressing against her. She started fighting, clawing at him, trying to push him away. His hands came up and pinned her shoulders to the pillow and now his voice was harsh and the whiskey breath was hot against her face. "Don't play games with me," he said. "You were married for two years. You're used to getting it regular. Your husband's been dead a year. You want it as bad as I do." He was pressing against her and she felt his hard manliness against her naked thigh. "Love me, Opal," he said. "Love me."

What does this have to do with love? she thought wildly. *This is rape!* A vision of that poster Fenton had shown her flashed across her mind. WANTED FOR ATTEMPTED RAPE. She twisted her body to avoid him, and she shoved against him with all the strength she had. She wasn't whispering now. She heard her own scream ringing in her ears. "Rance! Leave me alone!"

She kicked and scratched and shoved, and he fell off the bed and hit the floor hard. He was on his feet, coming toward her, but his legs were tangled in his own trousers which had dropped around his ankles. He lunged toward her and the door flew open and Larrabee Stone was there. He was in his stocking feet, and he was naked to the waist. She saw his muscles bunch as he threw himself forward.

Larrabee grabbed Rance with his left hand and jerked him upright and in the same motion his right hand smashed into the center of Overton's face. Rance staggered back, blood spouting from his nose. He was clawing at his pants, pulling them up. Larrabee went after him, hitting him again. Rance slammed back against the wall with a crash and now Larrabee was going for him, his hands outstretched.

Instinctively, Opal turned up the lamp. The glow hit Larrabee's face and she had never seen such naked hatred in her life. He was going to choke Rance to death. She knew it . . .

Shug's voice was like a pistol shot. "That's enough, Tex," he said. Larrabee felt the prod of the six-shooter against his spine. He straightened.

There was blood smeared all across Rance Overton's face. His lips were pulled back from his teeth. He said, "Give me that gun, Shug. I'll kill the son of a bitch!"

"Get the hell out of this room, Rance," Shug said. "What is it with you? Every time there's a woman around it's trouble. I've damn near had to horsewhip you to keep you away from Lorella. If you're so hard up, why don't you ride down to the nearest whorehouse and pay for it like a man. Now get out!"

Opal stared at the backs of the three men as they left the room. She saw Larrabee close the door. She thought, *Oh my God, is that all it is to men?* And then the thought came, *Did I bring this on? Was it my fault?*

She buried her head in the pillow and her body shook with her sobbing.

When Larrabee closed that bedroom door the rage was still seething in him until he knew no reason. He whirled to look at Rance who was holding a towel to his face, and Shug was there, the six-shooter still leveled at Larrabee's belly. Only then did he miss Baker. He glanced toward Baker's bunk. It was empty. His inner rage clouded his reason. He said, "Where's Baker?"

There was a faint smile tugging at one corner of Shug's lips. He said, "What did Smith do, Tex? Change his name during the night?"

Larrabee tried to cover his blunder. "Baker . . . Smith . . . Jones . . . What the hell. He called himself a dozen names. We settled on Smith."

"That so?" Shug said. He was smiling fully now. He still

held the gun in his right hand, pointed directly at Larrabee, and his eyes never left Larrabee's face. With his left hand he reached into his pocket and brought out a piece of metal. He tossed it on the table and it landed with a loud clank. Larrabee looked at it. It was a deputy U.S. marshal's badge. "Time to quit playing games, Tex," Shug said. "Who in hell are you?"

"I told you," Larrabee said.

"You know this Smith or Baker or whatever you call him was a lawman?"

"I don't ask questions," Larrabee said. He glanced around the room. Will Baker's boots were still there under Shug's bunk; his heavy, sheepskin-lined coat was hanging on the deer horns near his gun belt and holstered gun. "Where'd he go?" Larrabee said.

"Decided to take a walk along about midnight," Shug said. "Figured maybe he was going to the outhouse so I didn't pay much mind."

"Without his boots or his coat?" Larrabee said.

Shug was looking directly into Larrabee's eyes. He said, "Cold as it is out there, I think that was damn foolish. Don't you, Tex?"

"I'd say damn foolish," Larrabee said. Larrabee had played a lot of poker in his time; he hoped his expression didn't betray him now. Inside he was churning. Outside in this weather . . . Baker didn't have a chance.

"Never did think lawmen had much sense," Shug said.

"I've found that so," Larrabee said.

There was a sound of horses outside, tramping feet, the stomping of boots to free them of snow. The door opened and Fenton Hoover, bundled against the cold, came in. He was followed closely by Lee and the hulking Hubie. Larrabee was surprised to see the light spilling through the open door. It was near morning. He had slept longer than he had thought. Fenton said, "Heard a commotion over here. Everything all right?" He looked at Rance Overton and started to grin. "What horse tromped on you?" he said.

"Little misunderstanding," Shug said.

Fenton Hoover was fighting to hold back his laughter. He said, "I guess you would call an earthquake a little misunderstanding too."

Rance was getting up from his chair. "You want to try some of it, Fenton?" he said.

"Sit down, Rance," Shug said. "You've caused enough trouble for one morning."

Lee looked around the cabin. "Where's Smith?"

"Damn fool decided to take a walk," Larrabee said. "Without his boots or his coat." He turned to Fenton and his voice was casual. "How's the weather out?"

"Quit snowin'," Fenton said. "Colder than Billy-be-damn."

"That Smith, as you call him, was a deputy U.S. marshal," Shug said. "You know that, Lee?"

Lee looked at Larrabee, saw him shrug and gesture toward the table. He saw the badge lying there. Lee said, "All right, I knew."

"I don't much like you bringing a lawman here into the valley, Lee," Shug said. "Fact is, I don't like it at all."

Lee sat down heavily on the edge of Baker's bunk. He looked up at Shug and now he was just a kid, caught in a trap. "I couldn't help it, Shug. God knows I didn't want to come down here, but the blizzard in the north pass cut us off. Will Baker was a close friend of Opal's husband. Seems he promised Frank Sprague he'd look out for her. When I got out, Opal promised me a job driving those mules. It was part of the reason I got the parole. Will Baker had orders to stay with me until I got settled in Millerton, so it worked out that he could help Opal and keep an eye on me at the same time. As for Tex there, I don't know one damn bit more about him than you do. He was a drifter that Opal hired at the last minute." He looked up and his eyes were pleading. "That's the God's truth, Shug. Every word of it."

No one, not even Shug, could have doubted Lee's sincerity. "Will Baker," Shug said. "The famous man hunter. So that's who he was." He looked at Larrabee. "Me and my boys always worked over on the west side of the slopes so we never did run into him, but I sure heard plenty about him in the old days." He grinned. "Looks like we got us a big one."

"Why in hell didn't you just shoot him and get it over with?" Lee said.

"Me shoot a deputy U.S. marshal?" Shug said. "That could be big trouble."

Rance Overton got up from his chair. His nose was starting to swell. It was probably broken, Larrabee thought with satisfaction. "I'm going outside," Rance said.

"That's good, Rance," Shug said. "Cool you off. While you're out there, see to the horses." He still held the gun on Larrabee but his eyes were on Rance Overton. He said, "And, Rance?"

"What?" Overton said.

"If you're thinking about that rifle out in the shed, it ain't there. I don't want no damn shootin' here."

Rance Overton didn't bother to answer. He shrugged into his coat and went outside. The door opened and Opal came out of the bedroom. She was fully dressed. Lee said, "All right, Shug, what is it you want?"

"Lee, boy," Shug Purcell said, "I've known you ever since you were born. Did you ever hear me ask for anything unreasonable?"

"Quit stalling, Shug," Lee said. "Lay it out plain."

"Well, I was thinking about those fifty mules up there at the far end of the valley," he said.

"I told you," Lee said. "Those are Opal's mules."

"Sure they are, Lee," Shug said. "And they're gonna be delivered. At least some of them are."

Larrabee glanced at Opal. He knew she was hanging on to every word. Lee said, "What's that supposed to mean?"

Shug Purcell sat down at the table. He laid the gun in front of him. He wasn't playing word games now. "Just this," he said. "You and Opal are gonna deliver twenty-five of those mules. I'm keeping the other twenty-five."

"Those mules are for the government, Shug," Lee said. Larrabee was surprised at the control in the kid's voice. "You ever hear of the United States Army?"

"Sure have, boy," Shug said. "And that's how come me and Rance figured this thing out last night. If none of those mules are delivered, the Army might come to see why. That's the way with the Army. They got ten thousand soldiers and nothing to do with them, so they send them out to look for mules and deputy U.S. marshals and things like that." Shug shook his head. "That Army don't never quit. I wouldn't want to get tangled up with them."

"Then leave it alone," Lee said.

"No," Shug said, "I think Rance and me have figured out a way we can have our cake and eat it too." He seemed relaxed and confident. "The way I see it, it will work out real nice. You, Lee, and Opal too, you deliver half of them mules. You can explain how you got caught in a blizzard and all that. Even soldiers got sense enough to know that mules wander off and you could easy lose half of them."

"They know Will Baker was with us," Lee said. "There's all kinds of papers and they got copies. They'll wonder what happened to Will Baker."

"I reckon they will, all right," Shug said. "And if they go so far as to look for him, they'll find him froze to death. They'll think he sure was crazy to take off his coat and his boots like that, but then lots of men have gone crazy when they were caught in a bad blizzard."

Larrabee looked at Opal. Her face was white with tension. She was gripping the back of the chair. He tried to put a touch of admiration into his voice. He said, "Doggone me, Shug, you just plain think big, don't you?"

"Meanin' what?" Shug said.

"Well," Larrabee said, "compared to the way I had it figured. See, I always did plan on cutting out ten of those mules for myself." He shook his head. "But twenty-five of them? You think big, Shug."

"You figured on making off with ten of those mules?" Shug said.

Larrabee said, "Do I look stupid enough to risk my neck for a bunch of strangers just for day wages I might not even get?'' He laughed at the idea. ''Hell, I figured on getting a lot more than that out of this mule drive.'' He looked at Opal with what he hoped was a suggestive leer. He said, ''Just a whole lot more.'' He saw the utter disgust on Opal's face. ''I guess I just think small,'' Larrabee said. ''I wish I had met up with someone like you a long time back, Shug.''

''I think things out,'' Shug said. He turned to Lee and his smile was paternal. ''So there you are, boy. Simple as that. Opal don't get cheated none and you'll be a regular doggone hero, deliverin' what's left of them mules.''

''I won't do it, Shug,'' Lee said. ''I'm through with you and all the rest of it. I'm not going back inside those walls.''

''You telling me you ain't going along with my plans?'' Shug said.

''I'm telling you to take your plans and go straight to hell,'' Lee said.

Shug looked intently at the younger man for a long time, and then he turned to Fenton Hoover. Fenton hadn't moved from his place by the door. Hubie, with his vacant stare, stood near him. Neither man had said one word. Shug said, ''Fenton, go fetch Lorella. Maybe she can talk some sense into this stubborn jackass.''

Lee's face had gone dead white. He was trembling all over, and it showed in his voice. ''She's supposed to be in Millerton. You promised me you'd see her and her dad got down there . . .''

''Did I?'' Shug said. ''I must be slippin' in my old age. I don't remember saying anything like that.'' He turned and looked at Opal. ''Why don't you rustle us up some breakfast, Opal? It's been a long night and I'm plum starved.''

Opal moved toward the kitchen. Her movements were mechanical. She stopped once and looked squarely at Larrabee. He had never seen such unmasked disgust in a woman's face in his life.

CHAPTER SEVENTEEN

OPAL MOVED WOODENLY AROUND THE KITCHEN. SHE STIRRED UP the fire in the cookstove and while it flared into life she whipped up a mix for hotcakes. There was plenty of canned milk, and she made thick, creamy gravy. The hotcakes were almost the size of plates and when she had half a dozen of them stacked on the platter that was keeping warm on the back of the stove she took plates and utensils out and set them in front of the men at the table. She avoided looking at Larrabee, who sat between Lee and Shug. Hubie sat at Shug's right, where he always sat. He picked up his knife and fork and stared hungrily down at his empty plate. The rich smell of boiling coffee filled the room. It was full daylight now.

When she came back into the room with the platter of hotcakes, Rance was coming through the door. She caught a glimpse of his face, swollen out of shape, and she saw him stomp snow from his boots and shrug out of his heavy coat. Shug said, "Better have some flapjacks, Rance. Opal made 'em. Ain't none better."

"I'm not hungry," Rance Overton said. He went across and picked up one of the bottles and he stood there, glaring at Shug, daring him to say something, knowing he would.

Shug said, "Better take it easy on that stuff."

"Go to hell," Rance said. He tilted the bottle and drank deeply, then wiped his mouth with the back of his hand. That small flare of rebellion had helped some, but not nearly

169

enough. He sat down in a chair, away from the table, and he put the bottle down beside him.

He was a man who had long lived with hatred. He thrived on it. But the hatred inside him now was tearing him to pieces. He hated Shug for not letting him have a gun; he hated Larrabee for smashing his face; he hated Opal because of the indignity she had caused him. And he combined all those seething hatreds and focused them on Lee Kirby, his stepbrother. It was easy to do. He had always hated Lee. And in his mind he was positive that Lee had purposely killed his father. All the evidence that the killing had been accidental . . . the total conviction of everyone else that it had been an accident . . . meant nothing to Rance Overton. The words had seared themselves into his brain. *You son of a bitch, you killed my daddy!* If there were some way to get Lee to start a fight with him, he wouldn't need a gun then. He could kill him with his bare hands. He knew he could.

Watching the men shovel down food made Rance sick to his stomach. He picked up the bottle and took another long drink. He saw Hubie raise a fork piled high with hot cakes and gravy, saw him pause, looking to Shug for approval. He saw Shug nod and Hubie stuff the entire gooey pile into his mouth. The gravy ran down his chin. Rance Overton hated that damn dummy, too. The sound of approaching horses broke into his thoughts. He went to the door and opened it and saw Fenton Hoover and Lorella Merril approaching the cabin, their horses at a full run. Without turning, Rance said, "Lorella's here."

Larrabee saw Lee get out of his chair and turn toward the door. Rance was still holding it open and the cold, outside air rushed into the room. He heard the running horses slide to a stop, heard the squeak of saddle leather, and then the girl was running into the room, her arms outstretched, and Lee was running forward into those outstretched arms.

She was wearing jeans and a heavy coat, but it didn't conceal her firm, young body. Her coal black hair was wind-blown and tousled and clung to her forehead, and her eyes were tawny like the eyes of a panther, her body tight and firm like the body of a young animal that has run much in the wilds. She was clinging to Lee, smothering his face with kisses that were salted with tears. She kept sobbing his name over and over.

In time she pushed away from him and the words rushed out of her, piling over one another. She said, "Fenton told me what Shug wants. Do it, Lee. Please do it. We could get out of here together, the two of us. Oh God, I've missed you, Lee."

Larrabee saw the trap closing around young Lee Kirby. Will Baker, the wise old lawman, would have recognized this. Go bad once and there was no way back. The law pushed you on one side and the old associations came back to haunt you, and you couldn't escape them. Again he thought of Baker, out there alone, probably frozen to death by now, and he realized how much Baker knew about things like this. A man like Purcell couldn't afford to have a kid like Lee Kirby running around loose. Lee knew too much. Shug had to keep him under control.

Lee pushed out of the girl's arms finally and turned and sat down in a chair. He buried his face in his hands. He didn't look up when he said, "All right, Shug. You win."

"Now that's just a whole lot better," Shug said.

Lorella was looking at Opal, her eyes pleading, and Larrabee realized how young she was. Not more than eighteen, he was sure. She ran across the room and threw her arms around Opal. "Please don't hate me, Opal. Please!"

Opal turned the girl and led her into the bedroom, closing the door. She sat down on the edge of the freshly made bed, pulling Lorella down beside her. One hand went up and smoothed the hair from the younger girl's forehead. "I don't hate you, Lorella," Opal said.

It was as if Opal had cut a dam. The words poured out of Lorella, tumbling over themselves. "I didn't want you to lose part of your mules," she said, "but I had to get away from here, and I was afraid for Lee and I've waited for him for two years . . ." Tears were streaming down her cheeks. "Opal," she said, "you don't know what it's like being caged up here and not being able to get away, and watching them make a fool out of your own father . . .''

"Shug promised Lee he'd let you and your father go," Opal said. "That was the deal Lee made with him."

"I know that," Lorella said, "but he never had any intentions of keeping his promise, and Daddy didn't want to leave his claim . . ." She looked up suddenly and the bitterness was there in her face. "There wasn't any gold in that claim," Lorella said. "There never was and there never will be, but Shug kept talking and talking, and finally Daddy started believing he was getting the money out of the claim . . ."

"I don't understand," Opal said. "What money?"

"The money Shug gave him to buy supplies down at Pine Ridge. Shug told Daddy to tell everybody it was Daddy's own money, and folks down there around Pine Ridge got to saying that Old Man Merril must have struck a pocket, and Daddy liked hearing that, and he really got to believing. Oh, Opal, it was awful. Every morning he'd go out there and dig in that claim and he'd tell me how much gold he was getting. He never was real right in the head. You knew that. Everybody did. He had been looking for gold and not finding it for too many years and he kept getting worse and worse, and finally Shug didn't have to threaten that he'd harm me anymore. It got so Daddy was just as bad as Shug. When I begged him to leave, he'd threaten me and get mad and rave and say I was trying to take him away from the biggest strike ever made . . ." She buried her face in her hands. "It was awful, Opal."

"How is he now?" Opal said.

"Daddy's dead," Lorella said. "He died two weeks ago. I buried him with my own hands, out there by that worthless claim. I knew it was what he wanted."

Opal held the girl close. "I'm sorry, Lorella."

Lorella looked up, her face tear-streaked, her eyes pleading. "Now Lee and I have a chance and Shug is going to let you go with us, so I had to tell Lee it was what I wanted, and it *is* what I want. I can't stand it anymore, what with Rance putting his hands all over me, never leaving me alone. Rance just kept after me and after me . . ."

"Did he . . .?" Opal couldn't bring herself to finish the question.

Lorella looked at her and she understood. She shook her head. "No," she said. "But God knows he tried. He kept grabbing at me and telling me how good he'd be for me. He's a horrible man, Opal. Just horrible. Finally Shug told him he'd horsewhip him if he didn't leave me alone." She wiped the tears out of her eyes with the back of her hand. "I owe Shug that much." And now she was pleading again. "I didn't want you to lose those mules, Opal. But I have to get away from here. Can you understand that?"

Opal thought of herself, only two years older than this girl at the time, throwing herself at a lonely old man, telling him she loved him, going through that ceremony at the justice of the peace, sleeping in the same bed with the man for two years, living a lie, all just so she could get away from this valley. She held Lorella's head against her breast, holding her as close as if she were a little child. She stroked her hair. "Yes, Lorella," she whispered. "I understand."

Rance Overton sat in a chair in the main room of the cabin, looking across at Lee, the stepbrother he hated more at this moment than any other man he had ever hated in his life, and he had hated many. Lee Kirby was coming out on top again. He was going to have Lorella . . . something Rance hadn't been able to do. And he was going to have a respectable job there in town and get a new start in life. *If I could only get you to come at me,* Rance thought. *I know I could kill you with my hands.* Opal and Lorella came out of the bedroom, their arms around each other, and right then Rance Overton knew what he was going to do.

He managed a smile through his puffed lips and he looked at his stepbrother. "It's going to work out fine for you, little stepbrother," he said. "And I guess you and Lorella will marry-up with each other."

Lee was somewhat surprised at the gentle tone of Rance's voice. He said, "As soon as we can."

"Can't blame you for that," Rance said. "Bet you're looking forward to that wedding night. That gal's gonna be something else stripped down in bed."

Larrabee saw Lee tense and to himself he thought, *Leave it alone, Lee. He's baiting you.*

Rance had it going and he wasn't going to stop. He said, "You ever seen her naked yet, Lee?" He didn't wait for an answer. He slapped his knee. "Whoeee," he said. "She's really something. I've seen her naked lots of times. She takes a bath in that warm pool over near her cabin."

Lee started to get up from his chair, and this time Larrabee said aloud, "Leave it alone, Lee. He's drunk."

Lorella's face had turned scarlet. Opal looked at Shug and said, "We're going out back." Shug nodded.

Rance said, "Why is it women always go together when they go out to pee?" He looked at Opal and Lorella. "What do you do?" he asked, "Watch each other?"

"Damn it, shut up, Rance!" Lee said.

"Come on, Lorella," Opal said. They started toward the door. There was no way but to pass in front of Rance. As they did, Rance reached out and gripped Lorella by the seat of the pants. He squeezed her flesh, hard. She whirled and slapped him hard across the face, but it didn't faze Rance.

"How long since you felt that ass of Lorella's, Lee?" Rance asked. "Damned if I don't think that's the roundest, hardest little ass I ever did feel . . ."

Larrabee saw it coming. There was no way he could stop it. There was no way any man could. Lee lunged out of his chair and threw himself at Rance. It was what Rance had wanted. His fist came up from his knees and landed solidly against Lee's face. Lee went down hard, but he was up again.

It was no contest. Rance was bigger than Lee; he was hardened by outdoor living; Lee was soft from two years in prison. Rance smashed his fist into that face he hated, time and again. Lorella's screams were like knife blades in Larrabee's ears. He threw himself toward the two struggling men, down there on the floor now, and Shug Purcell's gun jabbed into his middle. "Leave it alone, Tex," Shug said. "It's a family squabble. It's been coming on for a long time."

"Stop it, damn you!" Larrabee said.

The gun prodded deeper. "When I'm ready," Shug said.

Lorella was screaming, "He's killing him!" and Opal was looking at Shug, begging him with her eyes to stop it. Larrabee said, "You're ready now."

He wasn't even aware of what he was doing. He just knew that fight had to be stopped. He swung his fist with all his weight behind it and it landed on the upper side of Shug Purcell's jaw.

He might as well have slammed his fist against a brick wall. Shug Purcell didn't even wince. A trickle of blood came from one corner of his mouth and ran down his chin. He said, "You shouldn't have done that, Tex." He went across then and kicked Rance Overton in the ribs, hard. "That's enough, Rance," Shug said. "Goddamnit, I don't want him dead. I got lots bigger plans for him than just twenty-five mules."

Rance had his hands around Lee's throat. Shug kicked him again and Rance recoiled from the blow. "I said it was enough, didn't I?"

Lee Kirby had heard none of it. He lay there on the floor, his face covered with blood, and now Lorella was kneeling down by him, cradling his head, sobbing, "Oh, Lee, Lee darling, I love you so much. Do what they say, Lee. Please do what they say. All I want to do is get out of here and be with you. Oh my God, Lee, he's hurt you. He's hurt you so bad!" She had pulled her shirt out of her jeans and she was wiping Lee's face with the tail of her shirt, cooing to him, kissing his battered face.

Rance Overton stood there, looking down at them. "Sickening, ain't it?" he said.

"You ignorant bastard," Shug said. "Now get the hell out of here."

"I want my gun, Shug," Rance said.

"You'll get your damn gun when I'm ready to give it to you," Shug said. "And that will be when we're up there at the far end of the valley cuttin' out my twenty-five mules."

Hubie had been totally impassive throughout the entire moment of violence. He said now, "You want me to help you cut out them mules, Shug?"

Shug's voice became soft, fatherly. He said, "No, Hubie. I have another job for you."

"Sure, Shug," Hubie said. "Whatever you say."

No one was paying much attention to Lee and the girls except for Larrabee. Opal and Lorella had gotten Lee to his feet. They were supporting his sagging body between them. Lorella was still sobbing, still telling Lee how much she loved him. Shug turned to Fenton Hoover and now his voice was savagely rough again. "Get those women the hell out of here," he said. "Take 'em over to Lorella's place. By God, every time there's Rance and women around there's hell to pay." Fenton had started toward the door to help Opal and Lorella with Lee. Shug's voice lashed out at him. "And Fenton?"

Fenton turned. Only then did Larrabee realize how old the man was. His face was sagging, his shoulders slumped. "What do you want?" he said.

"Take Lee with you. He's no damn good here. Maybe if he's alone with Lorella he'll come to his senses."

Fenton only nodded. He moved toward the door, but Shug's voice stopped him again. "You make damn sure they're there when I bring those mules down. You understand that?"

"Sure, Shug," Fenton said. "I'll keep an eye on them." The four of them went outside and Larrabee could hear them mounting up.

Larrabee said, "Maybe I'll just mosey on over with them to make sure they don't get away."

"Maybe you won't," Shug said.

"You want me to go with you to help you cut out those mules?"

"I don't want that either," Shug said. He was looking steadily at Larrabee, the gun still in his hand. He said, "You made a bad mistake when you hit me, Tex. A damn bad mistake. I was beginning to like you. Now I ain't sure at all."

Hubie said, "You said there was something you wanted me to do, Shug. I'll do whatever you say."

Again Shug's voice was soft and paternal. "I know you will, Hubie." He clapped an affectionate arm around the shoulder of the hulking, dim-witted man. "I'm gonna give you a gun of your very own, Hubie," he said.

A broad smile flooded Hubie's usually vacant face. "I always wanted my own gun," he said. "You never would let me have one."

"But you know how to use one, don't you, Hubie?" Larrabee knew this was intended for him.

"I busted six bottles in a row, didn't I, Shug? And I made that tin can hop all over the yard, didn't I?"

"You sure did, Hubie," Shug said.

"You taught me to shoot real good," Hubie said. "But I ain't never had my own gun."

"You're gonna have one now," Shug said. Still keeping the gun on Larrabee, Shug went over to the deer horns and lifted Will Baker's gun from its holster. He checked it to make sure it was loaded and then handed it across to Hubie. "Here's your gun, Hubie," Shug said. "It's yours.

"To keep?" Hubie said.

"To keep," Shug said.

Hubie caressed the gun tenderly. "I ain't never had my own gun," he said. A puzzled frown creased his face. "You want me to shoot somebody, Shug?"

"No, Hubie," Shug said. "I don't want you to shoot anybody. But I want you to listen to me and do exactly what I tell you to do."

"Sure, Shug," Hubie said. "I always do what you tell me to do, don't I, Shug?"

"You sure do, Hubie," Shug said. "That's why I like you so much."

"You sure do like me, don't you, Shug?"

"Of course I do. Now here's what I want you to do. You sit down in this chair here. You take that gun and you cock it, and you keep it pointed right straight at Tex here. You hold that gun on him until I tell you to quit. But I don't want you

to shoot him, Hubie. Understand that? I don't want you to
shoot him unless you have to.''

"How do I know when I have to, Shug?"

"If he tries to get away. If he makes one move to get
away. Then you pull that trigger and let him have it right
smack between the eyes. You understand that, Hubie?"

"Sure, Shug," Hubie said. "I'll do just like you say." He
sat down in the chair, facing Larrabee, and he cocked the
gun. "I'm glad you like me, Shug."

"You're a good boy, Hubie," Shug said. "I'll be back in
four . . . maybe five hours. You just keep that gun pointed
right at Tex.''

"I'll do just like you said," Hubie said.

Shug was looking directly at Larrabee. "I know you will,
Hubie," he said. He took Rance's gun belt and holstered gun
from the deer horn rack, using his left hand. He turned and
went outside and Larrabee could hear him mounting up and
riding off toward the far end of the valley where the mules
were.

Larrabee looked at Hubie. Hubie was sitting there in the
chair, the cocked gun in his hand, that vacant grin on his
face. Larrabee eased himself in a chair across from Hubie. It
looked as if it was going to be a long wait.

CHAPTER EIGHTEEN

THROUGH THE SINGLE WINDOW IN THE FRONT OF THE CABIN Larrabee could see the morning sky. It hadn't snowed for some time and it looked as if it might even be clearing. Gray patches of clouds, driven by a wind that was unfelt here in the valley, scudded across the deeper gray of the cloud mass that still hung over the valley. Larrabee's thoughts wandered.

Will Baker was undoubtedly dead by now. Only a superman could endure the deep chill that had settled over the valley Will Baker was a tough old turkey, but he wasn't that tough.

He thought of Rance Overton and of the killer rage he had seen in him when he had finally baited Lee into a fight. He studied Hubie, trying to figure out the man's age, and he speculated a lot about that. Eighteen? Twenty? Twenty-five? With people like Hubie it was hard to tell. Their gentle, childlike manner made them seem younger than their years sometimes. He noticed the size of the man for the first time. He was built like a block of granite. A lot like Shug, Larrabee thought.

The thinking was all apropos of nothing, but when a man was trying to figure his way out of a death trap it was just as well to let the mind wander. Maybe, in its strange meanderings, the mind might settle in on something that would work. Looking at Hubie and at the steadiness of that gun that was pointed at his chest, it didn't seem likely. He thought of Lee

and Lorella and the obviousness of their love, and he thought
of Opal and was immediately sorry he had. Seemed like when
he thought of Opal there wasn't room for thoughts about
anything else. He shifted his weight slightly. The gun in
Hubie's hand moved with his movements. Larrabee grinned.
"Just trying to get comfortable," he said.

Hubie didn't say a word.

Larrabee was quiet for a long while and then he said
suddenly, "Suppose I have to go to the toilet, Hubie?"

Larrabee saw the cloud of puzzlement crowd Hubie's features. Shug hadn't said anything about that. He puzzled about
it for some time and then his face brightened. "I'd go with
you," he said. "I'd keep this gun pressed against your back
and I'd stand there and watch you until you were finished and
then I'd bring you back and put you down in that chair, just
like you are now." He looked at Larrabee for approval.
"You have to go?" he said.

Larrabee thought of standing there, trying to relieve himself with a gun pressing against his spine. He said, "No,
Hubie, I don't have to go."

He was getting no place fast, Larrabee knew, and time was
ticking away. He had thought if Shug and the others were
going to be gone for four or five hours that might work in his
favor, but it didn't seem to be going that way. He thought of
other times he had been in a tight spot. He even thought of
poker games and of that silly incident in Dolly Varden's
saloon. In a spot like that, you just figured out what the other
fellow was thinking and then you thought first. But how in
hell could you do that when you weren't even sure the man
sitting across from you with a gun was thinking at all. He
didn't have time to pursue the thought further. There was the
sound of a rider approaching, coming on fast. He wondered if
Shug had decided to come back. He wondered if it was Rance
Overton with a gun? It was neither. The door opened and
Fenton Hoover was standing there.

Fenton said, "Hubie, Shug wants you. He said to tell you
he's got to have you up there at the far end of the valley to
help him with those mules."

Total confusion was distorting Hubie's face. He thought Fenton was with Lorella and Opal and Lee. He knew for sure Shug had told him to stay here and hold that gun. His mind wasn't capable of sorting it all out.

"Shug needs me?" Hubie said.

Fenton's voice was soothing. "You know how much Shug depends on you, Hubie. He's having trouble with those mules and he knows he can count on you to help him. He can always count on you, Hubie. That's why he likes you so much."

"Shug likes me a whole lot," Hubie said.

"Sure he does, Hubie. He wants you to come right now. He even sent an extra horse for you to ride. It's outside there, all saddled up for you."

Hubie said, "He told me to stay here and hold this gun."

Fenton said, "I'll guard Tex for you. Just like Shug told you to do."

Hubie hesitated, still not sure, then he stood up. "You can't have my gun," he said. "This is my gun. Shug give it to me."

"I got my own gun, Hubie," Fenton said.

"Let me see your gun," Hubie said.

Fenton pushed back his coat. He lifted the gun from its holster. "I got one," he said.

"You're supposed to sit down in that chair and cock the gun and hold it on Tex. That's what Shug said."

Fenton followed the instructions to the letter, but Hubie still wasn't sure. "You sure Shug said he needed me?"

"He needs you real bad, Hubie. He's gonna be mad if you don't go up there and help him."

A quick change came over Hubie. "I don't want Shug to be mad at me."

"Of course you don't," Fenton said. "Now you just go out there and take that saddled horse I brought you and you ride up to the end of the valley and help Shug. He sure will be glad to see you."

"I like for Shug to be glad," Hubie said.

Hubie went to the door and looked out. He stopped and

turned and Larrabee was sure that whatever it was Fenton Hoover had in mind wasn't going to work. Hubie said, "There's two horses."

"You take the black one, Hubie," Fenton said softly.

Hubie said, "I like black horses." He went outside and Larrabee heard him getting into the saddle and there was the muffled sound of retreating hoofbeats in the crunching snow. Larrabee had gotten to his feet. Fenton turned the gun on him. "Sit down, Tex," he said. "I hold the cards."

Larrabee sat down. He said, "You mind telling me what's going on here?"

Fenton sat down heavily, still holding the gun. Fenton Hoover was a tired, old man. Fenton said, "You could have told Will Baker I was out there in Opal's barn that day. You didn't do it. There's a saying in our family that if someone does you a favor you owe him one back." He gestured with his thumb. "There's the door."

"How about Opal and Lee and Lorella?"

"They got horses and guns and enough supplies to get them down as far as Carson's Mill at least."

"It don't make sense, Fenton," Larrabee said. "Why didn't you just go with them?"

"There's posters up for me all over the west side of these mountains," Fenton said. "I reckon there's some on the east side now. I'm best off right here."

"It still don't track," Larrabee said. "Shug was going to let them go and at least Opal would have had twenty-five of those mules."

"You ain't got a real good case of the smarts, Tex," Fenton said. "You think Shug would let Lorella go? Hell no. That's the club he's got over Lee's head. All he wants is for Lee to take that job in there at the bank in Millerton . . . keep it a couple of months . . . get the layout of the place . . . maybe even the keys. As long as he's got Lorella, Lee will do any damn thing Shug says." He looked up and his face was tired and drawn. "I couldn't see that happen to Lorella. In two weeks she'd be as crazy as her daddy was. That or Rance would get to her. Even Shug couldn't keep Rance away from her forever, and maybe that would be even worse for her. That Rance is no damn good, Tex. He's rotten all the way through.''

''Why does Shug keep him around?''

''Look around you, boy,'' Fenton said. ''The famous Purcell-Kirby-Hoover gang. What's left? Time was there was fifteen men out there in the bunkhouse. Damn good men. They're dead or in jail. . . . Hell, man, Shug is an old man. I know he don't look it, but he's only five years younger than me. He's through and has been for five years, but he ain't got sense enough to see it. What's he got left? Clay and Garth and they ain't worth the powder to blow them to hell, and Rance Overton.'' Fenton looked up. ''Keep Rance away from whiskey and women and he's one hell of an outlaw.'' Fenton said it with pride. ''Good with a gun too, if it comes to that. He's all Shug's got except for Hubie, and Hubie ain't no good to anybody.'' Fenton spit at a crack in the floor. ''That's why he's got to keep Lee under his thumb. He wants to knock over that bank in Millerton. Shug dreams about that day and night. One last big job.''

''You sending me out without my boots and coat like Shug did to Baker?'' Larrabee said.

''Put 'em on,'' Fenton said.

''And my gun?''

''Take it,'' Fenton said. ''Ain't no bullets in it nor in the belt either. Shug saw to that.''

Larrabee glanced at the gun belt and saw that what Fenton said was true. He pulled on his boots. He took the empty gun and the gun belt down and strapped it around his middle. He had owned that gun for a long time. There was no sense leaving it here. He shrugged into his sheepskin-lined coat and put on his hat. ''Obliged, Fenton,'' he said. He went out through the door. He wasn't too sure but what he'd feel the smash of a bullet in his spine. Fenton's saddled horse was standing just outside. *What the hell?* Larrabee thought. *This is no time for scruples.* He started toward the saddled horse.

Fenton's voice from the doorway said, ''Don't push your luck, Tex. I'm gonna have to do me a heap of lying to explain to Shug why I sent Hubie up there and why you ain't here. If it don't work, I might need that horse a damn sight worse than you do." The old man grinned. "Besides, I don't owe you no horse. You didn't give me none."

Larrabee took one last look at the corral. It was empty. He started to run toward the timber, leaving footprints in the snow as plain as signboards. He knew it but he couldn't help it. He was panting by the time he got into the protection of the timber. He hadn't taken the altitude into consideration. He'd have to slow it down. He had one thought in mind. Get to Lorella's cabin. Maybe Opal and Lee and Lorella hadn't left yet. Even if they had, there might be guns and ammunition there.

Ammunition. What good was an empty gun? He stopped to get his breath and he fumbled in the pocket of his coat. His hand touched metal. He grinned. There were the three bullets he had put there when he had gone on the deer hunt. The shells would fit his Colt. He took the shells from his pocket and shoved them into the cylinder. Only three bullets, but it was a sight better than none. He plunged on into the timber. He was suddenly mighty proud of his Norwegian heritage.

The clouds were breaking up and there were small patches of blue sky here and there. The air was suddenly warmer and snow slid from the branches of the pines and dropped at his feet. He was panting again. He had to pace himself. And then he heard the voice, weak and trembling. It said, "Up here, Tex." He thought maybe he was starting to hallucinate. The voice sounded like Will Baker's.

Larrabee looked around. Nothing but pines and snow, and ahead a ways a thick clump of willow. He started to move on and again he heard his nickname. "Tex!" It seemed to come from above him, and he had an eerie feeling he was hearing voices. A man could take just so much tension. He looked up then, and clinging desperately to a low hanging limb was what had once been Will Baker. "Can't walk, Tex," Baker said hoarsely. "Feet gone. Had to get my feet off the ground. I pulled myself up here last night."

Larrabee stared unbelievingly at the old marshal, clinging

there to the branch of the tree, no more than four feet off the
ground. He was alive, that was certain, for he could still
speak. But that was about all. Larrabee saw his feet . . . cut
and bloody. They were swollen to the point where they did
not look like human extremities and they were purple-blue in
color. Larrabee went over to the tree. He held out his arms.
"Try to let go, Baker," he said. "I've got you."

Baker slid off the limb of the tree with less grace than the
clumps of snow that were sliding from the limbs of the pines.
Larrabee caught him and supported him, but when Baker's
feet touched the ground the stabbing pains that had probably
kept him alive distorted his features into a collage of sheer
agony. Larrabee laid him down on the snow. He stripped off
his coat and tossed it across the old marshal. Cold bit through
Larrabee's shirt. How in hell had the man survived?

Larrabee said, "Listen to me, Baker. Opal and Lee and
Lee's girl, Lorella, have gotten away. Fenton Hoover turned
me loose. If I can get to that cabin down the valley a piece,
maybe Opal and the others are still there. There'll be guns
and horses. We can make it."

"Go on, Tex," Baker said. "I'm done for."

"The hell you are," Larrabee said. "You're still alive.
Here." He struggled with Baker, trying to get the coat around
his shoulders. It was as if he was working with a piece of
cold clay. Baker's arms were stiff. He worked the coat around
Baker's shoulders, stuffed his arms clumsily into the sleeves.
"You're going too," Larrabee said.

He hooked his hands under Baker's armpits and started
walking backward, dragging Baker with him. He was glad for
the exertion because it made him forget the cold that was
biting through his flannel shirt. In a short time he was out of
breath and he had to stop. He looked at Baker and Baker was
trying to grin. "Coat feels good," Baker said.

"You're gonna be all right," Larrabee said. He didn't
believe a word of it, but he couldn't leave the man here
alone. He started out again, dragging Baker.

He had no idea of how long this went on but suddenly,
there across the clearing, was Lorella's cabin. Lee, Opal, and

Lorella, all mounted, all with rifles in their saddle scabbards, and all with bedrolls behind their saddles, came out from behind the cabin and spurred their horses into a run. Larrabee shouted, "Opal! Lee! Over here!"

The pound of the hooves of the three horses drowned out his words. He took hold of Baker again and started dragging him, knowing he had to get him into some kind of cover. He backed through the clump of willows and suddenly he was in water up to his knees. He had backed into a pool, hidden there in the willow clump. He fought for his footing, still clinging to Baker. He slipped and went down and felt the water closing over his face, and he felt the weight of Baker pushing him down. He had dragged Baker in after him. He fought free of Baker's weight and bobbed to he surface. He stood up and realized the water was only waist high. It wasn't until then he realized the water was warm.

He looked around. The pond was small . . . no more than twelve feet across. Water burbled at one end and tendrils of steam rose from the surface of the pond and quickly dissipated in the chill air. He remembered Rance taunting Lee about watching Lorella take her bath. This was the place. There were thick rushes and willows on this side of the pool but there was a grassy, gentle slope on the other side. Larrabee started dragging Baker toward that side.

"Don't take me out of the water, Tex. God, it feels good."

There was no need to remove Baker's dangling legs from the water. Larrabee walked around the edge of the pond, pulling Baker along until he had him over to the gentle slope with a carpet of grass, kept alive even through winter by the warmth of the water from the natural hot springs. He laid Baker down gently, his head and shoulders on the bank, his lower torso in the water. "I'm starting to get warm," Baker said. He kept fumbling at his shirt pocket and he took out the gold watch. "Tex?" he said.

"Yeah, Baker. Right here."

"This watch. I want you to take it. I want you to see it gets back to Dolly Varden."

"What the hell, Baker," Larrabee said. "You'll take it to

her yourself. I'm going over to Lorella's cabin. It's right near by. I think Opal and Lee are still there. We'll get you out of here."

Baker reached out and gripped Larrabee's pants leg. His grip was surprisingly strong. "Take your coat, Tex," he said. "I'll be all right. I'm gettin' real warm."

There was some logic to what Baker said. The cold was biting through Larrabee's wet shirt. He hesitated a moment, then started removing his sheepskin-lined coat from Baker's shoulders. It hadn't been in the water long enough to soak through.

Baker said, "My daddy gave me that watch. I was gonna pass it along to my son." He was having trouble breathing. "I had a son, Tex. Did you know that?"

"I'd heard."

"Sure you had. Everybody knew about Billy. But nobody would talk about it. Nobody except Dolly."

"Why don't you save your breath, Baker?" Larrabee said. It wasn't a rebuke. It was a piece of advice. He tugged at the coat, trying to get it free. He felt he was fighting time now.

"Like when somebody's got a sickness inside that's eatin' 'em up and they know they're gonna die and everybody else knows it. And what does everybody say? 'You're sure looking fine.' Nobody wants to face the truth. Why is that, Tex?"

"Just trying to be kind, I guess," Larrabee said. He got the coat free and was shrugging into it.

"You think it's kind not to let somebody talk about the thing that's tearing him apart inside, killing him inch by inch?" Baker shook his head. "There's no worse loneliness than that, Tex, and loneliness will kill a man as quick as anything else."

It left Larrabee at a complete loss for words. He tried to make his voice gruff. "I've got to get over to that cabin, Baker. I'll be back as soon as I can."

"I want you to take this watch to Dolly, Tex."

It would only waste time to argue with the man, Larrabee knew. He took the watch. "All right, Will," he said. "But there's no need of it. You're gonna be just fine."

Baker managed a twisted grin. "Don't be kind, Tex," he said.

Larrabee felt a blur in his eyes as he pushed out through the thicket, leaving the old marshal there alone. Damnit, there was nothing else he could do.

He pushed through the willows and a movement caught his eyes. Three riders were heading up a nearby slope. It was Lee and Opal and Lorella. Maybe he could still catch up with them. But there was Baker. He gave his surroundings a quick appraisal. The timber ended abruptly, right here at the end of the valley. There was a well-defined trail that Lee and the others were taking, and it led to a pass above them. There were huge granite boulders on either side of the trail. In front of him was a clearing that might have been a vegetable garden once, and less than a hundred yards across that clearing was the cabin. He started across the clearing and then he became aware of the thunder of hooves. He had been so intent on what he was doing he hadn't heard them before. He looked up and saw the riders, coming at a full gallop. Shug and Rance were in the lead, then the two outlaws, Garth and Clay, and Fenton Hoover was with them. Either he had lied his way out of another tight spot or he had decided to tell all. Larrabee had no way of knowing. Hubie was tailing along.

The riders were almost on top of him when he ducked back into the protection of low boulders and scrub brush there at the edge of the willow thicket. He didn't know if they had seen him or not. It didn't make much difference. He knew they had seen Lee and Opal and Lorella. They couldn't help but see them. They were in plain sight, just a few hundred yards up the trail on that exposed slope.

He threw himself down behind the rocks and lay there, breathing heavily. There were six of them out there and he had three bullets. He thought of Baker, lying back there in the warm water pool, completely helpless. He felt the gold watch in his pocket and to himself he said, *"Baker, I don't know for sure if I'm gonna get to deliver this watch or not, but I'm sure as hell gonna try!"*

CHAPTER NINETEEN

THE RIDERS RODE UP TO THE CABIN. SHUG EITHER HADN'T SEEN Larrabee or he was saving him for later. As a matter of fact, he acted as if he hadn't seen anything but that cabin. He threw himself from the saddle and headed straight for the door. Rance dismounted and was close behind him. Fenton sat there on his horse, head down. Some distance away, Hubie was having trouble with the big black Fenton had brought him.

Shug wasn't inside that cabin more than a few seconds. He came striding out and Larrabee could hear his voice clearly. He strode straight to Fenton Hoover's horse and he said, "You bastard, you lied to me!" He reached up and dragged Fenton from the saddle. Holding the old man with his left hand, he drove his right fist into Fenton's face. Fenton sagged and fell to the ground, and now Shug was kicking him savagely. His foot rose and fell with all his weight behind it. Larrabee started getting sick to his stomach. Shug was stomping the old man to death. "Damn you!" Shug kept shouting and then, "Garth! Clay! Get Lee and Lorella back here! Don't kill 'em, but I don't care what else you do to 'em. Just get 'em back or by God you'll get what Fenton got!"

Garth and Clay both spurred their horses. Garth was coming right toward Larrabee. He'd pass within six feet of him. Larrabee thought of Lee and the two girls. He stood up and gripped the gun, thumbing back the hammer. As Garth rode

so close Larrabee could see his eyes, he squeezed the trigger.
The Colt bucked against his hand and Garth seemed to be
suspended in air as the horse ran out from under him. Garth
hit the ground hard almost at Larrabee's feet. Larrabee felt
shaken. He had never killed a man before in his life and this
man had been somebody he didn't even know. He didn't have
time to give it much thought. Both Shug and Rance started
firing toward the rocks where he was hiding. Bullets whined
around him. Clay kept riding, straight up the slope toward
Lee and the girls.

Pressed against the ground, trying to avoid that hail of
lead, Larrabee couldn't see it, but up there on the trail Lee
had reined up sharply at the first sound of shots. He snaked
his rifle from its saddle scabbard and wheeled his horse. The
girls both had rifles in their hands now and all three opened
fire.

Shug and Rance made a dive for the open door of the
cabin. Hubie was still fighting the big black, well out of the
line of gunfire. The animal had panicked further at the sound
of the gunfire and it was pitching and rearing, and Hubie was
fighting to get it under control.

Riding at breakneck speed, down the slope, firing from the
saddle, Lee, Opal, and Lorella were hitting nothing except
the cabin, but it was enough to divert the gunfire from
Larrabee. He heard the shatter of glass as Shug and Rance
broke the glass in the cabin windows. Larrabee heard Shug
bellow, "Don't hit Lee and Lorella. Just turn them back and
then we'll get that bastard in the rocks!"

Larrabee risked standing up. He could see Lee and the girls
clearly now. He heard Lee's order, distant but clear. "Take
cover! Split up!" At the same time Lee threw himself from
the saddle and, gripping his rifle, he ducked into a clutter of
boulders on one side of the trail. Lorella rode out of sight into
the boulders on the opposite side. Opal kept coming straight
on, off the exposed slope, into the timber. She was quickly
out of sight. Hubie had gotten the black under control and he
was riding toward the cabin.

There was total silence as all firing stopped. Shug came out of the cabin and stood there on the porch, searching the slope. Larrabee might have had a shot at him, but with only two bullets left it was risky. He held his fire but Shug turned and looked directly in his direction. Hubie, riding up, momentarily blocked Shug's line of sight.

And then Larrabee saw Lee standing up, the rifle pressed to his shoulder. He was taking dead aim at Shug Purcell. Shug didn't see it, but Hubie did. He lunged out of the saddle, straight at Shug. "Shug! Look out!" he shouted. He threw himself on Shug at the exact second Lee squeezed the trigger. The bullet caught Hubie right between the shoulder blades. Hubie stiffened, and then his head snapped back and it seemed he was trying to touch the back of his head to his heels. His knees buckled and he slid down, still clinging to Shug, and he crumpled there at Shug's feet.

Larrabee could see the expression on Shug's face clearly. It was a distortion of anguish and pain and then it became twisted into a mask of rage more intense than anything Larrabee had ever seen in his life. He walked out into the middle of the clearing and stopped and stood there, staring up the slope, daring Lee to shoot him. There was no movement from up the slope. It was then that Shug turned and caught his first glimpse of Larrabee. He started firing wildly, the gun in his hand swinging from side to side. It was as if the man had suddenly gone mad. He started running, straight toward Larrabee. Larrabee fired. He was sure he had hit the man, but Shug didn't even stumble. He kept on coming.

Only one bullet left, Larrabee remembered. He couldn't risk wasting it. He dove back through the willows, back to where Baker was still lying in the water.

There was a moment of silence and through it he heard Shug reloading his gun. Larrabee stood there, waiting, his gun with one bullet leveled. He had assumed Shug would come through the thicket on the same path Larrabee had taken. He was wrong. The bushes parted a good twenty feet to his left and Shug was standing there, his gun in his hand.

The big man was staggering, Larrabee saw, and the front of his shirt was soaked with blood. Larrabee's first shot hadn't missed, but Shug, because of his massive size and because of the adrenaline of his rage, had refused to go down. He started firing erratically.

Larrabee threw himself full length on the ground. He rolled and a bullet from Shug's gun spewed dirt in his face. He rolled again and now he threw his left arm up as if to protect his face. He fired through the crook formed by his bent elbow.

He saw Shug stagger back from the impact of the bullet. But Shug wouldn't quit. He fired twice more, but he was losing his strength to hold the gun level. The bullets tore into the dirt, and then the gun slipped from his grip. He took three more steps forward and then he fell face forward, like the crashing of a forest giant uprooted by a storm. Larrabee got shakily to his feet.

He looked at Baker and he knew that Baker was still alive, and then he heard the movement in the willows. He turned, and Rance Overton was standing there. His gun was in his holster, but his hand was hooked over it, a man who liked to play with fate, sure he could outdraw and outshoot any other human being. Larrabee had no time to think. He thumbed back the hammer of his .44 and squeezed the trigger. The hammer fell with a click that seemed loud enough to echo through the whole valley.

Rance Overton's face was a swollen mask. Both eyes were surrounded by a deep purple green. His nose was swollen to twice its size and his upper lip was puffed out of shape. Larrabee's fists had left their mark. Rance's lips twisted into what was supposed to be a smile. He said, "What's the matter, Tex? Out of bullets?"

The poker-playing ability on which Larrabee had always prided himself deserted him completely now. His expression, his every movement, told Rance he had hit on the truth. Larrabee saw no sense in fighting it. He let the empty gun drop to the ground.

Rance said, "I like this. I like it real fine. Now I can take my time with you. I figure I'll bust your knee caps first, then maybe shoot off a couple of fingers. I want you to go real slow and easy, Tex."

He drew his gun then, and there was nothing histrionic about it. His hand didn't flash down and come up with a cocked weapon. He just reached down and slowly took the six-shooter from the holster. He cocked it, that smile still distorting his swollen lips. His black eyes glittered with hatred through the puffy, discolored lids. He raised the weapon. An unseen rifle cracked sharply. Rance Overton stumbled back. He dropped the gun and both hands were to his face. Blood seeped through his fingers. He kept staggering backward, fighting to keep his balance, and then he fell.

Opal Sprague rode out of the timber. The rifle she held in her hand was still trailing smoke from the barrel.

For a long time she sat there in the saddle, staring down at the dead body of Rance Overton, then she slammed the rifle against the ground and Larrabee thought of how Lee had thrown the rifle down the day of the deer hunt. Opal slid from the saddle. She ran to Larrabee and he put his arms around her and held her close. He could feel the trembling of her body. "It's all right, Opal," he said. "It's over."

"Hubie?" she said.

"He threw himself in front of Shug just as Lee fired," Larrabee said. "It was like he was trying to protect Shug."

"Maybe he was," Opal said. "Hubie was Shug Purcell's son. Everybody knew that, but Hubie being retarded the way he was, nobody ever spoke about it."

A low moan came from Will Baker. His lips moved and his words came out in a strangled sob. "That poor son of a bitch," Will Baker said.

Larrabee didn't know if Baker meant Hubie or Shug. He never would know. Not for sure. Baker's chin dropped to his chest. He rolled over on his side and lay still. Will Baker was dead. His battered feet, bloated to the point where they no longer resembled anything like feet, and his useless legs were still there in the warm water of the pond.

Larrabee was still holding Opal in his arms. He said, "I can't figure what happened. Lee had a clear shot at Shug. He just stood there, like he was asking Lee to shoot. And Lee must have seen Overton coming across that clearing."

"Maybe Lee's shot," Opal said.

"I've been thinking that," Larrabee said. He pushed her away. "I'd best go see. Will you be all right?"

"I'm all right now," she said.

Larrabee went out into the clearing. He took the first saddled horse he came to. It was the big black Hubie had been riding. The black started acting up, then realized he had someone on his back who knew what he was doing. He settled down.

Larrabee rode out through the clearing and out of the timber, then started up the well-defined trail. Lorella Merril rode out of the rocks and reined up beside him. "I'm going to see about Lee," Larabee said.

"I was just headed there," Lorella said.

It was then Larrabee noticed the body of Clay, the other outlaw, sprawled there at the side of the trail. He looked at Lorella.

"I shot him," Lorella said. "He was no better than Rance. He was always pestering me."

They rode up the slope together, toward the stone fortress where Lee had hidden out, and they dismounted and went in behind the boulders together. They saw the rifle then, its stock splintered, the sights knocked off. The weapon had been beaten against the rocks, time and time again, until the breach mechanism was beyond repair. Lee's horse was there, ground-tied, and Lee sat on the ground, his knees drawn up under his chin. He was holding his face in both his hands and there was evidence he had been violently ill.

Lorella ran to him and put her arms around him, and she cradled him close. "It's all right, darling," she said. "We're free. They can't hurt us anymore."

Lee raised his head and stared dully at Larrabee. He said, "Hubie. I never meant to harm Hubie. But he ran in there and it was like living it all over again . . . like it was my stepfather. I drew a bead on the deer and my stepfather stood up in a clump of brush, right there in front of me. I didn't know he was there. I squeezed the trigger and there he was."

His body shook with a violent sob. "My God," he said. "I didn't mean to kill Hubie."

Lorella was holding him in her arms, cradling him like a baby. Larrabee said, "You go on back down and you and Opal go back up to the cabin, Lorella. Build up a fire and get yourselves warm. You tell Lee I could use some help in the job I have to do."

He left them there together, knowing they needed to be alone for a while. He mounted the black and rode back down the slope. Opal was standing there in the clearing. She wanted open space. Larrabee said, "Lee's all right. Reckon Lorella will be down in a while. You and her go on back to the cabin. Lee and I will be along directly. We got some work to do first."

She looked at him and nodded. She knew the work he was talking about.

CHAPTER TWENTY

THERE WERE PLENTY OF SHOVELS AND PICKS IN THE SHED BEHIND Lorella's bullet-riddled cabin. Lee and Larrabee, working wordlessly, side by side, buried Hubie and Fenton Hoover. They dug a special grave for Will Baker, there by the warm pool that had kept him alive those last few minutes. Lee said, "He just kept riding me. He wouldn't let up."

"I got a feeling Will Baker thought a heap of you, Lee," Larrabee said. "He wanted you to go straight, that's all."

"He didn't have to ride me so," Lee said. "Whatever I did, I did for me and Lorella. She's my whole life, Tex."

"In time maybe I can explain it to you," Larrabee said. "It was just Will Baker's way. He was quite a man."

They left the other bodies there, just as they had fallen.

They came back to the cabin in time, and Opal and Lorella were there. They had stirred up the fire in the fireplace, and Lee and Larrabee stood in front of it, hands splayed out, soaking up the warmth. Larrabee went across to Will Baker's coat. There were some official-looking papers in the inside pocket. "We best take these," Larrabee said. "They're about your parole, Lee." He hesitated a moment and then said, "We best take his coat and his boots too. The officials will be asking a lot of questions."

Opal said, "I can't stay in this cabin overnight. I never want to see it again."

196

"I understand," Larrabee said. He looked at Lee. "You got any ideas?"

"Up at the end of the valley," Lee said. "There's a good spot to camp. What with the cliffs and the hot springs, it's always ten to fifteen degrees warmer up there and we'll be close to the mules so we can get an early start in the morning."

"Done, then," Larrabee said.

Larrabee and Lee got the pack mules and saddled them up. Without the whiskey and the carcass of the deer, the packs were light. The four of them rode up the valley, leading the loaded pack animals.

The upper end of the valley was fenced off at the open end. Sheer, granite cliffs closed it off at the other. There were pole corrals and spirals of steam rose from the natural hot springs. The mules were all there, looking fine, and Larrabee's own horse, Snort, was there. Larrabee went to the animal and put his arms around its neck. He pressed his cheek against the animal's hide. "Good to see you again, old-timer," he said. "You're lookin' perky, like you had yourself a good vacation." Snort nickered softly and nuzzled Larrabee's shoulder.

Opal was watching him. She remembered him arguing with the blue jay, and she remembered his arms around her, and she remembered his lips against hers and of how she had yearned for him. He was kind and tender and understanding. He was everything she had dreamed of, and he was a man she could have loved . . . Her thoughts enveloped her and swept over her, and she couldn't avoid them. *My God*, she thought, *I'm in love with him!*

But he was an outlaw. She had heard it from his own lips. He had planned to steal ten of her mules. She clung to that single thought, hoping it would drive out all other emotions. It didn't.

They set up camp and they sat there by the fire. Three of them had killed today, for the first time in their lives, and not one of them liked to think about it. Lee Kirby had killed twice, both times by accident. It made him sick inside. There were no words spoken among them as they ate a supper they didn't want. They got into their blankets and the clouds scudded above them, swept by an unfelt wind, and stars as big as frying pans appeared and hung there in the sky. The storm was gone.

Morning found them headed up the well-defined trail toward the pass. They had tried to ignore the sprawled bodies of Garth and Clay. Shug and Rance were in the willow thicket, out of sight, and Larrabee was glad for that.

The snow was belly deep on the mules in the pass, but Larrabee rode ahead, leading the pack animals. Snort was used to this sort of trail breaking. He lunged and plunged into the drifts and broke his way through, and the mule herd followed docilely along the newly broken trail. They went over the top and down the talus slope and into the timber. The sun reached down and touched them in the open spots, the chill was with them in patches of shade.

The valleys were splendid, more frequent now, and the timber increased in density. They passed by granite cliffs where waterfalls cascaded in two-thousand-foot drops to splash into foaming pools whose outlets were sparkling streams that meandered down through lush meadows, flowing westward, always westward.

They came to the slopes denuded of forest, and they heard the shouts of men and the thin whistle of donkey engines, and they saw oxen snaking logs down the steep hills, and they came to the place called Carson's Mill. The whine of the mighty saws was in the air. The bunkhouses and the cookshack itself were built on skids so they could be moved on to another location after the pristine forest had been raped to supply lumber for men who were building a new land. Ever building.

Up on a knoll was a big tent with a wooden floor and wood sides all around. Four girls were there, their skirts striking them just below their knees and black mesh stockings covering their calves. Their cheeks and their lips were painted, and they whistled and waved when Larrabee and Lee led the mules into the camp. Opal saw them and knew them for what they were, and she wondered how many times Rance Overton had been in that tent. The thought sickened her, and again she thought, *Must I always be wrong when it comes to men?*

They moved out of the camp and the air was pungent with sun and pine and scented cedar, and the majestic sugar pine rose here and there with cones two feet long. The woods were alive with birds and with plume-tailed gray squirrels, busily chewing away at pinecones to find the succulent pine nuts that would sustain them through the coming winter.

They passed out of the forest and into the scatter of gray bull pines and the scarlet twists of the sinuous-limbed manzanita and the gray of the chapparal, and they camped there by a quiet, sycamore-lined stream. The scent of alder and dampness was in the air.

Larrabee was moody as he sat with Lee there by the campfire. Opal hadn't spoken one word to him. She was avoiding him, and he didn't know why. She spent all her time with Lorella, and they seemed to be talking constantly.

Larrabee said, "What is it women find to talk about, Lee?"

"Men, mostly, I guess," Lee said.

"Well why don't they talk to us head-on?"

"It ain't a woman's way," Lee said sagely.

Larrabee looked at Opal and Lorella sitting there together. Opal was gesturing animatedly and Lorella was nodding, and then Opal got up and she came straight toward where Lee and Larrabee were sitting. Her hands were clenched, her arms straight down at her sides. She was walking as if her knees wouldn't bend right, sort of stiff-legged and bouncing. Her chin was jutted out and her lips were drawn thin, and there was outright hellfire in her eyes. She stopped directly in front of Larrabee and she looked down at him. Sitting, as he was, she looked three feet taller than she was.

She said, "All right, I want to know this. Just how did you plan to steal those ten mules? Just when did you intend to do it? Did you ever think that I might fill you so damn full of lead you'd never be able to pull your ass into a saddle again? Did you think of that, Larrabee Lucas Stone, or what the hell ever your name is?"

Larrabee just sat there. He knew his mouth was open, his jaw hanging slack. There was nothing he could do about it. He heard Lee chuckle, and then the chuckle got away from him and he was laughing, and then he became hysterical and he rolled on the ground, weak with his laughter.

"And what's so damn funny, Lee Kirby?" Opal demanded.

"You are," Lee managed to say through choking laughter. "Did you believe all that stuff Tex told Shug? Didn't you see he was trying to get on the good side of Shug so he could stall for time and give us a chance to get away?"

Opal's mouth was open now, and Larrabee looked at her and he thought, *My God, she looks beautiful when she's mad, and she looks beautiful now, and she always will look beautiful to me.* . . .

Opal said, "You mean you didn't plan on stealing my mules?"

"Never even dreamed of it," Larrabee said.

"And all those things you said. They were all lies?"

"I don't much like that word 'lie', ma'am," Larrabee said. "But maybe I did bend the truth a little."

"Then all that about breaking out of jail . . . being on the run?"

"No, ma'am," Larrabee said. "That part was the gospel truth. That jail back there in Gillette wasn't much more than a woodshed and I didn't cotton to being locked up that way, and I busted the whole side out of it. This Sheriff Harry Brockwell, well, he's as wide as a barn door and twice as tall, and he's got a temper to match, and he was plumb mad, and he ain't about to quit lookin' for me . . ."

She said, "I don't want to hear about it." She flounced off, her knees still not bending right, and she plopped down on the ground alongside Lorella, so hard her whole body shook.

Larrabee said, "I just plain don't understand women, Lee."

Lee reached over and patted the older man on the shoulder. "It will come to you in time, son," he said. "But don't think too hard on it. I don't want you to forget you owe me two dollars."

Lee crawled into his blankets, still chuckling. Larrabee sat there by the fire, staring into the coals. He saw Opal and Lorella getting into their blankets and there was a deep-down gut aching in him such as he had never felt before. He didn't know what it was, but it wouldn't go away. He didn't sleep worth a damn that night.

They made their last camp within sight of the lights of Millerton, and they delivered the mules the first thing the next morning. There was a cavalry major there, resplendent in his crisp uniform, and there were six troopers. They led the mules to prearranged corrals, and Larrabee was sorry to see them go. It was like the closing of a chapter of his life. There was a matronly but handsome woman with the major and he took her to be the major's wife, but he wasn't introduced.

"If you'll come on down to the house with me and my wife," the major said, "there's papers to sign. You know the Army. They're long on paperwork."

"Speaking of papers," Lee said, "I'm anxious to get up to the court-house and show them those papers Will Baker had in his pocket. I don't want anything to go wrong now."

"First things first," Opal said.

Larrabee felt as if suddenly he had no part in any of this. They all had things to do, a way to go. He watched them walk off together, the major and his wife, Lee and Lorella, arm in arm, and Opal, talking excitedly. He looked down the street and saw the hotel. He might as well go there, he thought.

He went to the hotel bar and tossed his last dollar on the bar and ordered a drink of whiskey. It was then he saw the town marshal for the first time. He was a short, blocky man with a seamed face. He was at the far end of the bar, and he was staring intently at Larrabee Lucas Stone. There was no expression on the marshal's face. He was just staring.

Larrabee downed his drink. It didn't taste half as good as he had thought it would. That town marshal was still staring at him.

He went into the lobby of the hotel and plopped himself

202   THOMAS THOMPSON

down in one of the easy chairs where he had a view of the
main street of the town. The six-horse teams hauling wagon-
loads of finished lumber went by in a steady stream. He said
to another lounger, "Must be a lot of building going on
around here."

"Down the valley a piece," the lounger said. "Town of
Fresno. Growing faster than fleas on a dog's back."

"Damn shame how things have to change," Larrabee said.
He didn't know why he said it. He had never felt so alone in
his life.

CHAPTER TWENTY-ONE

LARRABEE SAT IN THE HOTEL LOBBY A LONG TIME AND FINALLY HE couldn't take the inactivity any longer. He got up and went outside into the glare of sunlight, and there was the town marshal, standing there, just staring at him, not saying a word.

Larrabee started down the sidewalk, and he saw Lee and Opal and Lorella coming out of the stone building that was obviously a bank. They were hugging one another and giggling like three school kids. Opal looked up and saw Larrabee and she said, "Oh! There you are! We were just coming to look for you." Her voice was jubilant. "It's payday!"

She stood there, more confident than he had ever seen her. She was almost arrogant as she hauled a stack of money out of her purse. She counted out one hundred dollars and gave it to him.

Larrabee looked at the money and he looked up at Opal. "That's a lot of pay for less than a month's work," he said.

"I told you I'd pay you well, didn't I?" she said. She had drawn herself up to her full five feet four and she had such a swagger about her, he wouldn't have been surprised if she had pushed up her pants with the palms of her hands and spit in the dust. "Besides," she said, "I can afford it. Those mules brought top dollar."

Lee broke in. "Two dollars of that is mine," he said.

Larrabee gave him a fake scowl. "You're like a damn elephant," he said. He handed over the two dollars.

Lorella said, "Those papers Will Baker had were all in order. If Lee behaves himself for one year . . . and I'm going to see to that . . . he'll be a free man."

"And I got me a job," Lee said. "That banker is giving me a job, just like he said he would. What do you think about that, Tex? I'm gonna be a banker!"

"You'll be a right good one," Larrabee said. "You sure don't forget who owes you money." He stood there awkwardly, and then he said to Opal, "That hotel looks passably nice. Will you be putting up there?"

"The major and his wife asked Lorella and me to stay with them," Opal said.

"That's right nice of them," Larrabee said. "How about you, Lee?"

"The banker wants me to stay over at his house," Lee said. "He wants to talk to me about the job and all."

"Oh," Larrabee said.

Lee looked at him a long time and then he said, "Tex? I want to ask you a favor."

"I'm not gonna get in no mule-shoeing contest with you, if that's what you have in mind," Larrabee said.

"I want you to be the best man at my wedding," Lee said.

"You and Lorella?" Larrabee said foolishly.

"Tomorrow afternoon," Lee said.

"I ain't never been a best man," Larrabee said.

Lee laid an affectionate hand on his shoulder. "You'll pick it up fast, son," he said.

Opal said, "Lorella has asked me to be her matron of honor." She said, "I suppose you'll be going out to see about getting a job?"

"I thought on it," Larrabee said. "But I can't do it right off. I got to go back to Twin Pines."

"Oh?" Opal said.

"I promised Will Baker I'd take his watch back to Dolly Varden."

She started to say she could do that for him, and then she

bit her tongue. *Why do you always have to be so damn practical?* she thought.

"You couldn't very well go back on a promise to a dying man," she said.

"No, ma'am," he said. "I couldn't rightly do that."

"I'll be leaving the day after the wedding," she said. "I'll take one of the lower passes."

"I'd want you to go the safe way," Larrabee said. He rubbed his bearded chin. "I don't much like seein' you make that trip alone, what with all that money and all. I might just tag along. That is, if you don't mind."

"I don't mind," Opal said.

He stood there, feeling ill at ease. "Then I guess I'll see you at the wedding," he said.

"Yes," she said. "I guess you will."

He stood there watching the three of them move off together, Lee in the middle, Opal clinging to one arm, and Lorella clinging to the other. He saw Lee lean over and kiss Opal soundly on the cheek and he felt a quick stab of jealousy. *What the hell's the matter with you?* he thought. *They're cousins, ain't they?*

He walked back to the hotel, that loneliness he had never felt before gnawing away at him again. He got his horse who had been tethered there at the hitch rail and mounted and rode down to the stable at the edge of town. "Be here a couple of days," he said to the stableman.

"Be two dollars in advance," the stableman said.

Larrabee reached into his pocket, feeling his unaccustomed wealth. It was more money than he had ever had at one time in his life. He paid the stableman. "You take good care of that horse," he said. "Give him an extra bait of oats."

"I'll do it," the stableman said.

Larrabee went back out into the street and walked up toward the hotel. He saw the familiar red-and-white striped pole jutting out across the sidewalk and he went there. He had a shave and his hair trimmed, and he spent most of an hour just soaking himself in the tub and then doused himself with the froo-froo water that was there. He was a man who liked to smell good and to hell with anybody who said anything about it.

When he went to the hotel and registered, he felt someone was staring at his back. He half turned and saw the town marshal there. The clerk said, "Up the stairs, third room on your left."

The room was like a hundred others Larrabee had stayed in . . . Spartan, with a brass bedstead, a dresser with a marble top, and the inevitable pitcher and washbasin and the ornate chamber pot tucked discreetly under the bed. He went back downstairs and went into the bar and had himself a drink, and the town marshal was standing there at the end of the bar in his usual place, and he was looking directly at Larrabee. He went into the dining room and had some supper, and the feed wasn't very good. It wasn't anything like Opal had made out there on the trail. He ate only half of it, and it tasted like chalk.

He went back to his room, undressed, and got under the covers, but he didn't sleep well, and he was up at the crack of dawn. It was the day of the wedding, he reminded himself. He went downstairs and had breakfast. The ham was good and the eggs cooked just to his liking and the biscuits were fluffy enough, and the gravy passable, but it wasn't anything like Opal could cook. That woman sure had a way with a skillet.

He went down to the stable to see about Snort and he put his arms around the gelding's neck and said, "I'm sick, Snort. I don't know what it is, but there's something gnawing at my gut and I never felt like this before in my life." Snort nickered in sympathy.

He looked at his boots and he thought of that wedding, and he borrowed some saddle soap from the stableman. He took off his boots and gave them a scrubbing with the saddle soap and he polished them until they looked decent again. He put them on and went back outside.

He wandered up and down the street half the morning, thinking about Opal and that place of hers over in the Owens Valley, and wondering how she was going to make out alone over there. She needed a man to help her. A man could do an awful lot with that place, and she had a good start now, but she could lose it all. He pictured that cabin and he thought if maybe Opal had the time and somebody to help her, she could plant flowers out there in front and maybe a vegetable garden in back. He knew Opal would like flowers.

He came to a jewelry store and some hidden impulse drove him inside. The jeweler was a rooster of a man with a jeweler's loop screwed into one eye. He didn't take it out when he looked up and said, "Can I help you?"

"Just lookin'," Larrabee said.

"Help yourself," the jeweler said. He laughed then, and it was like the bark of a fox terrier pup. "Not to the merchandise," he said, "to the looking around."

Larrabee saw a plain gold band. He said, "How much is this one?"

The jeweler came over, the loop still in his eye. He looked down. "That wedding ring?" he said. "It's a fine one. Ten dollars. It's fourteen-karat solid gold."

"Won't turn a lady's finger green, will it?" Larrabee said.

The jeweler popped the loop from his eyes and there was hurt indignity in his voice. "I told you, sir," he said. "It's fourteen-karat solid gold."

"Reckon I'll take it," Larrabee said.

The jeweler's face lightened up. "Say," he said, "I heard there was to be a wedding today. You the groom?"

"Nope," Larrabee said. "I'm what they call the best man. But I don't see how you can be the best man when it's somebody else getting the girl."

The jeweler gave his fox terrier bark. "Never thought of it like that," he said. "Groom got so nervous he forget to buy the ring, that it?"

"Something like that," Larrabee said.

The jeweler put the ring in a velvet-lined box and Larrabee stuffed it in his pocket. He went back outside and suddenly he was aware of his clothes. His boots looked pretty good, but he *had* been sleeping in these clothes for quite a spell.

Wouldn't hurt to get a new pair of pants, he guessed. Lee deserved that much. He went into a clothing store.

"Want a pair of pants," he said. "Something kinda dressy."

"Of course," the clothier said. He brought out a pile of pants and Larrabee picked a pair of black ones with sort of western-style slash pockets. Something a dude cowboy might wear to a Saturday night dance, he thought. He looked down at his faded blue chambray shirt and said, "Guess this shirt wouldn't look too good with those pants, would it?"

"A white shirt, maybe," the clothier said.

"Sounds right," Larrabee said. "I'm goin' to a wedding."

"Then you'll need a coat," the clothier said. He brought out a black frock coat and had Larrabee try it on. It fit fine. It came almost down to his knees and he thought of a gambler he had seen once up in Montana.

"That's nice," Larrabee said, "but I wouldn't wear a thing like that once again in a coon's age."

"Rent it," the clothier said.

"Rent it?" Larrabee said.

"Of course," the clothier said. "I rent them all the time. For funerals and such."

"This is a wedding," Larrabee said.

"Two dollars rental," the clothier said. "And I'll throw in a silk cravat."

"What the hell ever that is," Larrabee said.

"A necktie," the clothier said.

"Oh," Larrabee said.

The clothier hustled around the store and came back with a pair of black shoes. They were high-top with no laces, and they had elastic inserts on the side. "Just what you need," the clothier said. "Gaiters."

"Not me," Larrabee said. "I just polished my boots."

"A hat, perhaps?" the clothier said. "A derby?"

"I got a hat," Larrabee said.

"Your funeral," the clothier said.

"Wedding," Larrabee said. "Got a place where I can change into these duds?"

"Of course," the clothier said. He led Larrabee to a tiny

curtained room that had a full-length mirror in the door. He pulled off his boots and slid out of his battered blue jeans, and put on the black pants. The shirt came next; he shed the faded blue and put on the new white one. He put on the frock coat then and looked himself in the mirror. *Not bad*, he thought. He pulled on his boots and stepped outside, the black silk cravat in his hand. "What do I do with this damn thing?" he said.

"Here," the clothier said patiently. "I'll tie it for you." He knotted the tie skillfully into a flowing bow. Larrabee stepped back inside the dressing room and took a long look at himself. He put his battered Stetson on at a rakish angle. It would do, he decided. He went outside.

"Three dollars for the pants, five-dollar deposit on the coat and tie," the clothier said.

"Five dollars?" Larrabee said. "You said two dollars for rentals."

"A deposit," the clothier said patiently. "You bring back the coat and the tie and you get your money back and then you pay the two dollars."

"If that's the way you do business," Larrabee said reluctantly. He handed over the money and went outside. It was past noon and he hadn't eaten anything since that breakfast that Opal could have made a sight better over a campfire. He wondered why in hell Opal came into his every thought.

Larrabee walked down the sidewalk, feeling somewhat ill at ease in his new tight-fitting clothes. He was conscious of the silk cravat knotted around his neck as a final bit of elegance. He saw a girl coming toward him, and he stopped dead still. It was Opal.

She was wearing a velvet skirt that clung to her with an alluring closeness. There was a sprig of lace at the throat of a snowy white bodice, ruffled down the front, revealed by a smart little jacket that matched the skirt. White ruffles protruded from the sleeves of the jacket at the wrists. With gloved hands she clutched a brand-new purse and there was a perky hat with a saucy feather perched on her well-coiffed hair. She stopped and Larrabee stared at her.

"You think I'm silly, don't you?" she said. "Splurging money on things I don't need." She looked up, her eyes pleading, "I always wanted to just once have an outfit like this."

"I don't think you're silly," Larrabee said. "I think you're downright beautiful."

"Do you mean that?" she said.

"That you're not silly?"

"That I'm beautiful."

"Always did think that," he said, "but those clothes sure do add a lot to what was already there."

She felt like kissing him. She had waited so long for somebody to tell her she looked like something. She didn't have a chance to say anything. Two men with badges on their vests were angling across the street toward their. It was that damn town marshal. He said, "You Larrabee Lucas Stone?"

"Been packing that name for twenty-six years so I can't very well deny it now," Larrabee said.

"You know a sheriff by the name of Harry Brockwell back in Gillette, Wyoming?"

Larrabee felt a sinking in the pit of his stomach. He looked at the town marshal, but mostly he saw the growing concern in Opal's eyes. He said, "Fine man, Harry Brockwell."

"I had a letter from him," the town marshal said. "He said you'd be coming this way and I was to keep an eye out for you."

There was near desperation in Opal's eyes. Larrabee said, "By any chance did he say why?"

"Yes, he did," the marshal said. "At some length. Said you had a going-away party and you and some of your cowpoke pals messed up a saloon real bad."

"Sheriff Harry Brockwell is a right honest man, so I can't dispute his word much," Larrabee said. "He say anything else?"

"Yep," the marshal said. "He did that. Said you busted a big hole in the side of his jail."

Larrabee wished Opal would quit looking like she was going to cry. He said, "Well, I was sort of anxious to get started on my way to Millerton."

"Mighty serious charge, breaking jail. Sort of makes you an escaped convict, don't it?" the marshal said.

Opal had buried her face in her hands. "I've thought a lot about it along those lines," Larrabee said.

The marshal said, "So what do you think I ought to do?"

"I don't rightly know," Larrabee said. He tried to grin. "You could send Harry Brockwell a telegram and tell him if he promises not to lock me up anymore, I'll promise not to break out of his jail anymore."

"I already sent him a telegram," the marshal said. "I asked him what I was to do with you."

Opal looked up, all hope gone from her face. "You get an answer?" Larrabee asked.

"Yep," the marshal said.

"What'd he say?"

"He said to tell you if you ever come back to Gillette and give another goin'-away party and get yourself in a mess of trouble, he's gonna lock you up in his brand-new jail which has got brick walls, and he's gonna forget all about you bein' there." The marshal spit across his chin and squinted up at Larrabee. "You're liable to be in that jail for a mighty long time, son," he said.

"Then I don't reckon I ought to go back there and get in trouble, should I?" Larrabee said.

"That would be my advice," the marshal said.

"That all?" Larrabee asked. He saw hope returning to Opal's face.

"Nope," the marshal said. "That ain't all."

The hope in Opal's eyes was fading. "You owe me six dollars for the telegram," the marshal said.

"Well," Larrabee said, "since I been paid recently, I reckon I can cover that." He dug in his pocket and fished out a five and a one. He handed it across.

"There's more," the marshal said.

Larrabee felt that sinking again. He said, "What might that be?"

Larrabee saw a twinkle in the marshal's eyes. He said,

"Don't you never give no going-away parties as long as you're in my town."

"I reckon I can live with that," Larrabee said.

The marshal and his deputy moved away and Opal stood there, just staring at Larrabee Stone.

Out of earshot, the deputy glanced at the marshal and said, "What about the damages to the saloon?"

"His friends paid for it," the marshal said.

"But busting out of jail," the deputy said. "That's a serious charge."

"Not in this case," the marshal said. "Harry Brockwell's an old friend of mine. I hear from him often and for seven years he's been fighting with the county commissioners to build him a new jail. When they saw the hole that Stone feller knocked out of the side of that wood shack Harry had been putting up with, they then and there decided to build him a decent calaboose. Harry's right happy about it."

The two men walked on and then the deputy said, "You didn't send no telegram, did you?"

"Nope," the marshal said. He jerked a thumb across his shoulder. "But he don't know that."

"But you charged him six dollars for it."

"Well, Harry Brockwell told me when this Larrabee Stone got here, which he knew he would, I was to hassle him around a bit. Harry being such a good friend of mine, I did it. I waited until I saw him with that lady friend of his, and then I worried him just a mite."

"But the six dollars?"

"I figured you and me ought to get ourselves a good steak supper out of it, don't you?"

The deputy grinned. He said, "Marshal, the longer I work for you, the better I like your style." They moved on down the street.

Larrabee and Opal still stood there on the sidewalk. Opal searched his face and said, "And that's the full extent of your criminal activities?"

"Yes, ma'am," Larrabee said. He looked up sheepishly. "Guess it don't amount to much, does it?"

She didn't have a chance to answer. A two-hundred-pound woman squeezed into finery purchased in that long-ago time when she had weighed a trim hundred and eighty puffed up and stopped alongside them. "You going to the wedding?" the woman asked.

"Yes, ma'am," Larrabee said, "we are."

"So am I," the woman said. "Wouldn't miss this one for a million dollars."

"Oh?" Opal said. "Friend of the bride or groom?"

"Never heard of either one of them," the woman said. She reached up suddenly and gripped her nose between her thumb and forefinger and ducked her head. When she looked up again her eyes were moist. "Ain't missed a wedding in seven years," she said. "Not since my third husband passed on. Weddings make me cry." She seemed to notice Opal for the first time. A look of sheer wonderment flooded her face. "My," she said. "Ain't you the pretty one though." She looked at Larrabee. She said, "Are you two the bride and groom?"

"No," Opal snorted. "Of course we're not."

"Oh," the woman said. There was disappointment in her voice. For a moment she had thought she had found a couple of celebrities. She waddled on up the sidewalk toward the little church on the knoll.

"You didn't have to be so doggone positive about it," Larrabee said.

"About what?"

"About you and me not being the bride and groom."

"Just what are you talking about?"

"I been doing a lot of thinking the last couple of days," Larrabee said. "You and me, making that long trip back together, just the two of us. Well, you know how the folks in Twin Pines are. They talk. They talk a whole bunch. And that barber." Larrabee expelled his breath. "What he don't know for sure he makes up. I don't care so much for myself but it would be right wrong for folks to talk about you."

"So?" Opal said, puzzled.

Larrabee said, "What I was thinkin' was, we got to go to

that wedding and stand up there in front of all those people. We can't get out of that. We promised Lee and Lorella we would."

"I had no intentions of trying to get out of it," Opal said, "Did you?"

"No, ma'am, I didn't," Larrabee said. "But I was thinkin' as long as the preacher is already there and you and me got to be standing up there and the church is all sort of decorated . . ." He felt downright miserable.

She said, "Larrabee Lucas Stone, are you asking me to marry you?"

"Yes, ma'am," he said, "I reckon I am, in a way. But if you want to say no I sure will understand . . ."

She put a hand on either side of his face and forced him to look at her. Her eyes were brimming with unshed tears. "I don't want to say no," she said. "I don't want to say no to you ever in my life."

There were a whole bunch of things Larrabee wanted to say right now. Like maybe they should think it over, and about the ring in his pocket. He had mostly wanted to tell her about that, but there was a lump the size of a goose egg in his throat and the words just couldn't get past it, so he just stuck out his elbow and she looped her arm through it and held on so tight he thought she might never let go of him, and he hoped she never would.

They moved off the sidewalk together and walked right up the middle of the street. Larrabee Lucas Stone felt forty feet tall, with the most beautiful girl in the world hanging onto his arm and everybody seeing him.

They walked right on, unmindful of the shouts of the teamsters who had to pull over to let them by. As they neared the church on the knoll they heard the first wheezing notes from the little foot pedal organ inside the sanctuary.

AUTHOR'S NOTE

This is a work of fiction. So far as I can determine, there was never a state prison in the Owens Valley. No attempt whatsoever has been made to chart an actual trail across the Sierra for the purpose of this story. There are many. And there was never a town of Twin Pines.

But perhaps a modern counterpart can be found in the town of Lone Pine, there at the foot of Mt. Whitney, the highest peak in the contiguous forty-eight states, where literally hundreds of motion pictures and television Westerns have been filmed in the rockbound splendor of the ancient Alabama Hills. Or in Independence, with its Civil War history and its tiny imposing courthouse that looks down on busy U.S. Highway 395 where RVs of every description stream by each summer loaded with city folks seeking the relief of the coolness of the many government campgrounds offered to them on the slopes of the magnificent Sierra. Or in Big Pine. Or Bishop, there at the north end of the valley. The mountains are still there, unchanged, and in hidden valleys, high up in their vastness, hot springs bubble unexpectedly and jewel-like lakes reflect the image of the towering granite peaks. And in winter the cars still move up Highway 395, tops loaded with skis, and bubbling young people move down the slopes of Mammoth or June Lake or take out cross-country through the startling silent vastness of the heavy snows.

Yes, the mountains are still there.

And the mules? They, too, remain. The railroad, long gone now, came up through the valley and mules helped build it. The Owens River still runs, diminished now to slake the thirst of the megalopolis that is Los Angeles. And mules dragged lengths of massive pipe for that aqueduct that still takes the water into the city and they pulled the scrapers that cut the grades through the unyielding hills and they dragged the sleds and eased along the wagons that hauled the endless supplies for the sweating men. The Lorax mines of Death Valley flourished and the twenty-mule teams moved into written history and into legend.

Yes, the mules, too, remain. And each year, the last week in May, the city of Bishop holds its famous Mule Days with its parades and mule racing and rodeo and packing contests, and mule-shoeing competition . . . and the patient mule, that hybrid cross between a mare and a jackass, the animal who is denied even the joy of reproducing his own kind, still does his work, packing tourists into the high country to the hidden lakes in pursuit of the fighting rainbow and the elusive Dolly Varden. Cantankerous, unpredictable, letting loose with voices that grate the ears, they are still one of man's most dependable servants. And the city of Bishop celebrates that fact each year, and the Grand Marshal of the Mule Day Parade has included such notables as a youngish actor with political ambitions by the name of Ronald Reagan and many others. Bishop, California, is proud to call itself the Mule Capital of the World.

And perhaps a lonely young widow, somewhat like Opal Sprague, and an aimless drifter, not unlike Larrabee Lucas Stone, had some part in getting it started.

Who's to say?

Thomas Thompson
Newbury Park, California

About the Author

THOMAS THOMPSON's first Western novel, RANGE DRIFTER, was published in 1948 and his newest one, OUTLAW VALLEY, forty years later in 1988. In the 1950s Ballantine published TROUBLE RIDER, KING OF ABILENE, and THEY BROUGHT THEIR GUNS. Thompson wrote scripts for the television series WAGON TRAIN and THE RIFLEMAN and was for fourteen years (1959–1973) writer and associate producer of BONANZA. He also wrote the screenplays for Western films including SADDLE THE WIND and CATTLE KING for MGM. Thomas Thompson was twice winner of the Western Writers of American SPUR AWARD, The Levi Strauss SADDLEMAN AWARD and was honored by the Cowboy Hall of Fame as a lifetime member. He was cofounder of the Western Writers of America and served as its president for two terms.